Hi, Josie,
Happy reading!
and Merry Christmas!
~Erica Kiefer

LINGERING

ECHOES

Erica Kiefer

Clean Teen Publishing

Lingering Echoes
Copyright © 2013 by: Erica Kiefer

Clean Teen Publishing
PO Box 561326
The Colony, TX 75056

www.cleanteenpublishing.com

Content Discolsure

For more information about our content disclosure,
please utilize the QR code above with your
smart phone or visit us at
www.cleanteenpublishing.com.

For my husband, Dan, for always believing in me and rescuing me from self-doubt.

CHAPTER 1

Standing on the weathered dock, I stared into the shadowy lake. The water seemed darker today, sloshing against the pontoons beneath the platform. With each rise and fall, anxiety tore at the lining of my stomach like acid. I pulled my eyes away from the water, wondering if it would ever cease to be my enemy.

"There you are, Allie!"

I turned around to see Brooke Cannon adjusting the straps of her bikini as she approached. Though I'd only met her two days ago, I was not surprised to see her sky-blue eyes decked out in makeup, each careful stroke of mascara sweeping through her long, doll-like lashes.

"Today is going to be so chill," she said, joining me on the dock. "I haven't been on a boat in years. That was nice of your family to invite me."

"It's no big deal," I said with a shrug. I wished Dad had given *me* the luxury of an "invite" because I would have said no. But when you're seventeen and visiting your dad, some choices just aren't up to you.

"I can't figure out why you gave Mr. Collins such a hard time about coming," Brooke continued. "Who

1

wouldn't want to begin the summer cruising on a boat?" Her cheeks flushed with enthusiasm, a natural blush to accompany her fair skin.

I didn't elaborate on why the situation was more complicated than not wanting to wakeboard. Glowering, I watched Dad maneuver the rental boat into position with help from his wife, Clara. I let out a deep sigh. "It's overrated in my opinion."

Aaron's voice interrupted my gloom.

"Hey, how's it going?"

Brooke's attention gravitated to Aaron's approaching form. Whispering, she said, "You are so lucky. I can't believe you sleep under the same roof as he does! I guess I'll have to settle for staying three cabins down from you."

Luck had nothing to do with it. He was the best friend of my stepbrother, Nick, who invited Aaron to tag along for the summer. I tried not to roll my eyes at Brooke's infatuation with Aaron. She'd been ogling him since we ran into him playing basketball the other day, gushing about how she and six-foot-one blonds were meant to be together. Personally, from the way she scoped out every boy that crossed her path, I was pretty sure Brooke had an obsession with all boys. But maybe college freshmen were at the top of her list.

"And just what are you ladies gossiping about?" Aaron asked, throwing an arm around Brooke's shoulders. She gave him a look of playful disgust, craning her neck to match her eyes with his.

"Just because we're girls, we have to be 'gossiping?'" That's a stereotype if I ever heard one."

"Hey, stereotypes have to come from somewhere. I grew up with four younger sisters. Trust me. I know what juicy gossip looks like when I see it." He flashed a charming smile, while Brooke failed to hide her giddiness.

"Ok, the boat's ready! Let's go!" Dad called from the dock.

I sighed. Let the battle begin.

We walked over to the open-bowed ski boat, Brooke and Aaron chatting at my side. I stared at the swaying boat, resistance anchoring me in place.

"Come on, Allie," Dad said.

I gritted my teeth. My voice was low. "You know exactly why I don't want to go."

Dad was relentless, proof that stubbornness is, in part, genetic. "You don't have to get in the water. Just come spend the afternoon with us on the boat."

"What's the hold up?" Nick hollered from the backseat. Stretched out with his arms folded across his chest, he didn't hide his annoyance.

Shuffling my feet, I glanced behind me, desperate for an excuse.

Without warning, two strong arms wrapped around my waist and hauled me over his shoulder.

"What are you—Aaron Jackson! Put me down!" I kicked my legs in fury as he pulled me with him into the boat.

He chuckled as he seated me between Nick and

3

Brooke on the back bench. Surrounded by laughter, I glared up at Aaron's lean form. The top of his unzipped wet suit hung from his waist, his bare, golden torso gleaming at me.

"If you ever pick me up like that again—"

"Whoa! Calm down fireball! I was just trying to help speed up the inevitable." Aaron zipped up his suit over his defined abs and then threw a life jacket my way. Catching it before it hit my face, I frowned at him. He winked back and then broke into a wide smile.

"You better listen to her, Aaron," Nick chimed in. "I wouldn't try that stunt again if I were you. She might throw your back out next time." He laughed at his own joke.

"Nick, be nice," Clara said to her son. She smiled at me apologetically.

Indignant, I removed my own shirt and fastened the life vest over my swimsuit. I thrust the shirt into the bag at Brooke's feet.

"Ah, quit your sulking. You're ruining the day."

I didn't have to turn my head to know the rude comment belonged to Nick, but I faced him anyway.

"Sulking? That's what you think this is about? You don't know anything about me, Nick!" The high volume of my voice attracted every head in the boat.

Dad intervened, pushing his sunglasses on top of his head so I could catch his brown eyes reprimanding me. "It's going to be a long two months if you keep this up," he warned. He put a hand around Clara's shoulders.

"All we're asking is that you at least try to get along. Allie, I know it will be difficult for you to be up here after... after what happened. But it's for the best."

What do you know? I wanted to say, but instead, I held my tongue.

Breaking up the awkward silence, Aaron snickered, "Nick, why haven't you invited me on more trips with your family?"

"*She's* not part of my—"

"Nicholas!" Clara cut in, cautioning her son with a stern expression. But we all knew what he was going to say, and I couldn't agree more. I was not part of his family, and he wasn't part of mine. It was going to take a lot more than our parents' legal union to bond the two of us.

"Well, guess we're all ready now, right?" Dad called from behind the wheel. He made brief eye contact with me, looking away when he saw the resentment in my hazel eyes.

Strapped into the wakeboard, Aaron ripped across the water as he jumped from wake to wake. Flying through the air and pulling tricks, he even landed his 360 without fail. We watched him in awe as he maneuvered a tantrum, catching the wake and flipping in the air.

"He's amazing," Brooke admired, not taking her eyes off him. Nick murmured something about Aaron being a showoff and turned his back. Nick was, no doubt, still upset about the face-plant that occurred during his earlier attempt.

"You and Aaron just completed a year in college, right?" Brooke asked him.

Nick sighed, not hiding his blatant disinterest. "Yep. UC Davis."

Brooke rested her cheek on one hand and looked up at the sky. "College sounds so cool. I can't wait until I can go next year."

Whipping his head around, Nick raised an eyebrow. "Oh you're planning on going? Huh. Wouldn't have thought you were the college type."

I caught sight of his mocking grin just before he turned away again. Brooke's mouth fell open, though no words formed.

"Just what is that supposed to mean?" I ignored Brooke's hand on my shoulder.

"Allie, forget it," she murmured.

A wave of superiority washed over Nick's face. "All I'm saying is that college isn't for everyone. It takes more than just a pretty face to get in. And, well, some people got it—" He flicked his eyes back at Brooke. "—and some people don't."

Glancing with caution at Dad's back, I lowered my seething voice. "You're a real jerk, you know that? What's your problem anyway?"

"I don't have a problem. Truth of the matter is, I've worked hard to get where I'm at, to pay my own way." Leaning towards me, he pointed his index finger.

He lowered his voice in return, though both Dad and Clara seemed oblivious to the building feud behind their backs. "Unlike some people, I didn't sit around and let *Daddy* pay for everything. I know what hard work is like. And let's face it—neither of you spoiled princesses knows anything about the real work it takes to get to college, or to do anything worthwhile for that matter."

"Oh, really? Well, it sure hasn't stopped you from milking my dad's money this past year, and I don't care how hard you've had to work. Just because your dad left you and your mom when you were little, it doesn't give you the excuse to grow up into a despicable, self-absorbed pig!"

Looking at the floor, Nick gave a cool shake of his head. His eyes flashed back into mine. His words were quick and hateful. "Are you anything like your mother? If so, I completely understand why your dad walked out on her. Kudos to him."

My hand lashed out and slapped him across his face.

Brooke gasped. Her fingers flew to her gaping mouth.

My eyes cast downward, while heat seeped from my cheeks. From my peripheral, I could see Nick watching me, not moving to touch the sting on his left cheek.

I expelled warm air from my lungs with an agitated sigh. Unbuckling my life vest, I wrestled out of it. Standing up, I reached across Brooke for the bag beside her. "I think my shoulders are burning. Can you hand me my T-shirt?"

Bending over without hesitation, she rifled through the bag as though relieved for the disruption.

"Let's see how Aaron handles a double-up," Dad called over his shoulder, unaware of my movement behind him. He turned the boat without warning, looping back across our previous path. I stumbled against the back of the boat, falling against Nick as the boat maneuvered across the bumpy wake.

"Hey, get off!" He shoved me backwards with unnecessary force.

My momentum threw me off the rear of the boat. I yelped, somersaulting into the bubbly lake. The shock of the cold water jolted my body, swallowing me whole. As I surfaced the choppy waves, I cried out, inhaling water.

I thrashed my limbs, spluttering and disoriented. Hacking against the fluid in my airway, panic tightened my chest with an invisible weight, sheathing me in fear.

"Allie! Allie, you ok?" Aaron threw a long arm across my ribs. "Hey! Relax. You need to calm down!"

I struggled against him. The water was still the enemy and Aaron was trying to drag me down with him.

"Stop, Allie. I've got you!" Aaron leaned back, hugging my back against his chest, while he towed me with his free arm. Catching some air, I finally quit thrashing and allowed Aaron's solid strokes to haul me towards the boat.

"Are you all right?" Dad reached down and offered

his hand to help me up the ladder.

I ignored it. Refusing to look at him, I stepped inside and pushed past him to the front of the boat. Drenched and dripping, I sat down, hugging myself with the towel Brooke offered me. Smoothing back the dark brown waves of my hair, I cleared my burning throat.

"What happened?" Clara asked, throwing a second towel around my shoulders. "I didn't even see you fall."

"I think it was my fault," Dad admitted. "I was trying to give Aaron a challenging run and I turned too fast." He spoke to Aaron. "You've sure got some talent out there."

Aaron brushed off the compliment, looking back and forth between Nick and me with an uncertain expression. His eyes stopping on Nick, he said, "It looked like she had some help falling overboard. What's going on, man?"

All eyes followed Aaron's, resting on Nick's unconcerned expression. Leaning back into his seat, he put his hands up.

"Hey—I didn't do anything. It's not my fault if the girl's a little clumsy." He covered a sly smile behind one hand.

I turned away, loathing his very being. The twinge of guilt I felt for losing my temper was mingled with the satisfaction of seeing the red stain on his cheek.

And yet, I didn't want to deal with it anymore. Already, I was tired. I hated conflict and the draining emotions it evoked. I could sense it would get worse, festering like an infection the longer I remained at our summer cabin.

I turned to Dad, the man responsible for bringing me here, and for pressuring an implausible merger. I looked at him in earnest.

"Why did you bring me here, Dad? I told you I didn't want to come—not to the cabin and not on this boat. Why can't you ever just listen to me?" My eyes moistened.

"Well, Allie, I just thought it might help you to—"

"No, Dad! I don't need your help. And besides, there's nothing *to* help. She's dead!"

CHAPTER 2

My hand brushed against the coarseness of the tree trunks, tracing the lines and curves of the bark with my fingers. Haunting laughter filled my mind, bidding me towards the river I knew too well. With an aching heart, I followed. I kneeled by the river's side, collecting the fallen pine needles and cones. I tossed them in, watching the ruthless current drag them along. The leaves glanced off protruding boulders before they were sucked underneath the surface.

I let out a long sigh and glanced upwards, allowing drizzling rain to kiss my face. A silent flash of light lit up the darkened sky, followed by a mumble of thunder. As the sky shed its heavy tears, I remained huddled on the muddy soil, staring up into the grayness.

The abrupt rumble of a motor caught my attention, clashing against the sounds of nature. I stood up, straining my eyes through the curtain of rain to find its source. Across the river I could make out a figure on a motorcycle. He was dressed in dark clothing, his head sheltered with a helmet.

He seemed to be staring at me.

Curious, I stared back. Neither of us moved.

What was he doing out in the rain? He was probably wondering the same thing about me, wondering what I was doing outside all alone. Wiping water from my eyes, I took a step backwards, not taking my eyes off him. Why was he was still staring? I stepped backwards once more, assessing this stranger.

He revved the motor, once, twice, three times. Then he seemed to come to a decision. His bike roared towards me, closing the gap between us. The bridge was off to my right. I didn't wait to see if he was going to cross it.

Unsure of his intentions, instinct told me to run. I spun around, sprinting towards the cabins. Adrenaline fueled my blood, warming my cold limbs, as I dodged trees and bushes. I didn't look behind me, even when I was sure the motor was becoming louder, closer. I kept running.

The cabins were in sight. Only then did I dare to glance over my shoulder, my heartbeat thumping in my ears too loudly to hear the motor for sure.

He was gone.

Just as a shiver of relief coursed through me, I slammed into a body, shrieking as I beat at his chest. His strong arms grabbed me, holding me captive.

"What the—Allie! Stop!"

With wide eyes and a quick intake of breath, I stared up at Aaron. His arms were wrapped around me, pinning my forearms against his chest, ending my struggle.

"Let go!" I shoved against him, uneasy with his restraint, and he released me. Still panting, I glanced over my shoulder once more, swiping rain from my vision.

"What happened? Are you ok?" Aaron put a hand on my shoulder, turning me around to face him. This time I didn't shake him off, now welcoming the familiar face.

"There was someone—someone out there," I said, but except for the rain playing its unique melody against the pine leaves, the forest was quiet. Aaron raised an eyebrow. Drenched and hysterical, in combination with my outburst yesterday on the boat, I knew he thought I was insane.

"Come on," Aaron said, taking my elbow. I checked once more to be sure the motorcyclist had disappeared, and then I followed his lead. Aaron walked with me to the front porch of our cabin, and we sat on the covered steps.

"What were you doing out in the rain?" he asked.

I hesitated. "I was out by the river."

Aaron paused a moment before he said, "You were thinking about your cousin." It wasn't a question. Just a simple statement of fact.

He knew then.

Aaron caught me watching him carefully. He opened his palms and explained, "Your dad told us your little cousin drowned last summer."

I clenched my teeth, giving a simple nod of my head.

"I don't know what I can say to make you feel

better, but I'm sorry that happened. Do you want to talk about it?"

"No!" I didn't mean to snap at him. Frustrated at the little control I seemed to have over my emotions these days, I tried again. "Look, I'm sorry. It's just...that's all there is to say. Maddie drowned. No amount of talking can change that."

Quiet for a moment, Aaron then rose to his feet. "Well, in that case, I was going to grab some breakfast, but do you want to shoot hoops instead?" He put out his hand with understanding resting in his expression.

I almost laughed at his abrupt change in conversation, but I was more relieved—and grateful. I looked down at my dripping clothing. I probably should have changed, but I didn't really want to be alone. "Sure."

With one final glance towards the river, I put my hand in his, and he pulled me to my feet.

"Allie! Over here!"

A hushed, but loud, whisper caught my attention from where I stood behind the crowd. Brooke gestured with her hand, patting the empty space next to her on the log bench. I eased my way through the audience, slipping in next to her, and apologizing to the woman on my right when I kicked her back. She glared at me before returning her attention to the storyteller.

Aaron, sitting on the other side of Brooke, waved

at me. "What took you so long?" he asked. "Still soaking your muscles after your brutal loss this morning?"

I rolled my eyes. "Whatever. I was just off my game."

Aaron shook his head and returned my smile. "You can prove it to me next time."

"Thank you, thank you," the storyteller's deep voice bellowed from the stage as he bowed in appreciation. We turned our attention towards him. Clasping his hands against his black vest, he offered a gentle smile from behind his white goatee.

Brooke leaned over. "He just finished telling some of his favorite Aesop's fables," she whispered with excessive volume. "He was really good!"

"Shh!" The woman next to me threw another pointed look, scooting away. Brooke stuck out her tongue and scowled back. I suppressed a giggle, despite the immaturity of it all.

"And now," the man continued, quieting the crowd, "It is my great pleasure to introduce the lovely and distinguished Alina Ivanova." The audience gave a welcoming clap.

A middle-aged woman crossed the stage in a billowing skirt, dyed with purple, red, and touches of green ink flowing into each other. Her thin, long-sleeved yellow blouse swirled, belling out at her wrists as she curtsied. An olive-green scarf wrapped around her head, her hair tucked inside. Silver tassels decorated the fringe along her forehead, jingling together behind the gleam of the fire.

"Good evening," she began, and the crowd softened. Her husky voice hinted of an accent. "Russia, where my family originates, has many tales. As a young girl, I sat around the dinner table while my babushka told us story after story, filling our minds with morals and lessons she wished us to remember. And now, in her honor, I pass these tales on to you."

She paused, allowing the slight rustling of the trees to set the mood, the soft breeze twisting the dancing, orange flames. Her eyes scanned the crowd, now captivated into silence. I flinched when her eyes met mine, holding my gaze for an uncomfortable moment; a moment that tugged at my darkest secrets, my deepest fears, invading my privacy. I struggled to pull away, to resist her searching eyes. The woman released me, and then she began her tales, weaving in and out with descriptions that painted vivid pictures in our minds of the lessons and morals she wished us to know.

As the evening grew late, I stifled a yawn. The glowing embers flickered, a soft blush amongst the coals. Families shuffled out with sleeping toddlers gathered in their arms. As the numbers began to dwindle, the final storyteller played a gentle, concluding tale, rhyming and strumming on his guitar. Many from the audience stood up to leave, dusting off their pants as the final strum echoed a closing chord.

"Wait!" a dark-haired teenager called out, sitting with a few of his rugged pals. "No one told a ghost story.

You can't sit around a fire without a ghost story."

His protest caused murmuring of agreement from other kids, their shadowed faces illuminated by the dying light.

"You want a ghost story?" a familiar Russian voice observed. Alina Ivanova stepped back onto the empty stage. Her pale eyes pierced through the smaller crowd. She smiled, heightening her sharp cheekbones and pinching the crow's feet around her eyes. Those standing to leave hesitated, their interests peaked once more.

"I know a true one. It happened not far from here," Alina began, pointing a long finger towards the lake hidden behind the row of cabins. "Just north of the river and east of this great lake, there lived a family: a mother, father, and their two children. The boy was the age of many of you," she said, pointing at some of the teenagers present. A knowing look passed across her face.

"There was something evil in that boy, something dark festering inside of him. He was always in trouble. Always," she emphasized.

The boy who requested a ghost story squirmed in his seat as she gazed at him before continuing.

"He trusted no one, and no one trusted him, especially not his father. His parents were protective of their little girl, whose age barely touched ten. She was a sweet girl, who adored her brother and saw the small spark of good inside of him. But she was the only one who could see it, and even that did not protect her from his malice."

My body mimicked those around me, sitting with my back straight and tense. We waited with eager ears.

"For one day, the boy, furious with his father for threatening to send him away, burned the house to the ground. Trapped, with no hope of escape, the blackened walls collapsed upon themselves, burying the family in a fiery prison. Heavy, hazy smoke circled the remains like vultures." There were small gasps from the crowd.

"Yes. Mother, father, and sister. All three suffered a vicious, painful death, unable to escape from the sudden bursts of flames that engulfed the house in the quiet night—a night that broke the silence with screams of terror and agony as their skin was seared from their bones."

I shuddered, my face grimacing in distaste for the story.

Truly, it could only be a story.

Brooke gripped Aaron's arm with her left, holding my hand with her right. She stared straight ahead with a look of horror on her face.

"At night," Alina continued, "if you listen, you can hear their wailing through the trees, the mourning of a family lost, murdered by the callous hands of their only boy. But sometimes," she concluded, voice just above an audible whisper, "it might only be the angry wind whistling a haunting tune. That is for you to decide."

CHAPTER 3

In answer to the insistent knocking, I flung my cabin door open. A bright light flashed into my hazel eyes.

"Hey!" I protested, blinking away the glare. There was a quiet click and the light disappeared. When I could see again, Brooke awaited me with two teenage guys flanking her sides.

"So, are you ready?" she asked.

"Err, ready for what, exactly?"

Brooke's eyes brightened as she held up a large flashlight. "For an exciting adventure, that's what! Come on!" She grabbed my arm, tugging me after her. I dragged my feet and released myself from her hold.

"Hang on a second, Brooke. What do you mean?"

"Will you please just be spontaneous and—"

A voice behind me interrupted Brooke's pleading.

"Did I hear someone say 'adventure'?" Aaron stepped out the door, stretching his arms behind his head. The veins in his biceps bulged, attracting Brooke's attention.

"Uh—Brooke? You want to explain?" I said,

nudging her from her smitten stupor.

"Huh? Oh—right." She beamed at us with a mischievous glint in her eyes, looking around before she spoke with a low voice.

"So I was just sitting on my porch when these two happened to stop by and say hi." She gestured towards the guys beside her. "Adam and his brother...Brad, was it?"

"Brett," the shorter of the two corrected, appearing disappointed in her memory lapse.

"Yeah, that's what I meant. Anyway, they were at the storytelling last night, and Adam says the ghost story is true!"

Adam nodded emphatically.

"Ghost story—ha!" Nick scoffed. I turned around in surprise, not realizing my stepbrother had joined our small circle. "If that's the best she's got, *I* could be a storyteller. That was the lamest thing I've ever heard."

"Well, it really did happen," Adam affirmed.

Nick looked at him with mockery on the edge of his lips.

Adam stepped forward. "I've heard the rumors before about the fire. Last year, I checked it out with my friends. We drove up to the location of the fire close to midnight. The remains of the house were still there. Just when we started walking around, a windstorm picked up out of nowhere. I swear we could hear a little girl's voice in the wind, like crying."

Everyone became silent. I wrapped my arms around myself, looking at the ground with uneasiness.

Slow, rhythmic clapping disrupted the mood. All eyes followed Nick's clapping hands. "Bravo," he said, looking down at Adam. "I suppose I should congratulate you on your efforts to pick up on girls with made-up stories, but if that's the best line you have, maybe I should be offering my condolences."

Adam glared at him. "It's true," he defended again. He puffed up his chest and crossed his arms.

"Why don't you come with us if you don't believe us?" Brett interjected. "We're going right now."

Nick prepared to object.

"Not a bad idea," Aaron said. "We've got nothing better to do tonight, anyway." He put a hand on Nick's shoulder. "What do you say, man? Are you up for some teenage drama?"

Brett and Adam scowled at them while Brooke, equally insulted, put her hands on her hips.

"You're not that much older than us," she stated, upset by Aaron's demeaning slight.

Aaron put his hands up. "Hey, I didn't mean anything by it. Come on, we're ready. Lead the way."

After parking outside a large circle of trees, we walked passed a "NO TRESPASSING" sign that had obviously been ignored on numerous occasions. Spray-painted profanity stared back at us in bold, fiery letters across the warning. Following the trail of empty beer cans and cigarette butts, we noticed how the lush grass abruptly turned into dirt. Cracked, blackened branches littered the ground and, in the center of it all, were the remains of what was once a large home with exquisite design.

Of course, imagination was required. It helped that the southern portion of the house was mostly intact with its lavish, log exterior. The fire must have been stopped before it had destroyed the house in its entirety.

As my eyes roved along what should have been the rest of the home, my heart fell heavy. Burnt rubble was piled high on top of one another. It looked like a forgotten tomb.

"So it does exist," Aaron spoke, disturbing our awed silence.

"Told you," said Adam.

"Why hasn't it all been torn down and removed?" I swallowed, envisioning the burning flames that had destroyed the home and left it like a grave. It seemed to be a vivid and gruesome reminder of what occurred here. "They at least removed the bodies...right?"

Brooke and I glanced with uneasiness at the debris. I looked away, almost fearing I might see a charred hand emerge from within. I chided myself. That was what too many cheap horror films will do to one's mind.

Adam smiled at our reaction. "Yeah, don't worry. No way would they leave the bodies. Rumor has it, the kid who burned it down refused to let anyone clean it up. It was his home and his property—after he had killed his old man that is. He could do whatever he wanted with it. And for some reason, he chose to leave it as is."

"He probably wanted to leave it as a souvenir," Brett suggested. "The kid was sick. He killed his entire family. It wouldn't surprise me if he wanted some kind of trophy or memento of what he had done."

I grimaced. "Do you know what happened to him?"

Adam shrugged. "Nah. I didn't look that much into it. I'm betting he's just your local psychopath now." Adam laughed at his own joke.

Unsettled, I turned away, observing the trees surrounding us. It was close to dark. I didn't like how the old tree branches all seemed to hunch over, like they were ready to enclose around us at any minute. A shudder slid down my back and I spun in a quick circle, looking around me. A hand touched my shoulder blade, and I jumped.

"You all right there, Allie?"

I shook away from Aaron's touch with a sharp inhale. "Don't do that!" My comment came out brusquer than I intended. Everyone looked at me in surprise.

"The ghost story is really getting to you, isn't it, little sister?" Nick laughed at me.

"And don't you ever call me that," I snapped at him. With my arms still crossed, I stalked a few feet away, turning my back on all of them.

"What's her deal?" I heard Adam whisper.

"I don't know...."

I listened to the silence behind me, embarrassed by my reaction. But I couldn't help it. Talking about death only reminded me of how Maddie had drowned. They wouldn't understand. Nobody could.

"Well, we're here. Now what?" Nick said. He walked up to one of the standing walls, his flip-flops crunching against the glass particles beneath him. He peered into one of the cracked windows. "Well, I can tell you what other people have been using it for. I'm going in."

We followed Nick around the corner of the building and stepped inside a short hallway that led us to a bedroom. Nick gave a low whistle, while Brooke crinkled her nose in distaste.

There was a battered, queen-sized mattress lying inside a weathered bed frame. Next to it was a dresser, positioned on its side like a bench. Formulating the rest of the circle were tree stumps, a large boulder, and other miscellaneous items that seemed to have been brought in and used as chairs. In the middle of the configuration were gray ashes and fragments of wood.

"This is apparently the place to party," Brett said, kicking aside a beer can and seating himself onto one of the tree stumps. "Not bad for a makeshift campsite. Anybody have a match? I say we make a fire of our own."

I shook my head in disgust. I looked around at the graffiti-covered walls and the ransacked furniture. This room was one of the few remaining from the disastrous fire. A fire that had taken the lives of an unsuspecting family: a mother, father, and an innocent little girl...

A surge of emotion flooded my chest, taking me by surprise. "This isn't right. We shouldn't be here!"

Everyone seemed to be judging the expression on my face. I tried to hide my moistening eyes.

"Allie, this happened a long time ago. We're not doing anything wrong," Brooke said. She seemed embarrassed by my objections, smiling in apology to Adam and Brett.

"Yeah, we're not doing anything worse than what's already been done here," Adam said. "We're just trying to have some fun."

I shook my head again. "Fine. Do whatever you want. I'll wait by the car." Stepping over a block of wood, I marched out of the room and hurried down the destroyed hallway. Escaping the awkwardness I had created, I breathed a heavy sigh.

Outside, night had fallen and the temperature in the air continued to drop. Now I wished I'd brought a sweater to impede the growing wind. I rubbed my bare arms to make my goose bumps disappear, but something else kept causing my hair to stand on end.

I thought about the boy who had killed his family and shuddered in revulsion. Yet my heart also felt an odd sense of remorse for him, for reasons I couldn't quite figure out. What happened to the boy that made him so hateful, to drive him to do something so cruel? And what happened to him after his family died?

He was probably locked up in some juvenile

detention center or circling through state custody from one foster home to the next. How long ago was this anyway? Maybe he was a grown man, locked in prison for theft and other murders, just waiting to get out so he could strike again.

I fought against a wave of apprehension, observing the gloomy silhouettes of the trees, searching for watching eyes or whatever it was that urged me to leave. Closing my eyes, I pressed my forehead against the cool window of the jeep, struggling to contain the overwhelming sadness and panic.

Minutes later, reluctant footsteps and quiet voices approached from behind me, leaving the burned ruins standing alone.

CHAPTER 4

Brooke and I weaved through the crowds, trying to stay close to each other's sides, despite the young children who shoved past us in their haste. The mass of people inhabiting Hidden Pines never diminished before the conclusion of the three-day festival, making the crowds busier and pushier by the hour.

One such incidence ended with a double-scooped, strawberry ice-cream cone smearing onto Brooke's shoulder and absorbing into the ends of her hair.

"Ugh!" Brooke cried out in disgust. "Rotten, spoiled children," she grumbled over her shoulder, as she used her fingers to pinch off the sticky cream.

"Speaking of children, how's work going?" I asked, pulling off pink clouds of cotton candy and letting them melt in my mouth.

She made a face. "Well, I'm glad I have the day off. I *so* need a break. I wanted to ring those kids' necks yesterday!"

"Why, what happened?" I didn't know why I asked. As I had learned over the past week, the story was already on the tip of her tongue anyway.

"I was just doing my job and making sure all the

kids had life jackets on. Then this eight-year-old started running along the dock. He wouldn't listen to a word I said! And then—you'll never believe this—as soon as I turned my back, he pushed me into the lake! My makeup and hair were ruined!"

Brooke ran her fingers through her pale hair in memory of the awful incident. "This is the last time I ever work at a youth camp, that's for sure. I could not believe someone would do something like that."

"Brooke, you did say he's eight, right? And a boy?"

"Well, yeah, but—that is just so rude!"

I laughed to myself, while Brooke continued to frown at the absurdity of it all. Glancing over her shoulder again, her expression changed.

"What is it?" I asked, waiting for her to expel more of her frustrations over the wild children of today's world. Her steps came to a halt.

"I thought I saw someone," she murmured, still looking behind her.

I followed her gaze.

"Hm. Maybe not," Brooke said, more to herself than to me. She shrugged.

We walked passed a book sale a few minutes later. Brooke looked with disinterest at the used books lined up before us, while I ran my covetous hands along the covers of classic novels. I ignored the slew of fictional romance, evident by the scantily clad figures decorating their cover. I had decided long ago that it was a worthless genre. Passionate summer romances never played out like that in real life.

"Allie!" Brooke's hushed, but urgent, voice caught my attention. She was facing me, arms rigid at her side.

"What—" I began, confused at the brusque change in her demeanor.

"Shh. Just listen to me," she ordered. "Do you see that green tent behind me with the polka dots on it?"

I flicked my eyes over her shoulder with discretion. My eyes searched around the booths and multi-colored tents. Through a haze of sweet smoke billowing from a grill, I found the tent and nodded.

"There's a guy standing there. He's tall, has dark hair, he's wearing jeans… See him?"

My eyes flew across the throng of people passing by me in every direction. Young families, teenagers, a few elderly…I focused on the tent, inspecting its surroundings. Squinting my eyes, I shook my head.

Brooke made a sound of exasperation and turned around. She surveyed the scene, eyebrows crumpled together. "Where'd he go?" she demanded, hands on her narrow hips.

"Brooke, what's going on?" I was growing impatient with her game.

Still scanning, she said, "This guy has been watching me all day. I keep seeing glimpses of him, but whenever I try to get a good look at him, he disappears."

I had not told Brooke about the motorcyclist who chased me in the rain. I tried to hide the slight edge in my voice. "You think we're being followed?" I folded my arms across my body and rotated a full circle, watching the whirlwind of people pass me by. Despite the hum of the harmonica and the strumming guitars from the folk band, their jovial tune did little to ease my apprehension.

She nodded. "I know it was the same guy. He looked a few years older than us. He had this creepy stare in his eyes when I caught him looking at me." She paused in thought. Then she turned to me, her own eyes wide and a hand at her open mouth.

"Allie, what if he's some homicidal maniac? Some stalker who targets his prey during festivals, when people are unaware of danger—and then BAM! He snatches them right up into his cold, murderous hands. I can hear it on the news right now: *Teen girls go missing at Hidden Pines. Their bodies have yet to be found.*"

She exaggerated a shiver. "Or worse: *Their severed remains resurfaced weeks later from the depths of the lake.*"

I stared at her for a long, silent moment.

"Ok, now you're just being ridiculous." I whirled away from her, my quick steps distancing myself from Brooke and her theatrical headlines. I stopped and looked back at her in disbelief. "You truly are a drama queen, you know that?"

She threw her arms in the air with a raise of her shoulders. Her final response was a simple statement. "You just never know."

I removed my shoes and tread east along the shore, stepping away until the music was a low buzz behind me. Despite Brooke's efforts to drag me to the center of the dance floor, it had only been minutes before I tired of the jostling crowds and the over-friendly hands grabbing me from behind. I didn't feel bad ditching Brooke, or the bright lights that lit up the late evening. Last I saw, Brooke had her head on Aaron's shoulder, and her arms comfortably latched around his neck during a slow song. That's when I made my escape.

My brisk walk carried me towards the grove of evergreens growing a short distance from the lake. With Hidden Pines located in the heart of the Sierra Nevadas, the mountain was full of pines, cedar, and Douglas fir— but with purposeful steps, there was only one specific pine tree that I was looking for. Dropping my flip-flops, I rubbed my hands along the thick tree trunk before me, feeling small pieces of bark peel away in my fingertips. Wrapping my arms around the trunk, I leaned back and hung my head, staring up at the intricate details above me. I loved how the branches grew out in circular patterns higher and higher, making perfect layers for climbing.

A cracking noise caught my attention from an indistinguishable area behind me. I whipped my head around and stood up straight. I listened for a minute, my eyes struggling to make sense of the shadows that leered behind the trees. Despite straining my vision, I could not see anything through the quiet darkness. Yet I felt certain that something was watching me.

If Nick is trying to scare me, he is going to regret it! I turned my back on the trees, remembering the cute brunette last seen in Nick's arms as I fled the dance. He wouldn't leave her for something so dumb.

But someone else might have followed me.

I felt a sudden urge to get off the ground. Bracing myself on the branches above my head, I pulled myself up. More cracking noises from behind me caught my attention, this time closer—like twigs snapping under pressure. I threw a wary glance over my shoulder, biting my lower lip, but the sounds were buried again in quiet eeriness. I blew out a breath of air, unaware that I had been holding it.

I tried to reassure myself that it was probably just an animal. But then I thought of the crazy motorcyclist from that rainy morning, and Brooke's fear of the strange guy watching her today at the festival.

What if it's him, out there right now?

Images of a dark-haired maniac raced in my mind. My speeding heart urged me upwards through the spiral of branches. I ignored the pull on my hair, where it snagged on twigs and flaking bark.

I climbed higher. Perspiration dampened my palms.

I felt a presence boring into the back of my head. There was no doubt now. Heavy, shallow breaths caught in my chest. I scrambled through the thicket of limbs. An instinctive fear fueled me upwards.

In my haste, my foot slipped off the next branch

as I reached for the one above my head with clammy hands. I lost all footing, swiping in vain for anything to grab onto. Gravity pulled me down, my back colliding with the branch below me. The propelling movement slammed the back of my head onto something solid as I continued my speedy descent.

In seconds, I hit the ground on my side, my thigh landing on top of a thick root jutting out of the ground. I tried to cry out, but my breath caught in my throat. My chest felt weighed down with pressure. Quick, shallow breaths were all I could manage, pinching pain racing along my back. Squeezing my eyes shut, I laid my head on the dry dirt beneath me. My right thigh throbbed right down to the bone. I laid a hand on it, gripping the muscle.

Someone approached me in hasty, heavy steps.

This is it. Please let it be quick, I pleaded in my mind. I kept my eyes closed, yet sensed a nearby presence.

A rough hand slid under the side of my face and an arm swept my legs around, moving me into a sitting position. My aching back rested against the tree trunk. I grunted in protest, sucking in more quick breaths, unable to convey how much I opposed moving any part of my body. I chanced opening my watering eyes.

A dark-haired young man stared back at me with striking gray eyes. His disheveled black hair hung just over his ears, matching the day or two of shadowed scruff framing his face. His mouth was closed tight, lips pressed against each other. Heavy eyebrows curved above his eyes, though at the moment, they were pinched together. I watched him scan my body from head toe, kneeling a mere foot from me. My face grimaced in discomfort.

"Try not to move," he said in a deep voice.

It took another minute for me to regain some control of my breathing. I forced slow, even breaths. Groaning once more, I adjusted my position. "You're the one—agh—that moved me," I accused, grumpiness settling in to replace my fear. Placing a hand on the back of my throbbing head, I winced at the sharp pain that coincided with my touch. "Who do you think you are, sneaking around in the dark? What are you, some kind of pervert?"

The young man continued to stare at me for a few moments with an amused look on his face.

Curious, I took the chance to examine him. He looked like he could be nineteen or twenty, wearing a fitted, solid blue T-shirt against his broad chest and thick arms. A hint of a tattoo was visible, black lettering not quite hidden under his left sleeve. Small tears spread along his faded blue jeans. Returning my eyes to his, I noticed the gray was tinted with a light blue, like those belonging to huskies. It was hard to tell with the stray strands of hair falling over his eyes and, with him staring back, my nerves got the better of me.

He spoke with a soft, low voice. "I think I liked it better when you were having a hard time breathing."

I glared back at him, daring him to say more. A hint of a smile deepened a small dimple in his right cheek.

"I'm sorry I scared you. That wasn't my intent," he said.

I tried moving again, feeling less resistance from my throbbing limbs. With hesitancy, I kicked out, testing the dead-leg in my right thigh. Frustrated at the embedded knot in my muscle, I scowled at him again. "Just what was your intent?" I inquired, blowing a strand of hair out of my own eyes. This time, he was the first to drop his gaze. In an instant, he stood to his feet.

"Come on," he said, approaching my side and throwing a strong arm under my shoulders. He paused, turning his head towards me so that our faces were inches apart. "Do you think you can stand up?"

His breath was warm as it touched my face. With his face so close to mine, a sudden shyness erupted with a flush of red throughout my cheeks.

"Uh—I'm fine. Just fine." I winced as I leaned forward, trying to get up on my own. The sudden sharpness returned and I sank back down, letting out a disgruntled huff. Succumbing to his aid, I leaned back against his steady arm, feeling his bicep tighten while he supported me to my feet.

"How do you feel?" he asked, keeping his arm under my own, though I didn't think it necessary.

"Like I just fell twelve feet out of a tree and was stomped on by an elephant in the process," I grumbled. I gave him a sideways glance and caught another small smile at his lips. "Oh, so this is funny now?" I snapped.

He paused, calculating the irritation on my face.

"No, I would not dare think one bit of this was funny. Now let's get you home." With a gentle push, he encouraged me to take a step.

"I can walk without your help." I released myself from his grip and stooped in quiet pain to retrieve my flip-flops from the ground. Taking a tentative step, I silenced a groan, feeling my body resist. Fortunate for me, stubbornness runs in my family and I leaned on it to carry me forward, my right leg limping in protest. I managed a few quick, short steps, trying my best to walk with dignity, when I heard a low chuckle behind me.

Apparently, I was failing in my efforts.

No sooner had I turned my head around, ready to battle him on his sense of humor, when I was swept up into the air by two strong arms.

"Hey! Put me down!"

With a full smile, he exposed his white teeth lined up next to each other, as his dimples teased me again. "With the pace you were making, you'll never make it back before sunrise."

Resisting the idea of being carried, I tried another tactic.

"You're not supposed to move someone who's fallen, you know. Everybody knows that. I could have a broken back or a broken neck—"

He cut me off. "Well, there's obviously nothing wrong with your mouth."

I fumed in resigned humiliation, though not before cursing at him under my breath. Breaking the awkward silence, I asked, "Who are you, anyway?" It was a few moments before he responded.

"Damien."

Neither of us said anything more on our trek back to the cabins. My thoughts remained focused on the strange circumstance I found myself in. Had this Damien been the one watching me, or had he seen me fall and decided to play the "good Samaritan"?

Tall lampposts ahead of us signified our approach to the cabins. Looking to the shore, I noticed the stage was still surrounded with quite a few people, hip-hop carrying through the air. I wondered if Brooke was still out there. Recalling Aaron's arms around her, I figured as much. We reached my doorstep.

"Ok, ok. Now put me down—please," I added. My efforts to hurry back onto my feet were less than graceful, and I stepped on his foot in the process. He grunted but made no comment. I had my hand on the doorknob, ready to flee inside. But I managed to pause and turn around.

"So, thanks, I guess, for helping me back to the cabin. I mean, it was sort of your fault I fell in the first place, with you spying on me and all. If that's indeed what you were doing. Because to be honest, I'm great at climbing trees, so there was no reason for me to—"

"Allie," Damien interrupted, taking a step towards me and closing the gap between us. I stopped my rambling, somewhat grateful for the disruption in my nervous speech, yet uneasy at the closeness of his body with mine. He looked down at me from the five or six inches that he towered over me, blue-gray eyes staring back.

Moments of silence passed. I swallowed.

He leaned his face close to mine.

"Good night." He paused, a breath away. Then he straightened and turned his back, heading east along the cabins.

It was only after the shadows of the evening masked his silhouetted form that I realized two things: I had not told him which cabin was mine, and I hadn't mentioned my name.

CHAPTER 5

"*A*llie! You have to tell me everything!"

Squinting awake, I felt someone plop down on my bed beside me, with a hand shaking my shoulder with earnestness. Brooke's blue eyes were wide and alert with excitement. I grabbed my cell phone off the nightstand, flipping it open to discover the time was just past seven AM. I rubbed my sleepy eyes.

"Brooke, what are you talking about?" I tightened the covers around my shoulder, curling up on my side.

She beamed at me and leaned closer, her voice just another pitch higher than usual. "I saw you last night! I was walking with Aaron when I saw you all wrapped up in that guy's arms. And wow, he's got big arms! Where were you hanging out last night after you left the dance?" She frowned. "And why didn't you invite me?"

Attempting to sit up, I let out a groan as every muscle in my back ached like a thousand bruises. I massaged my stiff neck. "I wasn't 'wrapped up' in his arms. At least, not how you're implying. Can you move?"

I gave her a nudge with my knee, and she bounced up off my bed. She crossed her arms across her chest, appearing skeptical while she studied my face. Flipping my comforter off me, I reached for my toes and exhaled in pain. I felt like a battered piñata.

"Holy cow! Look at the side of your leg!" Brooke, mouth open, was pointing to a four or five-inch splotchy surface that looked like spilled blue ink on my thigh. "And what's with that scratch along the side of your face? Don't worry," she said, pulling out her purse. "I always carry concealer with me. It won't even be noticeable." She dabbed her finger and reached for my face.

I stepped back, putting my hands up. "No, no! I don't need that. Can you just stop for a second?"

Brooke paused with a pout. She shrugged her small shoulders, returning the makeup to her purse. She crossed her arms again, rocking back on one heel, and stared at me with a frown.

"Ok, look," I said, pulling the chair around from the desk and sitting down. Brooke followed suite and plopped back down on my bed with her legs crossed under her. She leaned forward with a satisfied grin.

"So I went for a walk along the edge of the lake. You know, where the lake curves and there are all those trees on the hillside?"

She nodded, absorbing every detail.

"There's this great tree for climbing. It's a tree I've often sat in when I've needed to get away. But when I got there, I felt like someone was watching me, and I kind of got scared. So I started climbing the tree—"

Brooke's eyes widened. "He was spying on you!" she concluded. "Oh my gosh, that's so creepy! But wait—

why were you in his arms?"

I tried not to laugh at her childish excitement and even felt a little of it rub off on me, remembering the solid outline of his jaw, the intensity of his eyes...I shook my head and continued with my story.

"I was climbing too fast and I fell." I winced, just thinking about it. "And there he was, kneeling beside me...Then, even after I told him not to, he carried me home."

Brooke clasped her hands together, staring up at the ceiling. "Wow. And he is incredibly good-looking! So, did he ask about me?"

"Huh?" Her question threw me off guard. "And why would he ask about you?"

"Because," Brooke answered, running a manicured hand through her layered tresses. "That's him. That's the same guy I was telling you about. He's the one that I caught watching me at the festival. And since you were always with me, well, naturally he would go to you to find out more about me."

I cleared my throat, unsure how to proceed. "Well, uh, yeah. That—that makes some sense." I stood up, pretending to organize the miscellaneous items on my desk in no particular order.

"So..." she pressed, "What did you find out? What'd you tell him?" I was quiet for a moment before letting out a quick sigh.

"You know what, Brooke? He actually didn't ask anything about you. In fact, he didn't say more than a few sentences to me. All I know is his name's Damien."

I watched her reflection scowl in the mirror as I pulled my brunette hair into a high, messy ponytail as I often did. She hopped up, straightening her tank top.

"Well, he's probably just a weirdo anyway and not very interesting." She swung her purse over her arm and headed for the door, then threw her head over her shoulder. "The festival is closing tonight. Want to go look around one last time?"

I nodded and, without another word, she flounced out my door, long, blond hair swinging behind her.

The folk band was up on stage by late morning, filling the air with enthusiasm. A woman in blue jeans and tall, brown leather boots sang into the microphone, swaying her hips and tapping her foot to the rhythm. We came across a large, red tent, shadowed under the trees. In front of the tent, a table displayed itself with an array of silver and gold jewelry, each set with unique combinations of colorful gems and stones.

"These are beautiful!" Brooke cooed, holding up a v-cut bracelet with a wide, silver band. One large, oval sapphire was embedded at its center, with more tiny, blue gems decorating the band. Brooke hooked it onto her left wrist, admiring it with her slender arm held out.

"These look pricey," I murmured, scanning all the bracelets, necklaces, and rings. I held up a pair of silver, spiral earrings encrusted with green stones. Eying a mirror resting flat on the table, I held it up to my face. I shrieked at my reflection, catching a glimpse of a dark figure behind me. I dropped the mirror and spun around, my back pressing against the table's edge. Brooke jumped at my sudden movement, also twisting around in fright.

The Russian storyteller stood just a few feet from where we stood with racing hearts. She stepped towards us. "They are not so expensive," she emphasized, her Russian accent combing through her words. "Imitations. But very beautiful."

She caught sight of the mirror, now lying facedown at my feet. She frowned. I scrambled to pick it up. Turning it over, I caught my own reflection, split by the long crack down the center of the glass.

"I—I'm sorry," I stammered, offering her the broken mirror. "Uh, I can pay for it." I held it away at arm's length with trembling hands.

She put her hands up, shaking her head, not even looking at it. She turned her head to the left, and spat three times over her shoulder.

"Bad luck," she murmured, walking around the table. She stepped inside the open slits of her tent and disappeared inside, leaving me still holding the mirror. I raised my eyebrows at Brooke, who still appeared confused and startled.

"I thought that was an American superstition," she said.

I shrugged. "Well, we *are* in America...or maybe

it's a Russian thing, too." I jumped when a blond head popped out of the tent's opening.

"Come inside," the woman ordered, disappearing again behind the flaps.

Brooke and I exchanged a nervous glance.

"Quickly," her low voice called from within. I placed the broken mirror against the base of a tree. Brooke grabbed my hand and then pushed my shoulder, so that I led the way inside the red flaps.

The first thing I noticed was an overwhelming fragrance. The aroma burned the back of my throat as it traveled into my lungs. The suffocating smell made me cough several times. Soft music floated from the back of the room. It sounded like two guitars, one strumming at a quickened pace, while the other plucked away at a slow melody—a melody reminding me of carnival music, peculiar and intriguing.

Along the sides of the tent were a few short tabletops holding scented candles of varying sizes and colors. Deep reds, yellows, and orange. They all glowed, offering hallows of dim light to the remaining darkness. Next to the candles, bundles of dark-colored incense burned from within tall, porcelain vases. The combined fumes already made me dizzy.

In front of us, Alina hovered over a low, square table. "Sit down," she commanded, lowering herself to the ground and sitting cross-legged. Brooke and I obeyed. We watched her shuffle a black deck of cards, the backsides decorated with tiny, gold flecks and thin lines.

"We were just admiring your jewelry," I said, uneasy in the presence of this woman.

No response. Her long dress was dark today, a blackened-green cascading the length of her body, including her long arms. A faded yellow shawl hung across her shoulders, blending with her pale hair.

"I'm sorry I broke your mirror," I apologized again.

The woman met my eyes. "That is your problem. Not mine," she stated. She handed me the stack of cards. "Shuffle these seven times. Focus your mind."

Brooke's voice broke the silence, high and innocent. "We didn't actually come here for a—"

Alina jerked her head up at Brooke, silencing her with one look. Brooke closed her mouth, hunching her shoulders and leaning into me.

"Focus," Alina said again, her words directed at me. "Think about your life as it is right now."

The cards moved almost involuntarily in my hands, bending and mixing. Without even meaning to, my last year flew through my mind: Last summer here at the lake. Dad's remarriage. Nick and Clara. My life in Portland, running, always running. My mom's concerned face flashed through my mind. Here, at the cabin again. Resistance, reluctance. New friendships...

Alina removed the cards from my hands. I must have finished. She flipped the cards face up onto the red silk that covered the table's surface, placing them one at a time.

I counted the colorful cards that she laid out in

five rows. Small and square, they totaled twenty-five. In silence, Alina observed the pictured cards in front of her. I bent down for a closer look. Every card had four different images, with each image aligned along one edge. But the images were cut in half, so that only part of the image was visible. There were half-suns, half-trees, half-mountains, a half-clover...

"We must see which pictures we can make whole," Alina said, rotating the cards without moving them from their place. She turned the cards in a clockwise motion, seeing if she could align one image with a matching image of an adjacent card.

Minutes passed. Five pairs matched, forming five separate rectangles. In the center of each rectangle was now one solid, completed picture.

"Look here," Alina said, pointing to the first match. The completed picture was of a gray mountain with a blue backdrop, nestled on top of greenery. However, it was lying sideways from my point of view. "You must be careful," she explained. "The mountain in this position is a warning of physical harm or accident, but one that can be avoided if you take precaution."

Skeptical, I began to relax, deciding to play along with her game for now.

Next, she pointed to an old-fashioned scale with two gold baskets hanging from the post. The image was lying horizontal. "You are weighed down. You must find balance within yourself. Only then will you succeed in your life's pursuits."

I rolled my eyes at the generic statement. But I said nothing, deciding to suffer through the fortune-telling hoax in silence.

Third: A closed, black book with a gold binding facing my direction. "A secret. Something of importance is being hidden from you. Be wary of who you trust," Alina warned.

I caught Brooke watching me from the corner of my eye, but I suppressed the urge to look her way. My head starting to spin with the incense seeping into every pore of my body. Regardless, I followed the long, pointy, red fingernail that scraped across the cards.

A fourth match: A green, four-leaf clover with a short stem curling upwards.

At last, something positive.

Alina shook her head, staring at the picture longer than the others. "An upside-down clover...bad luck. Despair and unhappiness are likely to fall your way."

I frowned at the deceitful clover in front of me. The music in the background continued to play its eerie melody while I waited to hear my fate connected with the final card. I had to turn my head sideways again to grasp the image before me.

A brown, wooden bridge hovered over a blue surface, connecting two pieces of green land.

"Ah..." the woman's voice said. Her eyes gazed into mine with impossible understanding. My apprehension returned. Her low, raspy voice continued. "Your past returns, an emergence you must face! Do not shy away from it, for it will fight to consume you if not conquered."

I felt the silent tugging emanating from her presence, the same force from the night of the storytelling. But my obstinate nature was a force of its own, willing against her—a shield for my secrets tucked away in safety.

Her pull loosened and she spoke again, her voice hushed and urgent. "You *must* make that walk. Connect your past to your present." Her voice was even lower, a whisper that passed through my entire being. She traced the bridge with that long, red nail, emphasizing her next words. "Stop. Running."

Her fervent words shook me. I stared at her, unblinking, hardly breathing. The unwanted past crept into my thoughts, painful images relived in my memories. Shameful liquid filled my eyes, brimming full. I swallowed hard, shaking my head, slowly at first, and then with real desperation. The tears slipped over my lids, tumbling down my warm cheeks. My body shook without control, quivering against Brooke's hand that held my own.

I could see Brooke in my peripheral, despite the blur of tears. She looked back and forth between Alina and me, confused. She glared at the woman.

"That's enough!" Brooke stood up, yanking my arm and pulling me up with her. We bumped the table, sending an earthquake through the cards. We stormed out of the tent into the brilliant sunshine. We both shielded our eyes, grateful for the fresh air and natural light. Brooke marched us away, tromping across the dirt and brush. Lightheaded, I had no choice but to cling to her arm and follow.

"Wait!" Alina called, scurrying behind us. "Wait."

We paused, half-turned around.

Brooke fumed. "Can't you see you've upset her with your silly games?"

I didn't expect the protectiveness and anger that Brooke unleashed. She zipped open her purse and chucked a wad of cash at the woman's feet. "Here, take it! Is that what you want?"

Alina ignored the money. She reached for me and I flinched. The tips of her cold fingers touched my cheek before she spoke one last time. "You cannot hide." Her icy blue eyes bore into mine again, this time with a hint of sympathy amidst the intensity.

Brooke severed Alina's spellbinding gaze. She dragged me back towards the cabins, kicking the broken mirror to the side. Neither of us looked back, though we could feel Alina's penetrating gaze in the back of our heads.

CHAPTER 6

*T*owel, blanket, and novel in hand, I walked along the sandy shore, distancing myself from the crowds. I spotted Brooke, Nick, and Aaron zipping along the lake on their Jet Skis. No doubt they were racing. I could imagine Brooke squealing while holding onto Aaron, all disturbing thoughts of the mysterious fortune teller left behind. I hoped to do the same—just without getting in the water.

Alone, I reached my usual spot, not far from the curvy hillside where my favorite tree grew. Undressing to my swimsuit, I lathered myself in tanning lotion and flopped onto my blanket. I resumed my place in my novel, relishing in the warm sun on my back. My body relaxed under the heat, soothing my mind and body...

"Your back is burning," a deep voice informed me.

Startled awake, I rolled onto my side, peering up at the tall figure above me. It only took a moment to recognize the tousled, black hair, thick shoulders, and broad torso, and those blue-gray eyes matching my gaze. I sat up at once, grabbing my towel and holding it against my chest.

"What do you think you're doing?" I asked, unable

to mask my surprise. "Do you make it a habit to sneak up on everybody or just me in particular?"

"Do you make it a habit to be so defensive?" he countered in a calm voice. "Just trying to help you out. Your back's all red."

I placed a hand over my shoulder, fingers pressing against the warm skin of my back. I scratched the surface with one nail. Sure enough, the telltale mild sting warned of the first-degree burn that would present itself by the end of the day.

Fabulous. More pain.

"How long have you been standing there?" I asked, aware of the little material covering my body. I pulled my knees up to my chest, hugging them against myself. Straining my neck to look back up at him, I added, "And do you mind sitting down? It hurts my neck to look up at you."

Damien complied, sitting cross-legged in front of me. He watched me with a prolonged silence that made me uneasy. "Not long," he said, finally answering my question. He eyed my book. "What were you reading?"

I picked it up, flipping through the pages with my thumb. "Jane Eyre."

Damien made a face. "Well, I guess you can blame Charlotte Bronte for your sunburn. No wonder you fell asleep."

"Jane Eyre is a timeless classic!" I shook my head in protest. "Sure, it's not an easy read, which obviously explains your distaste, and it can be hard to get into...but how could anyone resist the romantic escapade between two unlikely lovers? It's full of passion, forbidden love, and—"

"It's no use," Damien said, cutting me off with a raised hand. "You will never convince me."

I shook my head in mock disappointment. "Well, refined taste in classic novels is not for everyone." I smiled at him, appreciating the dimpled expression he offered in return. "I assume you do something more exciting with your free time then?"

"I kill time driving around. That's how I found you, actually. I was just passing by and saw you lying there. Thought I'd make sure you didn't fall out of another tree."

I ignored his attempt at a joke. "Passing by? On what?"

Damien pointed about twenty feet behind me to an expensive looking, black and silver dirt bike resting on its kickstand. A black helmet hung from the handlebars.

I narrowed my eyes, the sight conjuring up a memory of that rainy day in the woods. My eyes widened with understanding. "It was you."

I leaped to my feet, dubious and wary. "You were the one chasing me on that bike in the rain."

He didn't move. I took a step backwards, glancing over my shoulders at the sunbathers in the distance. I whipped my head back around to study Damien. "My friend saw you following us at the festival yesterday. And that means you were probably spying on me last night when I fell out of the tree." I waited for his reaction.

Damien remained calm, which only irritated me.

"I have my reasons," he finally said.

I crossed my arms. "You better explain to me why you are stalking me before I call the cops. I highly doubt your 'reasons' will hold up in court."

Damien stood up, dusting off his shorts. "So you want a ride then?"

"What? Are you being serious right now?" I glared at his arrogance, looking back and forth between him and the bike. Despite my efforts *not* to be impressed, I couldn't help admiring its exterior. Its black sheathing on the silver body was sleek and shiny, and I could see the massive treads on the tires from here.

"Looks like a pricey toy," I managed to comment.

"It's a Honda CR 500." He must have noted the blank look on my face because he didn't elaborated. "It gets me around. And by the way, I wasn't chasing you."

Oh. So he *was* going to answer my questions. Unconvinced, I said, "Then what *were* you doing?"

"I was out for an early drive. I didn't expect it to rain so soon." He paused, as though waiting to see if I was going to argue with his response. When I said nothing, he continued. "I saw you by the river and you seemed upset. I drove over simply to check on you, but you took off. I only followed you to make sure you were ok."

"So at the festival when Brooke caught you watching us, you just happened to be browsing the very same areas?" I raised an eyebrow.

"It's not a big festival. People run into each other

all the time." Damien shrugged. "Maybe she was stalking *me*. Did you think of that?"

I let out a laugh, realizing that could very well be true. Not ready to admit I might have been wrong in my hasty accusations, I tried once more to defend my honor. "How did you know my name and where I lived?"

Damien's mouth opened, and a look I couldn't quite decipher passed over his face. But in an instant, it was gone, his expression smooth and composed. "Everyone knows who you are."

"What's that supposed to mea—?"

"Your family, I mean," he corrected. "All the locals know who you are. I was out by the lake when your dad was renting a boat the other day. The employees were saying how fortunate it is that James Collins is a dependable client and what a nice family he brings up every year." He paused before mumbling, "I can only assume they were including *you* in that comment."

I glowered at him. "Hey, I *am* nice." At least I used to be. The events of last summer seemed to be taking its toll on my usually friendly nature.

"Anyway," Damien continued, "I was curious and asked about your family."

"They're not really my family," I blurted out.

Damien appeared surprised by my choice of words.

"What I mean is, I live with my mom and twin sisters in Portland. I'm just out here vacationing with my dad. He married a year ago, so Clara is my stepmom and

Nick...I just have to deal with him until I head to college in the fall."

"How long's your vacation?" Damien asked.

I shrugged. "A month or so. My dad's an editor and a writer, so he's hoping to gain some inspiration for the new piece he's working on, or something like that. My sisters will be up here after their basketball camp finishes."

Damien motioned towards the lake. "Is your stepbrother the reason you're not out there with them?"

Again, he seemed to know too much about my agenda, but his question distracted me. "I just don't go into the water much," I mumbled, not seeing the trio on Jet Skis. I shielded my eyes with one hand.

"Kind of an odd place to vacation if you don't like being in the water."

I fidgeted, sensing where his next questions might lead. I never talked about Maddie and I wasn't about to start with a stranger.

Too perceptive for his own good, Damien asked, "So what happened?"

I narrowed my eyes, defenses rising once again. "Nothing!"

He raised his eyebrows at me.

Turning a heavy shade of pink at my swift response, I rubbed my temples with two hands while I gathered myself together.

Damien's expression blended between skepticism and curiosity. But instead of pursuing, he asked, "You have a headache?"

"Yes, actually, I do." That much I could answer without fibbing. "It's been hurting since I hit my head last night. You should remember. You were there."

Damien leaned his head to the side, catching sight of the large discoloration on my thigh from where I hit the tree root. His eyebrows creased together as he examined me, following the length of my body.

I shied away when he reached towards my face. His hand paused midair. But he persisted, touching his fingers against the side of my chin and softly turning my head, so he could see the long graze cutting across from cheekbone to jawline.

"You're a little banged up," he observed, tracing the scratch with a delicate gesture. His face eased towards mine for a closer look. I trembled while his finger glided along my face. Damien's hand hesitated by my mouth, his index finger resting on the corner of my lips.

I locked eyes with his, sure that my heart was beating audibly through my chest.

Damien seemed to be weighing something in his mind, his expression solemn. An almost-tangible silence expanded between us in the moments that he faltered. Then he pulled back his hand and looked away towards the lake.

I took a deep breath, clearing my throat. Scooting backwards, I distanced myself from him.

"I think your friends are looking for you," Damien said, breaking the awkwardness. He nodded in the direction of the cabins.

I twisted around and saw two familiar figures marching towards us, Brooke leading the way, just a step ahead of Aaron. She gave a frantic wave with her slender arm, and then turned to Aaron, pointing at Damien and me. Noting her spirited conversation, I could only imagine the notions she was conjuring in that vivacious head of hers.

When I turned around, Damien was jumping onto his dirt bike. I stood up and pulled my board shorts over my swimsuit. When I looked over at him again, he paused as we made eye contact for one long moment. Then, without another word, he kick-started the motor and sped away in the opposite direction, leaving a dusty trail in his wake.

CHAPTER 7

"Well, you're taking your time getting up today." Aaron's voice entered from the doorway, the smell of bacon drifting through the door. My stomach gurgled in response.

I sat up in bed as Aaron offered me a warm plate consisting of three strips of crispy bacon, two fried eggs, and buttered toast slathered in red jam. He placed a tall glass of orange juice on my nightstand.

"Wow. What's the occasion?" I asked. I crunched into the toast, spilling crumbs down my shirt. Aaron sat down beside my legs.

"No occasion. I can't take the credit for cooking it, though. Clara and your dad cooked together."

Dad helps cook now? Hmm. That's different.

"But," Aaron continued, "I did have to fight Nick off to save this plate for you. He said anyone who sleeps in past eleven doesn't deserve a breakfast like this."

I dropped my bacon. "What? It's after eleven?" I fumbled for my phone with my left hand, my right fingers too covered in bacon grease to be of any use. I checked the time. It was eleven-fifteen. I never slept in this late.

"Yeah, you even overslept *my* record, at least for this trip. And trust me; I'm a guy that likes my sleep." He assessed my features. "Rough night?"

In an instant, nightmares swamped my mind with images I didn't want, and memories I tried to hide. I remembered now. The first half of the night tortured me with its usual cruelty.

Aaron put a hand on my knee, leaning closer. "You ok, Allie? You don't look so good. No offense," he added.

"Um...I think I'm just coming down with something." I looked away. I didn't want to see whether he believed me or not.

"Well, it's a good day to be sick if there were any day to pick one. The weather channel says a cold front is coming through." Aaron patted my leg. "Your parents ditched out to do some shopping downtown. So the rest of us can all just hang out and play games or something. It'll be fun."

I felt like it was raining already. Spending an entire day cooped up with Nick around hardly sounded enticing, but I played along for Aaron's sake.

"Sure. That would be fun." I forced an encouraging smile.

"That's what I like to hear. Now, you better finish that entire plate or all breakfast-in-bed privileges just might be revoked." He winked at me with an attractive smile. He stood up, preparing to leave.

"Thanks for breakfast, Aaron." I waved at him as he exited my bedroom, his tall, lean figure barely passing under the doorframe unscathed.

"I'm here!" Brooke announced a few hours later, hanging up her wet umbrella. She was dressed in jeans and a tight, long-sleeved hoodie. She swung her hair, shaking off imaginary water droplets.

"Was it necessary to use an umbrella to walk over here?" I asked her with a contained smile.

She walked over to the dining table where the three of us sat, still running her fingers through her silky hair. "It's pouring outside!"

"Yeah, and it's a five-second walk from your cabin to ours," Nick chimed in.

She pushed out her lips. "Did you invite me over here to play games or to make fun of me?" She crossed her arms, standing at the edge of the table.

I laughed. "I'm sorry, Brooke. I was just teasing. I'm glad you're here." I patted the empty chair next to me. She sat down in a bit of a huff, and then scanned the game board.

"All right, what are we playing?"

"After ransacking the stash in the closet, we found a game called Hotels," Aaron informed her. She brightened when he looked at her. "It's an old board game, like Monopoly, but it's way better. You have to upgrade your purchased hotels to be as fancy as possible. That way you get more money when other players land on you."

We played for the next two hours, making it through a couple rounds of Hotels, and then started on a game of Clue. Just as I was deciphering whether it was

Mr. Plum, with the dagger, in the billiard room, Nick tried to cheat by lying about the cards he had in his hands. Something didn't add up and I caught on to his trickery.

"You can't withhold information," I complained, grabbing at his cards across the table.

He pulled away, shoving my hands back. "I'm not! I'm just playing the game." His dark eyes glared at me.

I was so sick of his attitude.

"You're cheating and that ruins the entire purpose of the game." I glared back at him.

"Hey, aren't we just trying to have some fun?" Aaron's attempt to mediate was futile.

"Don't look at me. Allie's the one ruining it for everyone, making a big deal out of nothing. But we all know that's just the way she does things," he added, his voice heavy with spite. "All the drama to be the center of attention." He stared me down.

My face flushed with anger. In my mind, I knew this discussion was worthless. But it wasn't about the game anymore.

"I don't like cheaters. They can't be trusted, for anything," I spat out.

"*I* can't be trusted? This is just a stupid game!" He threw down his cards, knocking game pieces all over the board. "You want to talk about trust? Hm. I wonder how your aunt and uncle must feel about that topic. I bet they're not going to trust *you* again. Oh, wait. From my understanding, they don't have anyone *left* to trust you with."

Nick's words sliced at my soul, and he knew it. His face was smug in comparison to my tortured expression.

My body shook but not with rage. With shame. A shame so painful my chest felt like it was being pierced from within. My eyes burned with tears that I refused to let fall.

Brooke reached a hand out to me, but I didn't wait. I shoved back my chair in one fast movement, bolting for the door.

"Nick, man, what is your problem?" Aaron's voice was the last I heard before the door slammed behind me.

The torment I felt could only be compared to the torrential rains that pounded on top of me. The cold front had released its fierce army, strong winds driving against me. My bare feet tore at the dirt, splashing through muddy puddles. I ran hard, plastered with incoherent thoughts and emotions. My lungs burned with the icy air, my heart heavy. I barely saw the trees that whipped past me in a blur. Swaying branches scraped across my face, tore at my clothing. I fell to my knees.

At last, I let out a strangled cry, a flood of tears mingling with the pummeling rain. The thunderous river shouted back, taunting and hateful.

"Maddie!" The throaty sob was mine. "I'm sorry! I'm so sorry." I shut my eyes tight, desperate to hold back the nightmares that remained my reality...

"Come on, Allie! Hurry up!"

"Madison, don't run off." I dodged a couple of trees, running after her while her blond waves of hair blew in the

wind. The gathering rain already made the ground slippery and unsteady. It was all I could do to keep up with her giggling, nine-year-old form. By the time I reached the river, Maddie was already stepping onto the rocks.

"Hey, get back here! Didn't you notice it's raining? We can't play here today. It's not safe!" I made a desperate attempt to snatch her arm, but that encouraged her to creep further out onto the large boulders sticking out above the current.

"You're going to get us both in trouble!" Despite my annoyance, a begrudged smile escaped at the liveliness of her blue eyes, the undefeatable laughter in her face.

Barefoot, I stepped into the water, already drenched from the downpour. "It's freezing!" I complained. The icy water sent chills through my body, a physical protest.

Maddie laughed at my failed attempt to catch her, two arm's lengths away. "How much do you want to bet that I can make it all the way across to the other side and back?" She asked me, judging the distance without fear, as she wiped the rain from her eyes.

My steps wobbled and I threw my arms out for balance. Maddie's motions mimicked mine, her steps becoming more hesitant from the middle of the river.

"Madison, get back here! The current is too strong." I had to yell to be heard over the sheets of rain and flowing water crashing against the rocks.

Maddie observed the rapid flow of the river beneath her. She frowned in admitted defeat. The wind swirled furiously, shaking the branches overhead. The rain continued to slice against our skin, pelting our faces heavily from the dark sky. She pivoted, taking a slow step towards me.

I leaned over, reaching my arm as far as I could. Our fingers were just inches apart. One more step. . .

In an instant, she slipped. Her knee slammed down under the water and I heard her cry out just before her body was swept into the water.

"Maddie!" I lunged back onto the embankment, sprinting alongside the river to keep sight of her. Her small body bobbed up and down in the water. She fought a fierce battle to keep her head up, but was sucked back down seconds later.

Frantic, I searched the river for my cousin. There, gripping a protruding boulder, I saw her, gasping for breath and struggling with all her might to hold onto the slippery surface. I grabbed a fallen branch, tugging hard to remove it from the thorny bush it had fallen into.

My body numb with cold and fear, I thrust the branch out, inches from within Maddie's reach. She swiped at it with one hand, straining to make the reach.

"Allie! Allie, please help me!" Her voice was withdrawn, choked with panic.

"Come on, Madison! You can do it! Just a little further!" The terrified, shrieking voice could not be mine.

Yet there we were, just the two of us.

I lay down on my stomach, desperate to close the gap. Maddie made a final, frantic dive. Her hands wrapped around the branch with a secure grip. Relief surged through me.

In that same moment, I leaned too far. My sudden

movement pitched me headfirst into the water. All rational thought was lost as my head submerged into the freezing water. When I came back up, I gasped for air. My empty hands flailed.

Maddie! Oh, Maddie!

I caught one last, fleeting glimpse of her, innocent blue eyes terrified, before she was dragged under once again, disappearing beneath the swirling surface...

CHAPTER 8

My body was lifted off the ground where I lay curled by the river's edge. Strong arms cradled me close, my eyes half-opened. Exhausted, my limp body did not resist. The rain had softened but the cold air lingered. My limbs felt numb, my clothing heavy and soaked all the way through. My teeth chattered inside my clenched jaw.

Within a minute, a warm voice spoke to me, still holding me against his chest. "Allie, I need you to sit up, ok?"

My mind felt as weary as my body. The words sounded a universe away, a soft hum that I struggled to understand. I didn't respond, but allowed him to adjust my body. My legs straddled the bike, a familiar black sheathing now splattered with mud. I slumped forward with sagging shoulders, my spinning head heavy and weighing me down.

Rough, yet gentle, hands cupped my face, lifting my jaw. My eyes struggled to focus...and then I froze in recognition.

Piercing, blue-gray eyes stared back into mine. A warmth of electricity jostled my body—a breath of life reviving my faded mind.

He released his hold, removing his black leather jacket, and pulled it around me. I slipped my arms into the dry sleeves, following his commands. Satisfied, Damien swung his leg over, now sitting in front of me. He tried to look at me over his shoulder, blinking rain out of his eyes.

"Can you hold on?"

I placed tentative hands on the sides of his wide torso. He put his hands on mine, pulling them closer together, wrapping my arms around his waist.

"You need to hold on tight," he ordered. It took a couple kicks to start the waterlogged motor. He revved the engine. The bike lurched forward out of the mud as we took off. I adjusted my grip, feeling my body slip backwards.

Driving parallel to the river, I laid my cheek against Damien's damp, cotton shirt. His back was warm, his body heat seeping through the thin material. I closed my eyes, feeling the tight muscles of his back against my face. I could hear his rapid heartbeat muffled through his clothes.

With the way we cut through the wind as we flew through the trees, time felt surreal in those moments. Were the cold not biting through my skin, I might have believed I was dreaming. But a dream like this was welcomed against my recent nightmares.

Damien pressed on the brake as we approached the wooden bridge. "We need to cross," he called over his shoulder.

His words sounded familiar, conjuring up a recent memory of colorful square cards laid out before me.

The red tent. The overwhelming fragrances.

And the fear. The hesitancy.

My eyes looked down at the rushing river below. I squeezed tighter against him, closing my eyes. Sensing my trepidation, he folded one hand into mine, his voice low and comforting. "Don't be afraid."

He waited until he felt me nod against his back. Then he drove across the bridge, crossing the arch at a slow speed.

We arrived at a small cabin. The construction on the outside seemed new; its smooth wood frame still intact with little chipping or weathering. Damien cut the ignition. I slipped off the back, while he locked the bike into place. My legs wobbled. In moments, Damien reached my side, securing me with one arm. We stepped through the doorway.

The interior was clean and simple in design. From the entrance, we stood in a comfortable living space. Directly ahead was a narrow kitchen with a small dining area. A bedroom filled the space next to the kitchen. To my left was a bathroom.

Finding my voice, I said, "Is this your home?" Damien led me to the long, leather couch and sat me down.

"No. But I live here." His distinction was clear with the sudden tartness of his voice. He walked to his bedroom, while I wondered about the change in his tone.

An involuntary shiver shook my body, reminding me of my saturated body. My sopping jeans left a trail of puddles from the doorway and continued to drip under my bare feet. Damien returned with a green towel and a handful of clothes. I accepted the thick towel, holding it against my face. I eyed the remaining clothes in his arms. He gestured towards me.

"It's not Nordstrom's or anything but it's warmer than what you have on."

Accepting the clothes, I murmured a thank you.

"You can use the bathroom right there," he said, pointing to the room beside me.

I hurried onto the cool tile floor, shutting the door behind me. I jumped in shock at the figure in the mirror.

Battered on the outside and broken within, I touched my reflection, watching the hand of the girl in agony reaching back. Her face was pale. Fresh scratches crisscrossed her face, almost masking one long, fading line stretching across the right side. Sorrowful green eyes gazed back, appearing darker with the dripping, wet strands along the sides of her face.

My face. *My* agony.

With a deep sigh, I stripped my clothes and observed the options Damien gave me. Throwing a red T-shirt over my head, it parachuted on top of me, reminding me of my favorite oversized pajama shirt at home. Slipping into the long, grey sweatpants, I experimented successfully with the drawstring. I gave up any efforts to tame the tangled layers framing my narrow face.

Abandoning my wet clothes, I opened the bathroom door and stepped across the wood flooring. The first thing I noticed was the glow of the fireplace, and then the large, steaming mug sitting on the coffee table. I looked over at the bedroom and stopped.

Through the door that lay ajar, I could see Damien. His black sweats appeared identical to mine, the back of his naked torso facing me. He slipped his arms into a long-sleeved, white thermal. Something about his back caught my eye. A darkened, discolored patch of skin covered from one shoulder blade to the other, though it was hard to distinguish next to his tanned skin. He finished pulling the thermal all the way over his long upper body before I could make out the distortions. Grabbing another T-shirt off the bed, he turned around. He stopped short, catching me watching him.

I turned away, but my eyes darted back to where he stood, pulling a short-sleeved gray T-shirt over his head. Damien met my gaze. Searching my face, he moved towards me. I noticed that the baggy sweats fit him just right, and the tight shirt outlined his upper body and the curve of his biceps.

"Oh, so is that how it's supposed to look?" I said to him, attempting to cover up my unease. "Somehow, I don't think I pull it off as well as you do." I threw my hands along my body, modeling my voluminous attire in jest.

He couldn't help but laugh a deep, low chuckle. His dimple accompanied his grin as he sat down beside me. "The shirt doesn't look bad on you." He eyed me up and down again. "The pants could use a little work though."

He motioned to the steaming mug on the table. "Go ahead. Drink up."

I cupped the heated mug, my fingers tingling as the heat seeped through them. I took a sip of sweet chocolate. Swallowing, I enjoyed the warm sensation that traveled down my throat, spreading throughout my chest, and then to the rest of my body. I sighed in contentment, leaning back into the leather couch. I noticed Damien watching me, empty-handed.

"Where's your drink?"

He shook his head, his expression serious. "I'm not the one who tried to drown myself in the rain."

Pausing mid-sip, I looked down into the brown murkiness of my drink. Somehow, it was not as appealing as it was moments ago. Pulling my knees up, I cradled the mug close to my chest. My fingers tapped the top of the porcelain, stalling.

"Will you tell me what happened?" he asked.

He wasn't asking if I *wanted* to tell him, but asking would I. They were two very different things.

It was silent for a couple minutes after that, neither of us saying or doing anything. Just sitting— Damien with his persistent inquiry, and me with my unyielding privacy.

I put the mug down and turned to face him, taking in his defined, dark eyebrows and the cut outline of his jaw. "I don't even know who you are."

He studied my face, observing me with his calm confidence. "But do you trust me?"

My mouth opened in surprise, taken aback by his question. How could I trust him when I barely knew him? Haunting words floated into my mind—Alina Ivanova's voice low, eerie, and so penetrable that I could almost smell the incense.

"Be careful who you trust..."

A brief moment of fear breached my emotions, tapping my senses. And yet an indiscernible force drew me towards him, summoning me.

"Something happened up here last summer. I've never really talked to anyone about it." I stared into the safety of his eyes, and he willed me to continue, securing me in his gaze. He gave a brief nod.

"Every two years or so, my dad's side plans a family reunion. My dad has two older brothers and a younger sister, Aunt Heidi. She's always been my favorite. And her nine-year-old daughter and I—we were close." The past tense pained my face.

"Maddie loved the river. We both did. Any chance we had, we'd run over there. We always took our shoes off at the same place, right next to this giant pine tree. We used to race each other to the river to see who could get across the fastest without falling in. It didn't matter that I was seven years older. She loved competition more than anyone I know." I gave a quiet laugh in bitter remembrance, followed by a sorrowful sigh.

Damien waited with patience while I wrestled with my emotions, preparing to voice details I'd never shared.

"It was our last afternoon at Hidden Pines, so, of course, we were playing in the trees. We were told to be home by dinner, especially since it had been storming the last couple of days. We lost track of time and it started raining again. Maddie ran to the river, wanting to cross one more time before we had to leave. I chased after her.

"She tried crossing the rocks to the other side of the river. And then it all happened in a split second. She slipped. The river was rushing fast, the current so much stronger that year." My voice picked up in pitch and speed, recalling the final moments with Maddie, aloud for the first time since that day.

"I—I tried to save her. Her hands were on the branch and all I needed to do was pull her in. But I fell. She was right there and I let her go!" The helpless tears that I thought were dried up resurfaced with the memory, cascading down my cheeks. I threw my hands over my face, hiding my shame, my guilt.

Damien circled me in his arms, pulling my head against his warm chest. He let me cry. He didn't hush me when I wailed with a grief so heavy I felt I was sinking in the river all over again. My body shook against him. My sobs tore at the wall I had built to barricade myself from my emotions—pain, misery, guilt, shame, sorrow, love—

until the floodgates were lifted, and I released them all on Damien.

At last, my cries subdued. All that was left was an occasional shuddering breath as I inhaled. Damien stroked my hair, his fingers brushing across the side of my face. I felt safe in his arms.

But tired. I was so tired.

He didn't move when I spoke again, my voice low and calm.

"I should have drowned, too. But someone saved me that day." My eyes met his with bewilderment. "Pulled me right out of the water. I don't remember much after that. I awoke in the hospital. My dad and sisters were there, and Aunt Heidi. I couldn't look at her, couldn't tell any of them what exactly happened, but of course, they knew. They found Maddie's body the next morning."

Sitting up, I rubbed my face and my burning eyes. Embarrassed, I focused on the puddle of tears that had absorbed into his shirt.

"I'm sorry that happened to you. Nobody should have to lose family like that," Damien said.

Silence carried us a minute more. My thoughts seemed to etch visibly in my face. With uncanny understanding, Damien concluded, "You think it's your fault."

Slowly, I nodded my head. "Everyone says it's not—that it was just a bad combination of an early spring and the rain that made the river run so fast that day. Everyone tried to tell me it was just an accident. And, of course, it was—just an accident. But it could have been prevented. I was supposed to be looking out for her. I should have stopped her, or at least saved her like I could have." I muttered the last words, looking down at my fingertips.

"You ever talk to anybody about it?" Damien asked.

I jerked my head up. "What, like a shrink?" I was more than a little offended at his words. My mom had hinted in the past that I go see somebody. My unwillingness to talk about the "incident" had her worried—it had *everybody* worried. I clammed up anytime they tried to pry into the details of that day. What else did they need to know? Maddie fell in and I couldn't save her. There was nothing more to it. And I didn't need anybody playing the sympathy card with me, or trying to get into my head, including the relentless school counselor.

Damien remained calm at the sudden flare in my eyes. "I didn't mean a psychiatrist or anything. I just meant your family. Or friends."

"No. I didn't see what good it would do. Only one thing seemed to help me, at least temporarily."

"What was that?"

"Running." I thought back to my senior year and the blur that became its memory. "Back in Portland, that's all I did. I was supposed to return to the varsity basketball team. We were expected to have a great season that year. And they still did, but without me. I just didn't care about it anymore. It all seemed so trivial. All the practice and emotional investment over winning or losing a game—who cares, you know? None of that matters." I shrugged my shoulders. "It's just high school, right? One necessary, tedious step towards college."

"That's one way of looking at it, I suppose." Damien was careful with his answer. He seemed hesitant to say everything that was on his mind. It was just as well. I wasn't sure I wanted to hear it, especially if it sounded anything like what my parents and school counselors tried lecturing me about.

"What is it about running you like so much?" he asked, after my silence.

I let out a sigh, reflecting on the sound of my sneakers pounding against the pavement, the wave of trees rushing by as I moved along the dirt trail, the fleeting ability to shut my mind off from relentless memories...

"It's peaceful," I answered. "I could just be myself without having to worry about being analyzed by all the curious faces around me. No probing eyes or listening ears trying to figure out if I was "ok" or not. No forced conversation. And it helped me sleep."

I met Damien's pensive gaze. He was judging me. And why shouldn't he, after everything I had just told him? I felt anxiety creeping up on me, followed by bewilderment. *Why did I just tell him all of that?*

Something occurred to me.

"Why were you there today? At the river?" It seemed more than coincidental how often his path was crossing with mine.

Damien sat up, turning towards me. He pinched his lips together before answering. "I was in the area. I heard your friends outside calling your name."

Brooke and Aaron had been looking for me.

"They seemed worried. I drove by the blond girl. She was pretty freaked out and said she didn't know where you were—that you had a fight with your stepbrother and ran off. I told her I thought I knew where you were and that I would take care of you."

Gesturing towards my cooling hot chocolate, he added, "I'd like to think I'm keeping my word." He stood up, putting a subtle end to our conversation.

I took my time rising to my feet, standing inches away from him. I cranked my neck to look up at him. My physical and emotional exhaustion seemed to remove my inhibition. With caution, I asked, "Damien, why...how did you know where I was?"

I waited for him to reveal something more— something from his own pocket of secrets. He didn't answer. Instead, he stared back, his expression careful.

Without reserve, I stepped into him, slipping my hands under both layers of shirts. He closed his eyes as they slid up along his sides. I could feel his body tense beneath my fingers. I felt the wide muscles of his lats, my hands ascending along his body with purpose. I reached the upper portion of his back.

He flinched, eyes open. But he didn't move away and I didn't stop. I allowed the sensors of my fingers to explore the skin all along his back. While smooth at the base, the texture changed right behind the top of his ribs and up to the base of his neck. The layer of skin felt worn and damaged.

I remembered what I'd seen when he was changing his shirt—that discolored area of skin that stood out against the smooth tan of his back.

Damien's hands seized my wrists. He met my imploring eyes.

No questions, his eyes seemed to say.

He pushed my hands down, my fingers sliding all the way down his back. He filled my hands with his.

I leaned my cheek into the small crevice between his pecks.

"Seems like you have some secrets of your own." My voice was tranquil and even, but I felt Damien stiffen against me.

He bent down, putting the side of his face against my cheek. I closed my eyes, feeling my body quiver in response. His mouth rested by my ear, his lips touching my lobe when he spoke.

"Time to get you home."

CHAPTER 9

*amien left me on the doorstep of my cabin, holding a plastic bag full of my damp clothing. *You'll be ok now*, he had said, driving off before I opened the door.

Would I?

I rubbed my heavy eyes with a deep sigh. The emotions of sharing such a personal experience from my life had taken a lot out of me. I wasn't used to opening up to people, and especially not to strange guys who showed up at random times during my vacation. How was it that Damien could draw that much out of me?

I shook my head, perplexed. Taking a deep breath, I twisted the doorknob and stepped inside.

"Allie! Allie, you're ok!" Brooke leaped at me from the couch, throwing her arms around my neck. Aaron hurried beside her, concern and relief on his face. Brooke glanced out the door at Damien's retreating figure. She whispered into my ear, "You better believe I want details." She gave me a meaningful look, followed by a wide, giddy show of her pearly teeth. "I have to go. Call me later!"

Dad pushed past them, two firm hands on my shoulders.

"Allison, do you know how worried we've been? Clara and I returned home, only to find out you've been missing for two hours. And in the pouring rain, of all things. We were about to call the police." He noticed the scratches on my face and my oversized attire. "What happened to you?"

I looked into the living room, where Nick slouched in the corner of the couch. I pursed my lips, not even knowing where to begin. I pushed Dad's arms off my shoulders, hurrying towards my room. "I just needed some time alone."

I entered the safety of my bedroom, turning to close the door. I jumped, seeing Dad's arm clutching the doorframe.

"We need to talk." He stood there, immobilized, waiting for a response, or maybe for me to back up and let him in. The tone of his voice made me feel like a child again. A feeling of dread wound around me like a spool of thread. Panic tightened in my chest, anticipating the subject of discussion. I couldn't do it twice in one day. And not with him.

I spun around and sat on my bed. "Talk? Now you want to talk? What have you been doing for the last four years, Dad? You and I—we do not talk. Sorry, but you happened to miss an important time in my life when I was learning how to do that! And I shouldn't have to apologize. *You* left *us!*"

My breaths heaved in my chest. I was shocked at the natural emergence of my anger—not feigned, as

I intended. I could feel it fighting its way out. The bitter resentment escaped my mouth as I continued. "And all for a selfish summer fling with some other woman."

I looked away, unable to face the hurt in his eyes, and not allowing him to see the pain in mine. It took another minute before he walked over to my bed. He hesitated before sitting beside me.

"Allie, would you look at me, please?" His tone was softer, no doubt displacing his own pain for the time being.

I was ashamed for losing the battle inside myself but still wary. Complying, I looked up. He reached out, then thought better of it and pulled back. He was silent for a minute, while I turned away again.

"I know you're going through a hard time. I expected this would be hard for you. And this time, I'm not just talking about getting to know Nick and Clara. I haven't forgotten what happened the last time we were here."

Of course not. How could anyone? My hands fidgeted.

"I know you haven't forgotten either. I see it on your face every day. You're hurting. That's actually a large part of why I brought you up here."

My eyes flashed over to his face. He reached out again, this time placing a tentative hand on mine.

"Your mom—well, all of us—have been really worried that you haven't talked to anyone about what happened. She said you spend most of your free time running by yourself and that you don't hang out with your friends much, or even talk on the phone. It's not healthy, Allie. The...therapist that Aunt Heidi is seeing suggested bringing you back to the scene where it all happened... with Maddie." He paused, perhaps testing my reaction to her name, or maybe because I was glowering at him.

I threw his hand off mine. The words that came out of my mouth were shrill. "Is that your idea of a sick joke? Just to throw me back into the scene of the crime so I can feel like a murderer all over again?"

Dad put his hands up. "Allie, it wasn't supposed to happen this way. We had a plan. We were letting you get comfortable up here first. We hoped you would get used to being around water again and make some new friends. The therapist emphasized helping you socialize again by creating a support group. And we're lucky that's working out so well, even better than I could have hoped. This therapist is scheduled to come up in a couple of weeks, and we were going to help you through the healing process together. Sort of an intervention—"

"An intervention? What, like I'm some lab rat you're experimenting with, seeing how much you could poke and prod me until I open up and spill my soul? And socialize..."

My eyes shot towards the door, remembering my new friend who was always around, always supportive. Realization and understanding cleared my head. It had been too easy. Angry betrayal lit up my face. "So, is Brooke in on this too? Just a personal chess piece as part of your ploy to help me 'get comfortable'? How much are you paying her, Dad? How dare you? How dare you!" I jumped off the bed and stormed out my bedroom door. I almost ran into Aaron, who was coming down the hall.

"Whoa! Allie, you all right?"

Another convenient ally.

I dodged past him, marching out the front door, and banging it shut behind me for the second time that day.

It was dim outside. The overcast clouds still shaded the early-evening light. Fuming, I tromped towards the outdoor court. It was quiet and empty. I grabbed a basketball lying against the wall, used and forgotten. I dribbled, the hollow thumping filling the still void in the air.

Who do they think they are? An intervention...Some know-it-all therapist...

I took a sloppy shot. The ball hit the backboard and bounced back towards me.

I thought of Brooke and Aaron, saddened by the artificial friendships.

Traitors! How could I be so naïve?

Another angry shot missed the backboard, the ball arching and hitting the ground with a useless thud. I scowled, walking to retrieve my ball, while hiking up the long, gray sweats that unrolled at my ankles. I stopped in my tracks, a sudden wave of nausea hitting the pit of my stomach. My thoughts turned towards Damien, sickened with total comprehension.

He was in on it, too. I thought of the compassion in his eyes, the warmth and tenderness of his skin on mine...

None of it was real. It was all part of this heartless scheme to help me 'open up'. It made sense now. *Of course*, he knew where I was by the river. And I trusted him. Told him everything.

"Try this one," a voice called, interrupting my heartbreaking epiphany.

I looked to the side, catching an orange blur in my hands.

"Nice reflexes," Aaron said, walking over to me. I squeezed the ball between my hands with a wary expression. I glared at him, shoving the ball as hard as I could at his chest.

He caught it with ease but looked at me in surprise. "Wow, what's with the hostility?" His expression melded into concern.

He was a very good actor.

They just won't give up, will they?

He bounced the ball to me. I stood there facing him, maintaining my glare. It didn't seem to faze him.

"Well, are you going to shoot it or just hold onto it?" he asked, looking to the hoop with anticipation.

Annoyed at his persistance, I let out a huff of air. I dribbled three times and took a third shot. The ball arched, falling with a satisfying swoosh through the net.

"There you go. See, I heard you could play. You just need to lighten up a bit." Aaron jogged to the hoop and picked up the ball. "What's with the silent treatment?"

Disappointment infiltrated my wall of anger. I longed for these relationships to be more than a strategic means to explore my past. I sat down cross-legged on the cool cement, sinking inside Damien's clothes.

I shut my eyes. The thought of him made me sigh.

"I want to know what's real," I said. Confused images drifted through my mind, reflecting on the events of these past couple of weeks. I felt a hand on my knee, and opened my eyes as Aaron sat down beside me. He waited.

"I want to know if you and Brooke are my friends or if...you're just a part of this ridiculous ruse to...I don't know what. I don't know what my dad expects me to get out of being here again. You can't change the past or just make it go away. No matter how much you want to."

Aaron was quiet in thought for a minute. Then he popped up to his feet, extending his right hand towards me. "Come on. We're going to play a game."

"What?" His response took me by surprise, but I clasped my hand around his and allowed him to pull me to my feet.

He picked up the basketball. "What do you say about a short game of 'PIG'? You start." He handed me the ball.

"Ok," I agreed with hesitancy, not positive I understood his intentions. I stood at the top of the key and threw the ball with a small hop. It fell through the net. Aaron retrieved the ball and mimicked my shot from where I stood. It hit the top of the rim and repelled away.

"All right. So I have a "P". And you get to ask me a question." He collected the ball while I stood there in thought.

I pondered my earlier statement.

I want to know what's real. I looked back at him. "Why would any friend of Nick's bother being nice to me?"

"Ah. Easy one," he responded. "Well, considering the awful picture Nick painted of you before we met, you turned out to be a pretty cool girl."

I grimaced, wondering what kinds of things Nick had said. What a rat!

"I think Nick has a skewed version of who you are in that thick head of his. He's a tough one to get to know. I mean, if I didn't grow up with the kid, I wouldn't like him either." Aaron laughed in thought. "Our first couple of months in the dorm, he got in more fights than anyone. He's bullheaded and opinionated, all of which you already know, I'm sure. But I'll tell you one thing. When Nick's on your side, he makes one loyal sidekick."

Ignoring the skepticism in my face, Aaron continued.

"So, to answer the question behind your question: No, I did not know anything about the, err...intervention idea. Neither did Brooke. How we treat you has nothing to do with it. We are not "chess pieces", as you put it."

I blushed, realizing with no surprise that he had heard me yelling at Dad. But I was flooded with relief, grateful that perhaps my new friendships might be genuine after all. Maybe even with Damien.

"All right. Take another shot," he said, rolling the ball into my hands.

I slid along the key, closer to the net. My angle was off and the ball rebounded. I shrugged. "Can't get 'em every time, right?" I picked up the ball and tossed it to Aaron.

He dribbled a couple of times, paused, and then gave me a sly smile. He sprinted towards the hoop, leaped into the air, and slam-dunked the ball. He hung onto the rim for a second longer, letting out a loud whoop. When he landed, he ambled back over with playful arrogance, to where I stood with my arms crossed.

"Do you really think that's fair?" I asked, sizing up my five-foot-seven height beneath his towering form.

"Hey, I didn't say we were going to play fair. You're up, little one." He laughed when I scoffed at him.

Oh, boy.

I pulled up against the baggy sweats, making space for my bare feet to touch the ground. I made a dash towards the hoop, preparing to thrust myself into the air. My pathetic efforts were squashed when I tripped on the sagging material underneath me. I staggered, catching my fall with quick footsteps before I lost the ball. I watched it roll away, letting out a loud laugh, despite myself. Behind me, I could hear I wasn't the only one that was entertained.

"Yeah, like you didn't see that one coming," I

accused.

"Hey, anything to see you smile again," he countered with a grin. "So, my first question: Who is the fool that supplied your supersized wardrobe?"

He tugged at my shirt, holding up a loose sleeve with distaste. "Or were you once a member of Jenny Craig? Because no offense, you look like a thug."

"Well, it's all he had, so I sported it the best I could," I said. "Not too shabby in my opinion."

Aaron's face was serious. "Yeah. Now that we're on the subject, who is that guy anyway?"

I sensed the mild criticism in his tone. "His name's Damien. He took me to his place to get a change of clothes and warm up. I sort of got drenched sitting in the rain."

"You went to his place? Do you even know this guy?" His alarmed tone caught my attention. "Allie, you shouldn't just take off with random guys. It's not safe." He shook his head at me again. "It's obvious you didn't grow up with a big brother. If you were my sister, you can bet I'd be keeping a closer eye on you."

"Well, I'm not your sister so you can just back off, ok? I've met him before. It's not like we're complete strangers." I didn't know why I felt so protective but I didn't apologize. I didn't need someone else trying to play the missing dad or older brother role in my life.

"Look, all I'm saying is you can't blame me for worrying. I saw him talking to Brooke while we were out looking for you. Let's be honest—he doesn't exactly look like your average boy scout. You need to be careful who you trust these days. It would make *me* feel better, anyway," Aaron concluded.

His words rang familiarly in my mind. That was twice in one day that the Russian woman's words were brought to my remembrance. I tried to shake her memory away.

"Let's just play, ok? How about a little game of one-on-one?"

With a disapproving sigh, he agreed. "You're on."

CHAPTER 10

*A*t 8:30 the next morning, my alarm sounded. I rolled over and turned off my phone. With limited service throughout Hidden Pines, it wasn't good for much else, though we did get some reception in parts of our cabin. My body moaned in response to the sudden movement. With a long stretch, I pulled back my curtain, squinting out towards the lake. The sun shone, no longer shielded behind a mass of clouds. It sprinkled its light across the water, even making the lake seem somewhat appealing to me again.

A blond head popped behind the glass of my window. I jumped back with a muffled yelp, dropping the curtain in my surprise.

"Allie! Allie, open the window!" a soprano voice called, followed by rapid tapping against the glass.

I threw the curtains open, revealing Brooke leaning against the windowsill. Releasing the latch, I slid the window to the side, allowing in a fresh breeze of air.

"Thanks for scaring me half to death," I chided. "How are you?"

"Well, I was going to ask you the same thing. After yesterday's ordeal, I thought I'd give you a little space—

space meaning less than twenty-four hours, of course. But Aaron did fill me in with some details. I'm glad you know I'm not a spy for your dad or anything. That would just be weird! Besides, I don't think I could keep a secret for that long. Oh, unless *you* wanted me to keep a secret. Then I totally would."

She paused to catch a breath. "So," she continued, with failing nonchalance, "Anything new lately?"

I watched her struggle to keep the casual expression of disinterest on her face. Unable to maintain a straight face myself, I sputtered a laugh. She broke down.

"Oh, ok fine. You know I'm dying to know the details! Move over!" I stepped to the side as she clambered into my room, jumping to wedge her small form through the window. I offered her a hand so she wouldn't fall on her face, and then I gave her a rundown of yesterday afternoon's events: Damien rescuing me from beside the river, driving to his cabin, wearing his clothes...

"Then I saw him changing in his room," I told her. When Brooke's eyes widened, I was quick to clarify, "No, not like that! He had sweats on but no shirt. I think he has some kind of scar on his back. It was a darker color and the texture felt different. I think he's—"

"Whoa, whoa, whoa. Hold on. I think you flew over a significant portion of your story. *Felt different?* You had your hands on his naked back??"

Brooke's mouth opened with disbelief, followed by a mischievous smile. "He kissed you, didn't he?"

My blushing cheeks took me by surprise. "Well, no. He—"

"But you want him to," Brooke concluded, nodding her head in satisfaction.

"Brooke!"

"Ok, ok. Sorry. It's just exciting, that's all."

"Nothing even happened," I protested.

Nothing, except that I shared intimate details about my life—details that I refused to share with anyone else.

But I wasn't about to tell Brooke that. It was hard enough yesterday. I waved a hand at her. "So don't get your hopes up for a juicy story. I don't even know if I'll see him again."

Brooke looked confused. "Why wouldn't you?"

I opened my palms with a shrug. "I don't know. The better question would be why *would* I see him again? I don't have any reason to; although, I'm sure he wants his clothes back."

Brooke made a derisive noise. "He made an effort to find you yesterday. I think that means *something*."

"Yeah, or he was just being nice," I argued. "It was a one-time thing, which is all the better because what am I supposed to do with a, uh..." I faltered with my words.

Brooke chimed right in. "A summer fling?" Her smile teased me. "Why *not* enjoy a summer fling?"

My mouth opened and closed with indecision. "Because—it's just—there's no point in them! Why waste time and emotion on something that's not going to last? People are so ridiculous about those kinds of things."

Brooke's jaw dropped. "So you think I'm ridiculous?"

"What? I didn't say that."

"Yes, that's exactly what you're saying! Because *I'm* not opposed to such things. I think it's all part of the fun and learning experience of dating. You'll never know what can happen if you don't give it a try."

I shook my head at her in disbelief. "Yeah, I know what happens: you love, laugh, break up, cry, and in the end, realize once again that it's not worth it."

Brooke looked out the window in disgust, while I folded my arms with resolution.

"Huh." Brooke leaned closer to the window as she peered through it. Satisfied, she continued, "Well, I guess you better explain your theory to yesterday's hero." She smirked at me.

"Uh, what are you talking ab—" My jaw dropped. Not twenty-five feet away was a familiar looking dirt bike. Straddling it, Damien leaned into his handlebars as he watched Brooke and me.

I gasped, yanking the curtains closed. I ran a startled hand through my unkempt hair, widening my eyes at Brooke. The corners of her mouth twitched with hidden laughter.

"Looks like he wants his clothes back sooner than you thought."

Through a gap in the curtains, I eyed Damien with uncertainty. He lifted his hand in greeting with an even expression. I jumped back again, out of his view.

"There, you see? He just waved at you. Now go out there and talk to him. I, on the other hand, am going to go back home—through the front door this time—and think about how jealous I am of you right now." She smacked my behind. "Go get 'em, tiger."

Brooke pranced out of the room while I rubbed my lips together. After a moment, I braved another peek out the window. Damien ambled towards me, wearing jeans and some kind of snug, motorbike jersey, which outlined his body. I cast a self-conscious glance behind me at my mirror, wishing I was a little more put together, but there was nothing I could do about my appearance. Resigned, I pulled the curtains open all the way.

Tugging down on my cotton shorts, I wrapped my arms around my baggy athletic shirt. I shifted back and forth on my feet, waiting for Damien to finish his stroll to my window.

Damien folded his arms across the windowsill. Recalling my bold encounter with him yesterday, a ripple of shyness swept over me. A trace of a smile developed on his lips.

"Hi." His warm voice tickled my stomach, and I resisted squirming.

"Um, hi." I looked over my shoulder at a plastic bag at the foot of my bed, hurrying over to pick it up. Walking back over to Damien, I handed him the bag. "Here. Thanks again for your clothes."

I dangled it in front him. He didn't take the bag.

"That's not what I came for."

"Oh." I put the bag on the bedside table. Baffled, I asked, "Well, what do you want?"

"Come with me. I want to take you somewhere."

Suspicious, I crossed my arms across my chest again, letting my natural defenses override my timidity. "Is it routine for you to show up at girl's windows and make demands? What makes you think I want to go with you?"

Damien leaned further into my window, drumming his fingers against the desk. He stopped and stared back at me with confidence. "Because—you'll regret it if you don't."

"Hmm. Well, I'm not ready to go anywhere right now."

"You don't need much. Throw on some pants and a T-shirt and you're all set. I'll wait for you in the parking lot." He turned his back and took his time walking back to his bike.

I stared after him. When he didn't turn around, I slid my window shut and pulled the curtains closed again, wavering.

I could refuse to go...and sit in the cabin wondering all day where he wanted to take me. Or, I could go and see for myself, eliminating any and all questions that my curiosity would otherwise torture me about.

I chewed on the inside of my cheek—a bad habit I was trying to break. Coming to a decision, I brushed my teeth, changed my clothes, ran a brush through my hair, and added just a touch of eye makeup. I blew out a nervous breath of air as I looked at myself in the mirror. With a light shrug, I walked out my bedroom door.

"Hey, nice to see you up, Allie," Dad greeted from where he sat on the couch. He was flipping through a magazine with a bowl of cereal on his lap. "You uh… feeling ok?"

By that, I knew he wondered if I was still mad at him about yesterday. I sort of was. I still hated the idea that he had planned on forcing a therapist on me and had his own plans for how to "cure me."

But with other things on my mind, I responded with, "Yeah, better anyway." Dad looked relieved.

Clara smiled at me. "Where you off to today?"

I rummaged through the kitchen cupboard for a granola bar. "Me? Oh, nowhere. Maybe just for a walk or something."

"If you get up just an hour earlier, you could come walking with me in the mornings," Clara offered, as she had already suggested a couple times this week. "I'd still love the company."

I nodded my head, noting the hint of hope in her voice. "Ok. Yeah, maybe I'll do that another day." I tore my granola package open and choked it down, followed by a small glass of milk.

"You seem like you're in a hurry," Dad commented, lifting up his reading glasses. "You sure you're ok?"

"Mm-hmm." I dumped out my remaining milk. "Yup. Just trying to get a start on the day." I moved to the couch to put on my running shoes.

"Well, you're doing better than the boys. They're still sleeping, as far as I know. I think they stayed up late playing video games. Oh, don't forget to check in with your mom later today. She'll be expecting a phone call now and then."

Shoes tied, I nodded my head. Mom wasn't crazy about me spending a chunk of summer away from her, with me leaving for Fresno State at the end of August. Dad had to work hard to convince her that I needed time with Clara and Nick—that, and time for his lame intervention idea. (No one bothered to weigh in *my* opinion on the matter.) I gave a brief wave. "Ok. I'll see you guys later." With that, I stepped out the door and into the fresh summer air.

I threw a tentative look towards the parking lot. A high-pitched motor revved to life. Damien drove the bike in a circle before he came barreling towards me. A tiny glimpse of the first time I saw him played in my mind.

Breaking abruptly, he stopped a couple feet from where I stood. Damien removed the thick, black helmet from his lap.

"Here. Put this on."

I took the helmet from his outreached hand, holding it in my own. "Do you always wear this?"

"No. But *you* have to. Go ahead and put it on."

I plopped the helmet over my head, almost drowning inside.

"It's a little big," Damien said. "But it'll do." His

97

gloved hand grabbed mine and pulled me towards the bike. "I believe you've ridden this once before."

Blushing, I swung my leg over the seat, locking myself behind Damien. He revved the engine once more, waiting for me to get situated. Unsure what to do with my hands I let my fingertips pinch the sides of Damien's shirt.

Damien placed his hands on mine and pulled them around his waist. "What'd I tell you about holding on?"

The engine roared, and the bike lurched forward. I gasped in surprise, squeezing my torso against him. I thought I felt Damien chuckle through his abs.

We charged through the canyon, flying around curves. The wind tore at our clothes and tossed the ends of my hair. I felt almost buoyant as we shred through the wind, not caring that we were surpassing the speed limit. I smiled, relinquishing myself to the feeling of freedom.

Too soon, Damien slowed the bike, pulling onto a dirt road. Leaving a cloudy trail behind us, I held on tightly as the path gradually inclined.

"You really need to hold on!" he called over his shoulder. I could feel my body slipping backwards, reminding me that the seat really wasn't intended for two. I clung onto Damien as we ascended up the trail. He leaned forward to control the jolting bike. Finally, the trail evened out and I could see some man-made jumps ahead.

Pulling up beside the jumps, Damien let the bike

idle, while I pulled the helmet off my head. I shook out my hair.

"Wow," I breathed. "Not a bad drive."

Damien smile, as though satisfied. "The real fun is the jumps," he explained, eyeing the ramps.

"So you're pretty good then?" I asked, a little wary of where this may lead.

"No, not really. These jumps aren't that big. They just take some practice."

I looked at the run. The highest ramp was about four feet. It looked scary enough to me. "Well, let's see you in action then." I slid off the back, handing the helmet back to Damien. He pulled it over his head before revving up the engine once again. He drove back the way we came, rotating around so he faced the ramps.

Damien kicked the motor into full gear. The bike sped along the flat part of the trail, speeding towards the first and smallest ramp. He easily popped over the jump. I held my breath as he rushed towards the next ones, landing each one effortlessly.

When he finished, he pulled up beside me, handing me his helmet. "You want to drive?"

I envisioned myself spinning out of control and crashing with zero grace. Adamantly, I shook my head. "No. No, I don't think so." I'd already had an emotional meltdown in front of Damien. I didn't need him to see me in a physical wreck, as well.

Damien laughed at my apprehension. "Here, give it a try. I'll help you." He slid back on the seat. Ignoring the sounds of my protest, he wrapped an arm around my waist, pulling me close. "Come on, sit in front."

I obviously had no choice in the matter. Tentatively, I threw my leg over the bike. Lightly placing my hands on the handlebars, I tested the rubbery texture. I felt Damien lean in behind me. He put his arms around me with his hands resting on top of mine. He squeezed my hands into a tight fist around the bars.

"Feel that? You need to have a firm grip on it, or you're going to lose control. You got the break right there." He tapped the lever along the right handlebar. "You know how to drive a stick?"

I shook my head. "I know it's sad, but I rely on automatics. Someone tried to teach me once, but it was a disastrous failure."

"Ok, that's not a problem," Damien said. I was aware of the closeness of his face to mine. I could feel the scratchiness of his day-old scruff scratching lightly against my cheek. I tried to focus on what he was saying, but the proximity of his body was distracting.

"We'll just keep it in first gear," Damien continued. "You ready?"

"I guess so," I said. Damien removed the helmet from his lap and slid it over my head.

"*Now* you're ready," he corrected. "Ok, she's all yours. Just gently pull back on the throttle and give it a little gas."

I twisted my right hand delicately, and the bike slowly gained momentum, shaking awkwardly while I tried to find balance.

"Don't be afraid to give it just a little more."

I overestimated the rotation of my wrist. The bike heaved forward unexpectedly.

"Whoa!" The handlebars wobbled in my grip. Damien, still holding on, easily compensated for my mistake.

"Sorry!" I said. "I told you I'm no good at this."

"Just keep going," Damien encouraged.

Nervous, I took a deep breath and then tried again. In moments, we were riding smoothly once more at a slow, even speed. Damien removed his hands from the handlebar and placed them along my sides. His hands pressed more firmly around my waist.

With growing confidence, I pulled back on the throttle. I laughed aloud, enjoying the acceleration. The cool air felt crisp against my skin. Silently, I noted the contrasting warmth of Damien's body against my back.

The morning passed by too quickly, and my stomach's low growl gave the time away. Not wanting to sound overeager, I didn't resist when Damien offered to drive me home.

Pulling into the lodge parking lot, I slid off the back.

"So, was it worth it?" he asked, wiping a hand across my cheek.

I could feel dust caked on my face and embedded in the cracks of my lips from our drive through the dirt trails. "Absolutely. Thanks for the ride and the lesson.

I'm glad I didn't wreck your bike or anything." I cringed, envisioning the almost-crash that ensued. Glancing behind me, I was startled to see Nick staring at me from a short distance away. He seemed to be returning from the lake and headed to the cabin, but now he watched me with what appeared to be critical curiosity.

"I better go," I said to Damien. "Oh wait. Let me get your clothes for you." I turned towards my cabin to retrieve the plastic bag, but Damien grabbed my forearm.

"Keep them for now. I'll get them next time."

I made a mental note of the words *next time*. "Ok," I said, retrieving my arm from his hold. "Thanks. So, I'll see you around then?"

Damien released an attractive smile, but he didn't answer. Instead, he put the helmet over his head, revved the engine, and spun his bike around. I watched him drive off with an uncertain smile on my face.

Nick was leaning against the side of our cabin, watching me. I squinted at him as I approached.

"What are you up to?" I asked, noting the scrutiny in his eyes. I hoped my cheeks didn't look as flushed as they felt.

"Should I be asking you the same thing?"

I folded my arms. "Now, why would you say that?"

Nick ran a hand through his brown hair, looking over my shoulder at the parking lot. "Oh, no reason."

I stared back at him for another moment. "All right. Well, I'm just going to go shower then." I started to walk past him to our front door.

"I wonder though," Nick's voice sounded behind me. I stopped in my tracks, noting the familiar callousness to his tone.

"What would your dad say if he knew his little girl was riding around on a motorcycle with a strange, older guy? And from what Aaron tells me—a guy that took you to his private cabin yesterday. What could be going on there?"

I spun around. "What do you care? Just mind your own business, Nick!"

"Oh. Found a sensitive spot, have I?"

"*What* is your problem? Why are you trying to cause trouble?"

Nick put his hands up in innocence. "Me? Cause trouble? I'm just trying to work on my role as a good older brother. I'm sure our parents would be quite pleased with my efforts."

I gritted my teeth together and lowered my voice. "How many times do I have to tell you? You are *not*, nor will you *ever* be, any brother of mine."

CHAPTER 11

"So, you're giving up?" Aaron asked.

Having threatened Nick to stay out of my way, and with Brooke working the day shift, it was just the two of us walking through the path of trees. I scrunched my eyebrows, not liking the mild hint of criticism in his voice.

"Nick's a jerk. He goes out of his way to make life difficult for me, and we barely know each other."

"Well, do you ever think that's *why* you both give each other a hard time? That maybe it'd be easier if you did get to know each other?"

Disbelief caught in my throat. "Oh, please. Now you sound like my dad, who wants everything to be just peachy, simply because *he* decided to get married again." I threw the question back at Aaron. "Did you ever think that I *am* getting to know Nick, and *that's* why I don't like him? Makes sense to me."

Aaron was looking at the ground as we walked, keeping his thoughts to himself for the moment.

"Why do you care, anyway?" I asked. "No offense, but it's not any of your business."

Aaron sighed. "Because—Nick is my best friend.

We've been friends since the seventh grade. Just because I'm a guy, doesn't mean I don't care about my friends' feelings."

"That's what I don't get," I interjected. "How did someone like you become friends with a grumpy kid like him?" For a full minute, the only sounds between Aaron and I were the crunching of pine needles beneath our feet.

"Nick's had it a little tough growing up," Aaron started. "You know much about it?"

"Just that his dad left him and Clara when he was little."

Aaron explained further. "When Nick showed up in seventh grade as a new kid, he didn't make the easiest transition. He was bad tempered and an easy target for some of the guys. Then he got himself into worse trouble. But once I got him to hang out with me after school playing sports and stuff, he turned around ok. And we became good friends from then on."

"What kind of trouble are you talking about?" I asked, my curiosity getting the better of me. Aaron shrugged.

"Why don't you ask him about it some time? Might give you something to talk about."

"Ha. Or fight about," I corrected. "Never mind. Basically, you're saying he has a sob story and I should be more sympathetic."

Aaron stopped walking. I took another step or two before I turned around.

"What?" I asked, noting the disapproval in his eyes.

Aaron looked confused. "You know, for someone that seems to have a sob story of her own, I'd expect a little more compassion or something."

I tried to bury the small mound of guilt growing inside me. "Yeah, well, maybe you should tell your boy the same thing. He's not winning any awards of empathy these days either. But to be honest, I don't think either of us cares about you playing the mediator between us, so you may as well stop wasting your time and energy. We'll survive the summer and then it'll be months before I need to worry about seeing him again."

Aaron looked at me with disappointment. "So that's it, huh? You're not even going to make an effort?"

I sighed, hating the way I felt, but unable to stop myself from continuing. "Some relationships are not worth the effort." I stared down at the ground, scraping at the dirt with the bottom of my flip-flop. I didn't dare look up at Aaron, and I wasn't sure he was still there.

But behind me, I could hear a motor growing louder as it approached. My stomach fluttered as I turned around towards the river. In the distance, I could see a figure approaching on a black and silver dirt bike.

"Is that him?" Aaron asked, moving to stand beside me. I could detect a shadowed hint of discontentment in his voice. I didn't answer. Instead, I watched Damien drive across the bridge and pull up alongside the river. Rather than approach us any closer, he waited and watched us from fifty feet away, without saying a word. The motor of his bike continued to drone, while Damien's eyes beckoned.

I took a step towards him, but Aaron grabbed my left arm.

"Allie, what are you doing?"

I looked up at Aaron in surprise. "I think he wants to talk to me."

"What—he doesn't have the decency to come over here to you? And why is he just looking over here like that?"

I met Damien's eyes, flushing as I noted the intensity of his gaze. "I don't know. I'm going to go talk to him, ok?" I didn't wait for a response, taking a few hesitant steps towards him.

"Allie—"Aaron began again, his voice a little more cross. "Remember what we talked about?"

"Remember how I said I didn't need a big brother?" I countered, without turning around. "It'll be fine." I continued to walk to Damien. His dark features were daunting at times and I felt self-conscious knowing Aaron was examining our interaction. At last, I stood just a foot away from Damien. He still didn't say anything, though his eyes didn't stray from my face.

"Hi," I started. "What are you doing over here?"

Damien leaned back on his seat. "I came to get you." His eyes flickered towards Aaron. "That guy isn't going to have a problem, is he?"

I looked over my shoulder at Aaron, who hadn't

moved, except to cross his arms across his chest. His blue eyes glared over at us.

"No. We were just talking but...that conversation is over."

Damien handed me his helmet and I accepted it with two hands.

"So where are we going today?" I asked.

"Hop on and see." Damien revved the engine and scooted as close as he could towards the handlebars.

"Always one for mystery," I murmured, but I slipped the helmet over my head, enjoying the excitement of uncertainty. I slid behind Damien, wrapping my arms around his waist. With a swift pull of the throttle, the bike took off. I took one second to look back at Aaron's thoroughly disgruntled face. A moment of guilt passed through me. Still, I couldn't help but smile as I wrapped my arms tighter around Damien's torso.

Neither of us spoke over the wind and roaring engine. Instead, we whipped over the bridge and through the trees, coasting next to the eastern shoreline of the lake.

Damien and I stood beside the water, surrounded by trees and a couple of solitary cabins in the distance. Across the water, I could just make out our cabin and the busy shore full of sunbathers and children playing on the water edges, as well as the usual Jet Skis.

"So what are we doing out here?" I asked.

"Does there need to be a detailed program? Because I can go home and create a brochure if you want."

I laughed. "No, but it seems like you have something in mind, even though you're trying to hide it."

"All right," he admitted. "I might have something in mind." He grabbed my hand and led me towards the water. I was so distracted by the feel of his warm fingers wrapped around mine that I didn't notice where he was taking me, but when we stopped moving, I realized that we were standing beside a canoe tethered to a tiny dock.

I pulled my hand away, staring at the canoe with a guarded expression. I looked over at Damien, who awaited my reaction.

"We're not going out on that, are we?" my small voice managed to say. I felt the habitual response from my body—my muscles tensed and my breathing became shallower. I could almost feel the ground becoming shaky beneath me.

"Why not?" Damien asked, grabbing my hand again and stepping into the canoe. I pulled my hand away.

"You know perfectly well why not," I stated with irritation, digging my heels into the ground.

"I didn't say we're getting in the water," Damien explained. "We'll just stay in the canoe. I promise I won't tip us over."

"There's no guarantee in that," I argued. "Canoes are unstable and can't be trusted."

Damien laughed. "Well, people say the same thing about me but here you are."

I opened and closed my mouth, struggling with a defense. Aaron's disapproving expression resurfaced to my mind. For a moment, I wondered why I resisted heeding his warnings.

"See, you got nothing. Come on over here," Damien coaxed. He moved to the rear of the canoe, bracing his arms along the edges. Heaving a sigh of frustration, I took a step into the canoe. The boat trembled beneath me and I stepped back.

"It'll be ok, Allie," Damien said. "I won't let it tip over. Do you believe me?"

I shook my head. "It's out of your control. You can't make promises like that because you can't control what the lake or people around us are going to do, or something *I* might do that would prove otherwise."

"Well, then you're just going to have to take a risk then, aren't you?"

Risk.

Something about his word choice made me hesitate further, but with nothing left to back up my argument, I put another foot into the canoe, bending over to hold onto the edges. The canoe rocked back and forth, threatening to tip. I slipped my other leg inside and turned around on the bench so my back was facing Damien.

"Ok, grab your paddle," Damien instructed. I stuck it in the water while Damien untied the rope. He pushed the canoe off the dock. We glided along the smooth water with the initial wobbling ceasing, but the further we ventured from shore, the more anxious I became. This felt worse than the other day on the speedboat. I didn't like being so low to the water, vulnerable to the waves that rippled our way from the motors in the distance.

Damien's voice broke the silence. "So, is that guy a potential boyfriend?"

I laughed out loud. "Hardly. He's a friend of my stepbrother, who likes to pretend he has to look out for me. He has a bunch of younger sisters and seems to think it's his duty."

"He seemed a little more concerned than the brother-type."

I looked over my shoulder. "Well, he's not. He's sort of into my friend Brooke. Although, I think he's into just about any girl that walks across his path, but don't tell *her* that. He's just kind of like that." I laughed again. "And so is she when it comes to guys, so I suppose they're perfect for each other?"

Damien didn't comment, but I could tell there was something on his mind. Wasn't there always? And I never seemed able to pry it out of him.

"What about you?" I asked. I turned around in my seat so I was facing him, laying the paddle across the canoe. Damien seemed wary.

"What *about* me?" He stroked his paddle through the water to keep our momentum.

"You haven't told me anything about yourself. I've seen you enough times that you'd think I'd know something about you. But I don't. Including why you keep showing up."

Damien seemed taken aback by my statement.

"Why I keep *showing up*? I didn't realize that was in question."

I was thrown off by the way his eyes ran across my face but, for some reason, it only added to my sudden crankiness. "Well, it is, actually. I feel like you have some secret agenda to carry out, like you're hiding something."

Damien shook his head, his eyebrows pinched together. With thinning composure, he asked, "What do you want me to say?"

"I want you to know more about you. You know more personal details about recent events in my life than even my own family knows. Yet, any time I ask you something about yourself, I get stonewalled. Why is that?"

Damien put his own paddle down in the canoe. "I'm just kind of a private person. I don't like to talk about myself."

"And you think *I* do?" I folded my arms. "That's not a fair answer."

"It's a little complicated."

"Whose life *isn't* complicated?" I retorted. "I can't figure you out. For example, why would you bring me out here in a canoe, especially after I told you I hate the water?"

Thinking about it again, I gauged our distance from the shore. If the canoe sank right now, it was a long swim back to dry land.

An instant wave of panic hit me. My hands jerked to hold onto the edge of the canoe and my abrupt movement knocked my paddle into the water. Making a swift grab for it, I rocked the canoe back and forth. I gasped as I almost fell overboard.

"Hey, calm down," Damien said. "Don't worry, I'll get it." I let him retrieve it for me, accepting the wet handle he passed my way. Embarrassed by my reaction, my irritation grew.

"And you thought I'd like this *why*?" I asked, not bothering to help row us any further. Damien laid down his paddle.

"You're a bit of a grump when you're nervous, did you know that?"

I ignored his insult.

"And I didn't say you'd like it."

Exasperation spilled out of my mouth. "Then why'd you bring me here, Damien? Why did you even show up today?"

"Are you about to the pull the 'stalker' card again?" Damien's stern voice was a new development. His demeanor changed. "You want the truth? I was just trying to get you alone."

His words startled me for a moment. His low voice sent a tremor up my spine.

Aaron's concerned face came to mind again, his eyes narrowed and worried. I swallowed, not daring to look into Damien's own eyes.

Looking around, I felt an overwhelming sense of helplessness. I was stuck in a canoe in the middle of a deep lake, with no one around us. And nobody knew where Damien had taken me.

"You seem worried," he said.

"I'm not worried. I just don't like the water and you know that." My throat tightened, making breathing more difficult. What kind of person would know those intimate details and still bring me here? It was insensitive and mean.

"Take me back. Take me back now," I said, my voice rising.

Damien's expression was calm. He didn't make a move. I turned my back on him and thrust my paddle into the lake, pulling against the water, but I couldn't turn the canoe myself.

He was in control.

I glared at him. "Help me row back to shore. Right now."

"I don't understand. What's the matter?" Damien said. "I just meant I wanted to spend some time with you."

"Why?"

Damien thought for a moment. "You intrigue me."

"Intrigue you? So, what—I'm a source of entertainment?" I frowned at the hint of amusement in his expression. "Is it fun for you to watch me squirm or something? You're sick, you know that?" The swelling panic rose up my throat. I battled it with anger. "I want to go home."

I couldn't read the thoughts behind Damien's darkened eyes, but he nodded. "Ok, Allie. I'll take you back, *if* that's what you want."

I nodded.

I couldn't shake the anxiety. Instinct told me something wasn't right. Whatever the reason, all I knew was that I wanted to be back on dry land, and back in the safety of my cabin.

Damien did as I asked. And neither of us spoke another word as he drove me back. When we passed the river and drove through the trees, I tugged on his shirt. "You can drop me off here." Damien slowed down but didn't stop.

"I can take you all the way back to the cabins. It's not a problem."

"No, that's ok. I can walk from here."

"Are you sure?"

"It's *fine*."

Damien pulled on the brakes. I hopped off and removed the helmet, handing it to Damien without looking at him.

"Thanks," I muttered. Without looking back, I strutted off towards the cabins, feeling Damien's eyes following me.

An hour later, I was sitting on the porch, still feeling confused and grouchy. Even *I* could recognize the reoccurring theme in my emotions, but I couldn't explain them or make them go away.

The door behind me opened. Aaron stepped out, pausing as he looked down at me.

"Hi." I looked back down at my fingernails. Aaron

took a step down and sat beside me.

"What happened to *you*?" he asked, leaning his forearms on his knees. Despite his words, there was little concern in his voice. More apparent was a shade of contempt.

"First, I see you gallivanting away with your mysterious motorcycle-riding hero, and now here you are looking depressed."

I met his gaze with a tentative raise of my head. "I'm sorry I ditched out on you like that. I don't know what I was thinking. But that was rude of me and I'm sorry."

Aaron shrugged. "Hey, I can understand. He's a handsome fella, I suppose. I'd probably ditch out on me, too. Maybe. It'd be a pretty close call."

I smiled at him, sensing his humor returning.

"You want to talk about what happened?"

"I don't know." I made a face. "That's just it. Nothing happened. I just got a little freaked out. All he did was take me in a canoe. But I got nervous, and wasn't sure if it was because of him or you know, 'cause of my phobia and all."

Aaron pieced his words together with care. "You know, Allie, people get those feelings for a reason. And you should listen to those. Personally, I don't trust the guy. Just the way he looks at you is creepy. And, while I didn't say anything to your dad, I'm pretty sure he wouldn't be thrilled about you hanging out with someone like *Mr. Mysterious* either. He just looks like bad news."

"Great," I commented with my dampened mood. "Now *you* sound like Nick, too."

"But it's out of concern, not spite or trying to get you in trouble," Aaron explained. "There are a lot of weirdoes out there, Allie. I mean, do you even know anything about him?"

"Mmm..." I bit my lip. "That's somewhat why I got upset. I've told him a lot about *me*. He doesn't say much about himself."

Aaron raised his eyebrows, letting me think about that one for myself.

"Ok, I get your point," I said. "But I guess that's in part what makes him exciting."

"And likely dangerous," Aaron added. "Will you just do me a favor and listen to your instincts?"

"But how do I know my instincts aren't tainted? That I'm not just screwing things up because of my crazy emotions?"

"I can't answer that for you," Aaron said. "But just trust yourself."

Trust myself. I hadn't wanted to do that in a very long time.

CHAPTER 12

Hiding behind a tree, I held my breath. My eyes peered through the foliage, searching for the flag. I smiled to myself. Despite my initial reluctance to play Capture the Flag, Brooke was right. It was a nice break from juggling my emotions about Damien.

I could see two teenage boys hovering within a fifteen-foot perimeter of a scraggily shrub.

Dead giveaway.

I jumped from tree to tree, hiding from their distracted view. Finally, I sprinted towards the shrub. My fingers fumbled around as I made a grab for the flag.

"Hey! She's got the flag!"

I took off towards the boundary line, sidestepping a lanky, blond girl. I heard frantic scurrying behind me. Too far behind me. Satisfied, I leaped over a fallen tree, a mere fifty feet from victory. Nothing like winning a game to ease my troubled mind.

Someone slammed into my side and knocked me to the ground. The flag slipped from my grasp. I grunted as my body made contact with the solid dirt beneath me. My bare arms grazed along the ground, opening fresh abrasions.

"Ow!" I searched for whoever had assaulted me and scowled.

Nick rose to his feet, dusting himself off. "Got ya."

I placed a delicate hand on my knee. Having taken the impact of my fall, I knew the swelling wasn't too far behind.

"Nick, are you for real? This is *tag*, not tackle!"

"Oh, don't be such a girl," he said, crossing his arms as he looked down at me. "I thought you could handle it. Considering how much your dad brags about you being some all-star athlete, I assumed you'd be tougher. My mistake, I guess."

"A simple apology would be nice. It's just a game. You didn't need to attack me."

"Boo-hoo, Allie. You look fine to me. Don't be such a poor sport."

I stood to my feet, testing the weight on my knee. I grimaced. "You know what, Nick? I don't need to deal with your ridiculous attitude."

"Oh. Now *that's* funny. You're talking to me about *my* attitude? Take a look in the mirror, Allie."

I stared back at him. "What are you talking about?"

"What am I talk—are you serious? From the moment we got in the car to drive up here, you've been nothing but self-absorbed in your own pity party. Ok, so that sucks what happened up here with your cousin. I get that. But you're so stuck in your "poor me" attitude that you can't even see how you're affecting anyone else."

My jaw dropped. Nick continued his rant,

ignoring the circling group of curious onlookers.

"This trip isn't supposed to be all about you, Allie. But you've made it that way from the start. You're oblivious to anyone else. Take my mom, for instance. It's obvious that she wants a relationship with you. But you won't give her the time of day."

My body was still. My voice monotone. "I have nothing against your mom."

Nick threw up his hands. "It's not what you've done to her. It's that you don't care. Personally, I'm not interested in the two of *us* getting along. But I know it's important to my mom that she gets to know you, for reasons I can't understand. But I love my mom. So when your indifference hurts her, yeah, that's gonna upset me."

I opened and closed my mouth, but no words formed. I wanted to tell him he was wrong. But I couldn't. Because I could see some truth in what he was saying. I *was* focused on myself: my feelings, my fears. And I was pushing everyone away.

Aaron stepped towards us, placing a hand on Nick's shoulder. "Come on, buddy. Let it go for now. This isn't the place for this conversation."

Nick shrugged him off, unconcerned about the crowd. He stared me down, waiting for my rebuttal.

But I had nothing to say. For once, maybe Nick was right. I walked back to the cabin alone.

I looked at my row of letters: T, M, J, E, Z, R, Y. What could I spell with those? I tapped my finger on the table in thought.

"You're taking for-ev-er."

I ignored Nick as I studied the scrabble board. Inspiration hit me. I picked up the letters J, E, and R. Borrowing the K from "RAKE", Clara's previous word, I placed my letters on the edge of the board. The word "JERK" stared back at me.

"Thanks for the tip. Couldn't have thought of it without you. Your turn."

Nick rolled his eyes. "Whatever..."

"All right, knock it off, you two," Dad said from across the table. He and Clara exchanged a look.

"The board game was your guys' idea, not ours," Nick said, placing his next word.

A rapping noise caught our attention. Brooke threw open the door with enthusiasm, looking as though she was trying to hide her glee.

"Hi," she said from the doorway, hesitating as she met our faces. "Um, Allie? Can I talk to you for a minute?" I wondered if anyone else caught the hint of urgency in her expression.

"Yeah, sure," I said, scooting backwards in my chair.

"You better hurry." Dad examined the letters in front of him, while rubbing his chin. "I'm going to have a good one by the time you get back."

Brooke motioned me to hurry. No sooner was I

at her side than she grabbed hold of my forearm and tugged me out the door.

"She'll be just a minute!" Brooke managed to call back into the cabin before she pulled the door shut. That left the two of us standing on my doorstep.

"What's up, Brooke?" I asked, folding my arms against the chill of the evening.

Her eyes widened as she prepared for her explanation. "It's Damien. I have a message for you."

I looked at her in confusion. "What are you talking about? When did you see Damien?" He hadn't come around for a couple of days now. But I didn't blame him after how I reacted on the canoe.

"Just now. I was out by the lodge clubhouse and there he was, walking towards me."

"And?"

"He wants to see you."

My nerves twisted inside, combining apprehension and excitement. But how could I talk to him after what happened?

Brooke seemed to sense me faltering. She grabbed my wrists. "If you could just see the way he was asking about you; how he can't stand to be away from you...

"That doesn't sound like him."

Brooke squirmed. "Ok, I might have made that up. The guy doesn't say much. But if he did, I'm sure that's what he would *like* to say!"

"You're unbelievable."

"Thanks." She smiled. "So, have I convinced you

to give him just one more chance?"

"Brooke, why do you care so much?"

"*Because*...this whole thing with Maddie—" She hesitated when she saw me flinch. She quickened her words. "Ok, it's not my business and I don't know all the details, but it doesn't take an expert to know you're too hard on yourself. And there's just something about this guy that seems good for you. You come back looking a little...brighter, I suppose."

I chewed on my lower lip, fighting indecision. "All right," I agreed. "Where am I supposed to meet him?"

Brooke clapped her hands. "He said he'd wait by the tree—you know, the one you fell out of the night you met him?" She laughed while I made a face.

"Ok, yeah, yeah. I remember. Oh, wait. What am I supposed to tell *them*?" I gestured towards the door. I was sure Dad couldn't wait to show me the word he'd come up with.

Brooke moved my hand from the doorknob. "I'll take care of it. Get going!"

Stepping with uncertainty, I walked towards the lake, moving to the cluster of trees I had not returned to since the night I met him. My footsteps slowed when I approached my tree, but I didn't see Damien. Maybe he'd changed his mind.

Stepping up to the trunk, I placed a tentative hand along the bark. I glanced through the quiet darkness for any sign of his presence.

No one was there.

With a sigh, I looked up through the branches. Familiar and safe, I knew I would find comfort within them. With a quick heave, I launched myself up through the tree, rising higher and higher through the branches. My bare arms chafed against the bark, and I ignored the slight throbbing from my right knee, reminding me of last night's altercation with Nick. Frowning at the thought, I came to rest on a thick, solid branch. I straddled it with my legs. Wrapping my arms around the trunk, I rested my forehead against it.

It was twenty-four hours later and I still didn't know why I cared so much about what Nick thought of me. It's not like I had any respect for the guy. Why would anything he said linger on my mind? Yet, last night I laid in bed with my mind repeating his cutting words over and over again.

With a sigh, I looked down at the quiet lake and the empty shoreline. The water lapped against itself, nudged by the cool breeze skating by.

"Allie."

His voice startled me. I looked below the branches. Damien was standing at the base of the tree, his hands resting on the limbs above his head. He peered up at me. The full branches shadowed his features, darkening his defined brows.

I held my breath, hoping he didn't hear how it caught in my throat at the sight of him. I tried to ignore the indistinguishable tremor that danced through me as my eyes met his.

"Mind if I come up?" he asked.

"No, that's fine," I said. He climbed without difficulty, pulling himself through the branches until his face was level with mine. He sat on a limb beside me, stretching out his legs to balance himself.

Recalling my panic-stricken reaction the last time we were together, I blushed in the dark. But somehow, now that I was with him again, I couldn't remember why I'd been so afraid.

"Thanks for meeting me. You all right?" he asked.

I broke his gaze. "Yeah. But, um, I feel a little silly about the other day."

Damien shook his head. "That's what I wanted to talk to you about. You were right. I knew you were scared, but I still convinced you to go out there with me. I pushed you too hard and I'm sorry." He put a hand on my arm. "It's just that, ever since that day at the river—"

Damien stopped, hesitating with his words. He looked out at the lake for a moment, as though caught up in an unspoken memory. "Sometimes I see you with this haunted look on your face, and I know you're still there, like you're trapped and can't get away."

My hands gripped the tree trunk, but I couldn't speak. How did he seem to know me so well?

"I find myself wanting to help you and somehow thought I could. But when I upset you the other day—" He paused with a pained expression. "I know now that's not my place. Anyway, I just wanted to apologize to you tonight and let you know I'll leave you alone from now on."

"Please don't." The hurried anxiety in my voice surprised me, but I couldn't stop it. "I want...I think I do need...some help." I met his questioning gaze again and continued.

"I got into an argument with my stepbrother." I let out a short laugh. "That's nothing new. But this time, he was right."

"What happened?" Damien asked.

I reflected on the previous night's musings, lying in bed and remembering how troubled I'd felt inside.

"I don't make it a habit of acknowledging anything Nick says to me, but last night, he made a point. He told me I'm self-absorbed with my own problems. No, it's all right," I said, preventing Damien from interrupting me. "I understand what he was saying. I've let fear control me. It happened with you the other day on the canoe." I sighed and debated whether or not to continue. Taking a quick breath, I released it with a rush of words. "I'm having a hard time and haven't wanted to admit it. And that's why I need you to stay around."

Damien tilted his head, preparing to speak. Again, I beat him to it, afraid that if I stopped now, I wouldn't be brave enough to continue.

"There's something about you..." My voice softened with bewilderment. "I don't hurt as much when I'm with you. And I don't know why." I avoided his eyes, afraid to read his expression, but I'd said all I wanted to say.

A deep silence filled the gap between us. I had said too much. Embarrassed, I knew it was time to leave.

Damien's warm voice penetrated the quiet air. "I'm glad to hear that."

I chanced a look in his direction, surprised and relieved. He offered a closed-mouth smile. Unsure what my confessions meant to either of us, I smiled back.

An intrusive breeze swung through the trees, wrapping its chilly hands around my bare arms. I shivered.

"We better get you back," Damien suggested. He started to make his descent. I followed after him with reluctance.

Just before I was about to jump to the ground from my final branch, Damien reached up and placed his hands around my waist.

"Here, let me help you with that." Catching me off guard, he pulled me off the limb. My body fell towards him, and I wrapped my arms around his neck to catch myself. Damien held me against him for just a moment, and then eased my feet to the ground.

I stepped back, brushing a hand through my hair. Not sure what to do with myself, I folded my arms. Damien's dimples returned.

"Come here," he commanded in a soft voice. He offered his hand. I placed my hand in his, and his fingers folded around them.

"You ready to go?" he asked.

"I don't want to go back yet." I hesitated. "If I go back now, I have to face lying awake in bed." I cringed at the thought of the torturous ranting that often awaited me. "I'm not ready for that."

"Ok," Damien answered. He lowered himself to the ground with his back against the tree. He took a moment to brush at the dirt beside him, sweeping away twigs, a few stones, and broken bark. He patted the empty spot.

I sat down and pulled my knees up to my chest, wrapping my arms around them. Neither of us spoke for a time, but the silence was comfortable.

Breaking the quiet hum of nature, Damien said, "Tell me about Maddie."

A trickle of reluctance made me waver. I scrunched my face together. "Why?"

"You said you have trouble sleeping, right? Like your mind doesn't shut off?"

"Yeah."

"Do you ever think it might help if you talked about it? So it's not all stuck inside your head?"

My lips rubbed against each other. "What do you want to know?"

"Anything. Who was she? What was she like?"

Nine years of memories replayed in my mind. Some made me smile, while the more recent ones made me cringe and sigh.

"She was a beautiful baby," I started. "I was seven at the time. But I remember going to the hospital and sitting in a big chair with her little body in my arms. She had wide, pretty eyes and this perfectly round head." I gave a small laugh. "She came so fast that Aunt Heidi barely made it to the hospital. It was like Maddie couldn't wait to come out and take on the world. That's always how she was though—a little blond fireball with just enough sass and sweetness combined to make her dangerously loveable."

The wind picked up its pace. Damien wrapped an arm around me and pulled me close. Content, we sat in silence, our body heat warming each other.

"She was their little miracle," I whispered.

"What's that?" Damien asked.

"Maddie. She was Aunt Heidi and Uncle Bill's miracle baby." I turned to face Damien. "My aunt couldn't get pregnant. She tried for eight years, with all sorts of expensive tests and procedures. The doctors told her it was pretty near impossible. So, Aunt Heidi and Uncle Bill stopped trying. They made peace and accepted their situation, making plans to travel the world.

"But then Aunt Heidi was pregnant. None of us could believe it. She was so happy, beaming every time we saw her. Nine months later, she held her beautiful baby girl in her arms."

I swallowed the determined lump developing in my throat. I bowed my head. "And nine years later, she was clinging to Maddie's coffin instead. They trusted me with her. She was their little miracle, and I didn't save her."

I clenched my teeth, refusing to acknowledge the burning at the back of my throat. I would not cry again, but my mind couldn't fight the memories of Aunt Heidi's grief-stricken face, with her red, swollen eyes looking helplessly back at me.

Damien's hand touched my cheek. With tenderness, he turned my face towards him, cupping my face in both his hands. "It is *not* your fault."

I let out a breath of air, inhaling again to consume the threatening sobs. I shut my eyes, desperate to block out the pictures in my head. I could hear Damien speaking to me, though his voice sounded miles away.

"*. . . Open your eyes. Allie, open your eyes...*"

The images began to fade, until they all but disappeared, and then I was looking at Damien, his face inches from my own. One hand slid down to the back of my neck, as he rested his forehead against mine. His marble eyes stared back at me.

"It's ok," he said. "I know you don't believe it, but I'll keep saying it until you do. *It is not your fault.*"

His lips lowered until they rested on my forehead, lingering for just a moment. I closed my eyes again, feeling the warmth and softness of his lips against my skin. My breathing settled, and I relaxed beside him. Huddled together, we both looked out across the dim lake.

Stifling a yawn, I turned my head and rested my cheek against Damien's shoulder, linking my right arm around his left. I felt sleep tugging on my eyelids. Mumbled words tumbled out of my mouth.

Damien's hand caressed my face. "It's all right,

Allie. You're safe. You can sleep now."

Sometime later, I was aware of my body being lifted off the ground. My arms wrapped automatically around Damien's neck, allowing myself to curl up in his arms. My body rocked back and forth, following the rhythmic cadence of Damien's footsteps.

"Allie, I'm going to set you down now." Damien's voice was soft, his words tickling my ear.

My eyes fluttered open when my feet touched the floorboards of the porch. Damien's hand wrapped around mine, and he guided me to the doorknob.

"You better get inside. I let you sleep a long time," he said.

"Thank you."

My hand twisted the doorknob. I looked back at Damien, but he was hurrying to the parking lot, where I knew his bike awaited him. I watched him leave with a thoughtful smile on my face.

The door pulled inwards, jerking me inside.

"Allie, where have you been?" Dad shut the door, and then crossed his arms across his chest.

Confused, I blinked back at him. "Dad, what do you mean? I was just out by the lake."

"It's two o'clock in the morning." The stern tone of his voice was one I hadn't heard in a very long time.

Still somewhat groggy, I squinted my dry eyes back at him. "What's the big deal? I'm seventeen and it's summertime—"

"It's a big deal when you disappear with some

strange older guy, who I hear you barely know. And apparently, this isn't the first time."

"What?" Awakened, my eyes shot towards the hallway leading to the bedrooms. "Have you been listening to Nick?" Dad's expression answered the question. I threw my hands up in disgust. "Unbelievable. I didn't realize you were using him to spy on my personal life. What did he say?"

Dad shook his head. "Enough that I don't want you hanging around his type. It doesn't matter what he said. I want you to listen to what *I'm* saying, and that's to stay away from that guy."

I glared at him. "I don't understand. You don't even know him."

"I know enough," Dad said with a gruff tone. "A guy like that doesn't hang out with teenage girls for nothing."

"Well, you're wrong. It's not like that. And what's with you trying to play this new role in my dating life? I'm about to go to college!"

"I'm your *father*, and you're not in college yet."

"Oh, *now* you want to play that card. Well, guess what, *Dad*—I made plenty of decisions over the last four years without you. I'm pretty sure I'm capable of making this choice, too."

My dad worked his jaw, looking angrier than I'd seen him in a long time.

"We'll talk about this later." He bolted the door before he stalked past me and into his bedroom. I watched him shut his door behind him, and then listened to the muffled sounds of Clara's voice mixed with his. She was in on this, too. Heaving a sigh, I stomped to my bedroom.

I ran a tired hand through my hair, glancing out my window. I jumped when I noticed the tall, dark figure sitting on his dirt bike some fifty feet away. Damien was watching me from where he sat, his hands gripping the handlebars. I couldn't make out his features in the dark, but he waved.

I forgot about Nick, Dad, and every other worry. Satisfied, I pulled the curtains closed. Still smiling to myself, I slid into bed and fell sound asleep.

CHAPTER 13

I kicked at the pebbles, dragging my feet and watching the dust swirl around my sneakers.

"I appreciate you getting up with me," Clara began.

"Sure," I mumbled, letting my jaw fall open with a yawn. Shoving my hands into the pocket of my sweater, I peeked at her from my peripheral. She had shaken me awake at six am, cheery and unyielding that I walk with her. After last night, I figured she was up to something.

"So, who won the Scrabble game?" I asked, breaking our silence.

"We didn't finish."

"Why not?"

Clara laughed. "Well, after Brooke came in, she was determined to tell us all about her day, and kept avoiding the question about where you went. Then Nick said he thought he had an idea." I frowned at the mention of my nemesis. "He didn't have a whole lot of good to say about the guy you left to hang out with."

There it was—the true purpose behind this morning's walk.

"And, of course, everyone just believed Nick, right?"

Clara raised her eyebrows at my bitter tone.

"Clara, I'm sorry. I know he's your son, and you and my dad both had high hopes that the two of us would hit it off as newfound siblings or something. But the truth is—we can't stand each other. He goes out of his way to anger me, including lying about things or people he knows very little about."

"Nick's not the one I wanted to talk about," Clara said. When I clamped my mouth shut, she continued. "Your father's a good man, Allie."

I rubbed my lips together. "I know he is. And he seems happy with you. Doesn't mean he knows everything though, especially when he's only given bits and pieces of information."

"So about that. I talked to your dad last night, after you got home."

I didn't look at her. "Yeah, that figures. What about it?"

"Hey, now, no need to get defensive. I'm just saying we talked."

"Sorry," I mumbled. I tried to relax by paying attention to the crunching trail beneath my feet.

"I think your dad is concerned because he's never been around for the dating stage with you. It's a little new for him."

I laughed with bitterness. "Yeah, that's because he's not around much, like you said. That's not *my* fault."

"He's still your father. No matter what he's done in the past, it is his natural right to worry about you, even if that comes off as him telling you what to do."

I refused to comment.

"I think you should talk to him sometime—and I mean *really* talk to him."

I cringed. "Clara, we don't have that kind of relationship. We don't talk about sentimental things or have deep conversations about life. My sisters and I didn't even talk to him for an entire year after the affair with that woman. When we visit, it's always just been about vacation."

Clara was quiet for a time. "Do you think it's possible for people to change?"

Now it was my turn to walk in silence. "I don't know. I guess so."

Clara stopped and put a hand on my shoulder. She emphasized her next words. "Do you want to change your relationship with your father?"

I looked back at Clara with uncertainty. "I—I'm not sure. I'm sort of used to how it is. It's weird thinking about having a real conversation with him. I don't think either of us is very good at putting our thoughts into words—especially him."

Clara nodded. "I think it's easier for your father to put his thoughts on paper than out loud. He's a writer. It's what he does—it's what he's used to. That doesn't mean he doesn't care just as much, and it doesn't mean he can't change."

Change.

Clara's words ran through my mind all morning, but I wasn't ready to talk to Dad. I ducked in and out of the cabin without notice, remembering something else that had been bothering me since the night of the storytelling: The boy who killed his family in that fire. I had to know what happened to him, to feel some closure on the awful event. Could someone as troubled as this kid have the ability to change? If he could change his life, Dad and I certainly could, right? Either way, it seemed easier to direct my energy on this boy's story than my own life for the moment.

Disappearing into the clubhouse, I sat down in front of the computer and typed the following words into a search engine: *Hidden Pines, fire kills family.* Ten different websites popped up on the screen. My eyes scanned the short descriptions, looking for news reports.

There, the third site down, a bold headline that read: *Fire kills family of three in Hidden Pines, arson suspected.*

And another: *17-year-old son involved with the suspicious deaths of his family.*

There were more. I selected five articles and printed them. I clicked back on one of them, my eyes scanning the words: *Police are investigating the deaths of a family that took place while vacationing in Hidden Pines. 48-year-old Jonathan Michaels, his wife, Karen, 45, and their 10-year-old daughter, Jenna, died in a fire that burned down their cabin last week. Their teenage son is the only survivor from the tragedy. Police suspect foul play.*

It was true then. Minus some embellishment from the storyteller, the general facts didn't seem made up. I scooted out of my chair, hurrying to the printer. Flipping through the pages, one headline in particular caught my attention: *Son of Jonathan Michaels inherits 3.3 million in life insurance, despite being a person of interest in the suspicious deaths of his family.*

My fingers gripped the pages. Did this boy really kill his family for money? I shook my head, feeling sick in my stomach. But it was 3.3 million. A person could live for the rest of their life on an inheritance like that.

"There you are!"

I turned my head to see Brooke hauling towards me, an impish look on her face. She grabbed my wrists.

"Damien's looking for you!" Brooke pulled me after her, jabbering away as we exited the clubhouse. "I was laying out my towel when Damien drove by on his bike. And, I have to say, I know you have dibs on him and all, but a guy like him on a bike like that is an attractive sight." She whistled for effect. I gestured with my hand for her to continue. "Right. Anyway, he wants to talk to you."

"About what?"

"I don't know. I'm not his personal secretary! Although, all this running around trying to find you is giving me a workout. You better hurry. Your dad is taking everyone out on the boat again right now. I am supposed to invite you, and he expects you to come, even though we all know you don't want to be out on the water."

I could feel my heart beating just a little faster at the thought of spending the afternoon with Damien again. "Ok. I just need to put these papers in my room."

Brooke snatched them out of my hands. "I'll take care of it. Your dad is back there and, guaranteed, he will try to force you to go with us on the boat. All part of the 'intervention' you know." She said it with a roll of her eyes, emphasizing she was on my side.

Grateful, I said, "All right. Well, tell my dad I'm working out or something, and I'll catch up with you guys for dinner."

"Ok. Damien said to meet him by the tree again. Have fun!"

I walked the opposite direction of the cabins, towards the grove of trees. I could see Damien standing next to his bike. My stomach weaved in and out of itself at the sight of him. As I stepped closer, I admired how his fitted T-shirt enhanced the blue in his eyes, just surpassing the tint of gray. Strung across his chest was the shoulder strap of a duffle bag.

"Brooke gave you my message," he said.

"Yeah. You saved me from spending the day on the boat."

"The boat? Sounds like it was going to be a rough afternoon."

I picked up on his sarcasm and slugged him in the shoulder. "You know what I mean. My dad is still trying to get me back in the water."

I caught the sideways glance from Damien.

"What?" I asked.

"Nothing." Damien straddled his bike and

unlocked the kickstand. Suspicious, I stood my ground.

"What are you up to today?"

"I want to show you something, that's all. You ready?" He started the motor when I complied and sat down behind him. "You know you're going to fall off if you don't hold on like I told you."

I comfortably wrapped my arms all the way around him, latched against his torso, and enjoyed the ride. We followed the route towards his cabin. The river was alive today, awakened with all the rain it had gathered from the mountains. As it swished with playfulness along the embankment, a quiet fragment inside of me recalled why I once loved it so much.

Leaving the trees behind us in a northwest direction, we flew through a flat green meadow with the scorching sun blazing on our backs. Then we followed a dirt trail that weaved through a mountain. The trail opened up to mostly flat land again, fresh and green with small shrubs and bushes. We parked beside a huge hill.

"We have to walk from here," Damien said, offering his hand. I allowed him to guide me forward, his fingers wrapped around mine.

"Where are we?" I asked, leaning into his support as we climbed up the steep incline. He didn't answer for the next few minutes that it took us to trek up the hill. My muscles burned in protest of the hike, working extra hard to dig into the dirt with my flip-flops.

When we reached the summit, my breath caught in my throat, not only to catch my breath, but in awe of what awaited below. A beautiful, clear pool of water shimmered under the sun. The elevated landscape that we stood on created a natural, circular barrier that enclosed the water like a granite bowl. A small, graceful waterfall cascaded down the far side, opposite where we stood.

"Do you like it?" Damien asked, seemingly pleased with my reaction.

"It's gorgeous. I can't believe how clear it is. It's like a mirror," I observed, noticing the reflection of nature imprinted in the water.

"Not many tourists know of this place, so it's pretty well preserved. Let's go." Damien pulled me after him, sloping down a less-angled segment of the bowl. When we reached the bottom, there was a fifteen-foot wedge of land separating us from the water.

Damien dropped his bag under a small tree. He moved to the edge of the land, scooping up the crystal-clear water into his cupped hands, splashing his face with a satisfied sigh. I followed behind him, dipping my fingers. It was cool and refreshing as I threw it across my head, washing away the dirt that caked my hot, sweaty face.

"This is amazing," I said. The waterfall spilled down the precipice, white, bubbling water dancing its way down the rocks.

"You want to go in?" Damien asked, discarding his shoes by a bush.

I froze, no longer mesmerized by the span of water. "If I didn't like the canoe, what makes you think

I'm going to want to go in there? Besides, I don't have my swimsuit," I pointed out, as if that wasn't obvious enough.

And not having a suit was the least of my worries.

Damien chuckled. "Neither do I. That's never stopped me before."

I gaped at him and then scowled, crossing my arms across my chest. I took a step backwards, away from him and the water.

He seemed amused, reading the varying expressions on my face. His teasing eyes seemed to laugh at me. He stepped into the water with all his clothes still on. I breathed an audible sigh of relief as I watched him wade up to his thighs, with his shorts and shirt intact. As the water reached his waist, he inhaled a sharp breath.

"Whew! That gets pretty cold right here. There's only one thing to do." Without warning, he dove into the water, his whole body disappearing. Losing sight of him, familiar anxiety crept into my chest. Ten seconds. Fifteen seconds. I didn't realize I had stopped breathing until Damien resurfaced twenty-five feet away, treading water.

Damien swam back over to where he could stand in the water, waist deep again. He shook his head, throwing water droplets into the air. Then he ran both his hands over his face and through his thick hair, slicking it back. His pale shirt suctioned against his chest, outlining every muscle.

"It's not so bad once you get all the way in," he commented. He reached out with one hand, still a good ten feet away. "Come on."

I shook my head in defiance.

He persisted. "You said the other night you wanted help, right? This water is as calm as you can get. It's safe." Now it was his eyes that summoned me. His next words were slow, deliberate, his voice deep. "What are you afraid of, Allie?"

I stared at him with terror in my green eyes, barricading the tears that threatened to spill. Disbelief shrouded my face, my voice quivering as I spoke with an edge of anger. "What am I afraid of? Are you really asking me that?"

Damien didn't waver, his hand still reaching for mine. He waited.

I trembled, swallowing the burning lump in my throat. My voice was hushed, a whisper that exposed the aching in my soul.

"I'm afraid of how the water feels when it swallows you whole. It doesn't care who you are, or who you love. I'm afraid to sleep, to dream...to remember over and over again why I know how that feels." I was mildly aware that I had removed my shoes, my eyes locked on Damien's.

"I'm afraid of the hatred I feel inside myself, for surviving when she didn't." A single tear escaped the blockade, sliding down my cheek. One foot stepped into the water. I watched it disappear.

"Allie, you can trust me." Damien took a step towards me, beseeching my compliance.

In that moment, I wanted to believe him. I wanted to believe he could make all my fears and pains

143

go away, and release them from the snare inside of me. A shiver ran through me as I immersed the lower half of my body into the crystal pool. I waded towards Damien, reaching my own hand out to his.

My mind swirled with frightening memories of a cold, rushing river, but as the tips of my fingers touched his, the fear receded. His hand enclosed around mine, until my trepidation was all but forgotten.

Then he pulled me close, wrapping me into the sanctuary of his arms. Safe and secure, I held onto him like a buoy, the side of my face pressed against his solid chest. I could feel Damien breathing in and out, slow and relaxed, his chest expanding and contracting alongside my cheek. When I was able to let go and stand on my own, I cast my eyes across the surrounding water.

We were our own little island. I closed my eyes, listening to the waterfall, a constant trickling of water reminiscent to that of filling up a tub. Birds sang inside the trees above us, high-pitch chirping as they called to one another.

Damien brushed hair out of my face with a sweep of his hand. "You ok?" he asked.

My eyes opened and I nodded with a relaxed smile, despite the shiver that shook my body. I rubbed at the goose bumps on my arms.

"Sorry. The water's not as warm as the lake." Damien peered at the waterfall, and then back at me. "Feel like swimming?"

Another one hundred and fifty feet of water

distanced us from the waterfall. A small wave of anxiety returned, but I agreed.

Seeming in tune with my feelings, Damien took my hand. "Let's go. I'll stay by your side the whole time." He was true to his word. I kept my head above the surface, kicking my legs and pulling my arms against the water. Damien stroked beside me in our gradual pace, keeping his eyes on me. I offered a small smile, observing the peacefulness encircling us—the calmness of the water, the serenity of nature.

And then I felt it—an old, yet familiar, yearning to immerse myself in the water. I indulged the forgotten desire, plunging headfirst below the surface. For the first time in a year, I enjoyed the thrill of being engulfed by water. I twisted my body, swirling and pulling myself through the chilled spring until I could no longer hold my breath.

I emerged with a splash, breaking through the surface. Damien was treading afloat not far behind me, surprise and satisfaction on his face. My blood raced, warming my body.

"I'll race you!" I called back to him, laughing when he protested my lengthy advantage. We dove forward, kicking and splashing to one side of the waterfall. The weight of my clothes slowed me down, but the strong muscle memory of my limbs heaved me forward. I was within three arm's lengths away from the wall of rock, when a large hand grabbed my left ankle, anchoring me back. My head popped out of the water, and I gasped with laughter, fighting to break free of Damien's grasp. I splashed at him and he released me, taking off for the finish line.

"You're a cheater!" I hollered, wiping water from my eyes when he surpassed me. He rested against the rocks, his breaths heavy.

"You're the one that gave yourself the head start," he argued, laughing with me. He put out his hand, pulling me up beside him. My feet found the ledge he was standing on, elevating my torso above the water. Leaning against the rocks behind us, I caught my breath. I looked back along the pool of water.

"Wow. I forgot how good that feels. I can't believe I did it." I smiled at Damien.

"I knew you could do it." He took my hand. "Come on. Here's the best part."

He guided me across the natural bench beneath our feet, leading us under the overhang of the waterfall. We were enclosed in a small space, a blurry wall of tumbling water dividing us from the outside world. The wall of rock behind us was damp and cool, shiny and green with moss. We both became quiet as we looked at each other, our chests pulsing in and out as we caught our breaths. Moments passed without another word, with the sound of the falling water at our side.

Damien sighed and pulled me against him, placing his hand on the back of my head. I felt him tilt his head towards the concrete ceiling above us, debating his thoughts. His heart pounded through his chest, drumming in my ear. My beating heart resembled his, but I could feel his hesitancy, an unspoken indecision.

Keeping my face against him, with my arms wrapped around his back, I echoed his own question. "What are you afraid of, Damien?"

His response was slow, his hands clutching me against his body. "I'm no good for you. I'm afraid for you to know what I've done."

I lifted my head, twisting around to look up at him. His eyes met mine, a pale, somber glow in the dimness of our damp enclosure. We were both silent for a moment.

"Who are you, Damien?"

He turned his head, staring through the blockade of water. I felt a quiet sigh heave inside his chest.

"I'm not a good person, Allie."

My brow furrowed, studying his face. His expression hardened, shielding himself from my probing eyes, but he wasn't quick enough. I caught a glimpse of lingering despair—an emotion I knew all too well myself.

I shook my head, looking down at the rippling water. My voice was quiet. "I don't believe that."

"Well, you should." Damien's sudden movement took me by surprise. With one hand on my chin, he lifted my face. His eyes moved back and forth against mine, touched with a hint of anger. Yet, I knew the emotion wasn't directed at me. My breaths became shallow. I looked up at him with apprehension but didn't pull away.

In an instant, Damien's face softened. A gentle

hand caressed the side of my face in one motion, wiping the dripping water. Then his face lowered, his soft, full lips pressing against mine. His mouth opened, enclosing around the folds of my lips.

A shiver ran through my spine. My mouth moved with his, the insides of my stomach tingling. I put my hand behind his neck, pulling him harder towards me. Our bodies radiated warmth against each other, no longer chilled by the water.

And then Damien's gentle hands were on my shoulders, pushing us apart.

"I'm sorry. I shouldn't have done that." He ran a hand through his wet hair.

With my cheeks flushed, I turned away, trying to focus on the blurry veil crashing down beside us. "Why are you sorry?"

Damien seemed to struggle with his thoughts. "People might not think it's such a good idea."

"People? What people?"

Damien sighed in frustration. "Well, your dad for one. Don't try and tell me he'll be pleased you're hanging out with an older guy."

"You're not that old." I looked him up and down. "Are you?"

Damien laughed. "I turned nineteen in March. Not ancient, but old enough. Also, the people around here...well, the locals around the lake and from downtown, they all know me."

I raised an eyebrow. "So what? Are you betrothed

or something?"

"It's a small town. And they just like to talk. I wouldn't want to get you involved in any of that."

"Well, what do they talk—?"

Damien put his fingers against my lips, cutting me off.

"I have a better idea." He took my hand, and we exited the enclosure of the waterfall. I blinked my eyes at the brilliance of the sun.

"Where are we going?" I asked.

"I have something for you but it's in my bag." Damien's smile played with me, eyeing the distance we had swam once already. "You up for another race?"

I rolled my eyes but smiled. "Fine. You're on."

CHAPTER 14

Soaked and dripping, I stepped out of the water, leaning a hand on Damien's back for support.

"You're—a really good—swimmer," I said between breaths, laughing at my exhaustion.

"You're not so bad yourself," he commented. "Hey, don't sit down yet." He grabbed my arm, preventing my body from plopping on the ground.

"But I'm tired! I can't swim as well as I can run."

Damien picked up the duffle bag and unzipped it. Pulling out a blue blanket, he fluffed it out onto the ground. "Here you go. Now you can sit."

"What have you got there?" I asked, peering into the bag. Damien put a good-natured hand on my shoulder and forced me to the ground.

"Like I said. Have a seat."

"Oh, fine." I crossed my legs and waited. Damien sat down next to me and pulled out two brown paper bags. He handed one to me.

"Here you go."

I made a curious face, and then I took the bag from his hand, eying it with suspicion. "What is this?" The bag crinkled as I unfolded the top and peeked inside.

I laughed out loud. I pulled out a sandwich and waved it in the air.

"Did you make us lunch?"

Damien flushed. "Yeah. I made us lunch. But if you want to make fun of me for it—" He tried to seize the sandwich from my hand. I leaned away, laughing.

"No, no! I'm sorry! I want it; I do want it." I wrestled it out of his reaching arms. "What else do we have here...?" I stuck my hand in the bag, pulling out an apple and a small bag of Doritos. Damien wouldn't meet my gaze. I pinched a smile, feeling embarrassed myself at the thoughtful and unexpected gesture.

"Thank you," I said, putting a hand on his arm. "You didn't have to do that."

"Well, let's not get carried away here. It's just peanut butter and jelly." He tossed me a Gatorade. "But I thought you might get hungry."

"I am." I chewed on a sticky bite. "Mmm...You're quite the chef." A mischievous grin escaped my lips. Irritated, Damien folded his arms across his chest.

"Keep it up and see what happens."

I looked at him in mock disbelief. "Are you threatening me now?"

"Maybe I'll leave you at home next time." He tore open his bag of chips.

"Well, as long as you're considering a 'next time.'" I caught a trace of a smile along his lips, despite his efforts to ignore me. He picked up his sandwich.

"So," I continued. "I was wondering. Do I get to

know where you're from?"

Damien leaned back on one arm. "Hayward. Not far from Oakland."

"Hayward, really?" I dropped my jaw in surprise. "I grew up in Danville before my parents split. That's only thirty minutes away from you. If you were like my family, I bet your parents brought you up to Hidden Pines a ton, with it only being two hours away."

"We came up often enough."

"Huh. I wonder if we ever ran into each other?" I shook my head, softening my voice. "No, probably not. I think I'd remember you." I munched on my sandwich in thought. "So what do you do?"

"What do you mean?"

"Well, I can't imagine you just vacation up in the mountains all year long. Are you in college? Do you have a job? That kind of thing." I swallowed a mouthful of Gatorade while I awaited an answer.

"You're trying to figure out if I'm a bum or not," Damien stated.

I opened my mouth in protest. "Well, no, not exactly! It's obvious you're not a bum. You have a nice cabin and an expensive bike, and despite your constant scruff, you aren't carrying around the obligatory, overgrown beard. But unless you're living your life on credit, I was just curious what you do every day."

Damien crumpled up his bag of chips. I wondered if I offended him. Was it rude of me to ask? Maybe school and work was a sensitive subject. Maybe—

"I work at Eastridge Lodge," Damien answered, interrupting my guilty thoughts.

"Oh, yeah. I've heard of Eastridge. It's that huge ski resort, at least during winter. What do they do during the summer?"

"Some of the slopes are turned into water slides. And they have lifts for mountain bike runs or hikes, horseback riding, and, of course, shopping for the ladies."

"So are you the guy that sits by the lift and makes sure the riders don't face plant when they get on or off?"

Damien laughed. "I've done some of that. They make for some entertaining stories. But no, uh, I do more managerial stuff these days." His eyes no longer met mine.

"Managerial...well, that's impressive," I said. "That's one of the more ritzy resorts around these parts."

"It's something to do," Damien said, brushing off my compliment.

Curious, I eyed Damien, but he still wasn't meeting my gaze. I tried to appreciate that this was more information in one sitting than I'd ever heard from him.

My eyes ran across the transparency of his T-shirt, still wet from our swim.

"Hey...." I put down my food and leaned over his body, examining his left bicep. My fingers folded up his sleeve to expose the tattooed letters across his muscle. I traced the lines of the inked image with one finger.

"U-S-O? I've been meaning to ask. What does this mean?"

Damien took my hand and moved it away. "It's

nothing. Just a phase I was in when I was a kid."

Doubtful, I said, "Oh, come on. Everybody's tattoo means something." Damien's lack of response encouraged my intrigue. "Ok, let me guess, and you tell me if I'm hot or cold: You were in the military and it's a code for top-secret information—one you'd have to kill me for if you told me."

Damien rolled his eyes, but he seemed amused.

"Ok, I get it. Completely cold. Which is too bad because my next guess was going to be a secret agent for the government, but those two are kind of related so... what about a band you were in, or at least a crazed fan of? No? How about an old girlfriend's initials! Or worse...a one-night stand?" I made a face, hoping I was wrong.

"Really," he said, folding down his sleeve. "It's not a big deal. Just something stupid I did one night and haven't gotten removed yet."

The amusement was gone from Damien's face, followed by an almost irritated uneasiness. I decided not to press the issue anymore. Instead, I was quiet for a minute, my thoughts reflecting on the afternoon. I looked out at the shimmering water, still feeling a little surreal about the whole experience.

"Damien, why did you bring me here?" My inquiry seemed to catch him off guard. He stopped mid-chew, mulling over an answer.

"Well, I suppose it's the least I could do, considering you trusted me enough to tell me about last summer. I thought it'd make you happy to be in the water again, once I convinced you. You did say you wanted help, after all." His expression became somber. "And selfishly, I wanted to be the reason to make you smile."

The emotions of the day caught up with me all at once. "I never thought I'd go in the water again," I admitted. "Ever." I matched his gaze. "Thank you for helping me. I see now that's what you were trying to do the other day with the canoe."

Damien brushed a tangled strand of hair away from my face. His hand lingered along my jawline. "You deserve to be happy."

There it was again, a tiny shadow of heartbreak in his eyes.

"So do you," I said. My hand reached up to touch his. "Are you, Damien? Happy?"

The shadow dissipated. "I am with you," he answered. He kissed my cheek with a soft touch of his lips. He stood up and offered his hand. "Come on. We better get back before your family is worried."

Aaron, Nick, and Brooke were huddled together by the clubhouse when I found them. They were all dressed in damp swim attire, seated under the awning. Brooke's shoulders glowed a sensitive, sunburned red. Their attention was directed at a handful of pages that were sprawled flat on the table.

"Hey, there you guys are! Did you have fun on the

boat?" I asked, standing next to them. My smile dropped, seeing the expressions on their faces as they turned to me, a culmination of anger, concern, and relief. All except Nick, of course. He threw an apathetic glance in my direction, returning to the game he was playing on his cell phone.

Aaron stood up, gripping a page in his hand as he approached me.

"Are you crazy? You knew and you still went with him? And after what we talked about?" He didn't hide the anger in his voice as he loomed over me. Dumbfounded, I stepped back from him in surprise, my gaze resting on Brooke's guilty figure. She was hunched over, biting her lower lip.

"Allie, I'm sorry! I didn't mean for them to read it."

Aaron cut in. "Don't apologize! It's better that we all know."

Nick offered a comment of his own, still laid back in his chair, one leg resting on the edge of the table. "Man, Allie. I knew you were dumb, but I mean, come on. You got to at least be smarter than this."

I glared at all of them but stepped towards Nick. Aaron held me back with a hand against my shoulder. I flung him off, exasperation loud in my voice. "What are you all talking about?"

Aaron shook the page in my face. "How could you read this stuff and go off on your own with him again? Didn't you listen to anything I said the other day?"

I pulled the page out of his hands, scanning the

large words printed at the top of the page. There were also pages on the table. Headlines. They were all headlines.

"That's none of your business. I didn't even have a chance to read all of them. Why do you have these, anyway?" My eyes flew to Brooke's face. She was close to tears.

"I'm sorry," she apologized again. "Allie, I meant to put them in your room, but I left them on the dining table when I went inside your cabin. Aaron happened to see them and—"

"And we read them," Aaron finished for her, unrepentant in his approach.

"What is the big deal?" I asked, flabbergasted. "It was just a little research about the ghost story. Aaron, why are you so mad?"

"Maybe you should finish reading them," Nick said, a smug expression slithering across his arrogant face.

I studied the page in my hand, reading every word. The headline read familiarly: *Son of Jonathan Michaels inherits 3.3 million in life insurance, despite being a person of interest in the suspicious deaths of his family.*

I read on: *Three months after the death of his parents, Damien Michaels, recently turned 18, was awarded 3.3 million dollars, as indicated in the beneficiary clause of his parents' life insurance policy. Michaels' large inheritance continues to fuel speculation about his involvement in the fire that killed his parents and ten-year-old sister. Even close friends of the family are not convinced Michaels is unassociated.*

*Brian Watson, a neighbor of twenty years, stated,
"Damien and his father's relationship had struggled for a long
time. I have witnessed physical altercations between them
where Damien was out of control. It would not be far-fetched
to think he might have done this."*

*Initial reports from the fire marshal indicate an
accelerant may have been used to start the fire. Michaels
continues to be a person of interest in the ongoing investigation.
Hidden Pines Police Department declined to extrapolate on
Michaels' potential as a suspect.*

My eyes highlighted the name on the page.

Damien. Damien. Damien.

Stunned, I dropped the paper from my hands. It
fluttered to the ground, gliding back and forth until it hit
the ground.

"How...do we know it's the same Damien?" My
question sounded desperate, but I realized I didn't even
know his last name.

Brooke handed me another page with hesitancy,
her eyes full of pity.

I read the following report with dread, noting the
earlier date.

*Damien Michaels, 17, was admitted to the hospital
last night, suffering third-degree burns on his back from a fire
that destroyed the Michaels' vacation home. The percentage
of damage to the surface area of his skin has not yet been
determined.*

*On the night of the blaze, firefighters were unable
to reach the horrific scene in adequate time, due to the house's*

isolated location. When they arrived on scene, Michaels was outside the building with severe burns to his back. His ten-year-old sister, Jenna, was with him, lying on the ground unconscious. She died while in the ambulance. The initial coroner's report has not yet been released, but all indications suggest asphyxiation due to smoke inhalation.

Mr. and Mrs. Michaels failed to escape the flames. Their bodies were recovered from the rubble this morning.

Early reports from the police department do not indicate the source of the fire. However, Hidden Pines Police Department has not ruled out the possibility of arson.

A visual image of the dark discoloration plastered on Damien's back entered my mind. I rubbed my fingertips together, remembering the large, scarred surface area. I recalled Damien's words from just a couple hours ago:

I'm afraid for you to know what I've done...I'm not a good person, Allie.

My fingers touched my lips, and I shook my head.

Aaron's voice was gentler this time. "Don't you see, Allie? He's a sociopath. He's manipulating you. Tricking you into trusting him." His lips tightened, his eyebrows curved downwards. "You're not safe with him."

I turned to the table, my head beginning to spin. "Brooke, what else do the reports say? Was there a verdict?"

She nodded, picking up one more page. Brooke scanned the report once more before summarizing. "Well, there wasn't a 'verdict' because Damien was never formerly arrested as a suspect. The investigation is technically still open. Damien was always held under suspicion, but there was never enough information to continue pursuing him as a suspect."

"Doesn't mean the scumbag's innocent, though," Nick said, standing up and stretching his arms above his head. He held one page in his hand and waved it at me. His voice dripped with mockery. "You sure know how to pick 'em, Allie. Looks like you need to find yourself a new boyfriend."

I gritted my teeth, fighting the urge to react.

That's what he wanted. That's what he always wanted.

Snatching the page out of his hand, I gathered up the rest. I stalked away from them in quick strides, ignoring Brooke and Aaron's calls. I needed time to think.

CHAPTER 15

*I*t was early the next morning that I crept through the kitchen. Just past seven thirty, all else was quiet in the house. Even Clara, the earliest riser of us all, seemed to still be in bed. Being out on the boat must have worn them all out.

My hands slid along the counters, maneuvering around candles, potted plants, the fruit basket...I drifted over to the dining table and picked up magazines and a damp towel.

Nothing. Irritated, I shoved them away.

Where are they?

Moving into the living room, I checked over and under the coffee table with no luck. I started digging my hands between the couch cushions, crawling around on my hands and knees. A door shutting at the far end of the room caught my attention. I snapped my head up, my fingers still buried under the padding.

"Looking for something?"

Dad stepped away from his bedroom door. His wavy, brown hair, from where I inherited my own soft curl, was sticking up from where he'd slept on it, a disaster so reminiscent of how mine often faired in the morning.

He was still wearing his loose, checkered pajama bottoms and last year's family reunion T-shirt.

I stood up and rearranged the cushions into their proper places. "Um, yeah. I'm looking for the car keys."

"Oh. Where are you going?" He wandered into the kitchen and grabbed a mug from the cupboard. He gestured towards me, mug in hand. "Want some hot chocolate?"

"No, no thanks. I'm headed out. I couldn't sleep anymore so I thought I'd drive into town and pick up some groceries. Have you seen the keys?"

"You know Clara just went the other day, don't you? No need to make a wasted trip." He turned on the microwave, heating up a mug of milk.

"Oh." I dug my toes into the rug beneath me, silencing frustration. I tried again. "Well, I...thought I'd surprise Clara and make dinner tonight. There's something in particular I want to make and it requires some specific ingredients. You know, one of those Food Network meals that have odd spices here and there."

"Wonderful! That's real nice of you, Allie. I'm sure Clara would love that. Hey, maybe you two could cook it together."

I quit holding my breath and smiled back at him. "Yeah. Sure. So about the k—"

"How about I go with you? I've been meaning to go into town anyway. There's a bookstore I'd like to stop in. I bet you'll find something you like, too." He paused to retrieve his steaming mug. "You don't mind, do you?"

I grit my teeth. *Is he trying to be difficult?* I forced a good-natured shrug of my shoulders. "Nope. Not at all, Dad."

"Well, if you can hold your horses until I finish this mug, I'll grab the keys. I think they're in Clara's purse in the bedroom."

It was after seven by the time we jumped into the suburban and were on the road. The first ten minutes were quiet, while I tried to figure out how I was going to complete my agenda with Dad around. I hadn't been through the canyon since we arrived at Hidden Pines, and I realized my stomach was not much more at ease than it was on the way up.

"We missed you on the boat yesterday. You should have come with us."

So that's how it was going to be. Dad was still intent on getting me on the boat to "cure" me. Little did he know, Damien had already succeeded in getting me into the water, but I still didn't like Dad's plans to involve a therapist.

"That's all right. I was able to get some things done. Looks like you guys had fun though. Poor Brooke is sunburned, of course. You must have been out there for a few hours." I smiled through our forced conversation.

"Yeah, the boys enjoyed themselves. No one can compete with Aaron, but Nick's getting better. Even Brooke gave it a try—multiple times, actually, without ever getting up—but at least she tried it." Her failed efforts must have been amusing to watch because he laughed. "She's a good kid."

His next words were said with uncertainty. "I'm renting the boat again this afternoon. I don't suppose... you want to come out with us today?" He cleared his throat and awaited my slow response.

I tapped my finger against the steering wheel. Somehow, I no longer believed Dad needed this trip into town anymore than I needed my "special ingredients". If I didn't have other concerns on my mind, I might have been angrier at his cornering approach. As it was, I remained calm.

"Dad, is this about the intervention again?" I caught a look of guilt wash over his face before I returned my attention to the windshield.

"Am I that transparent?"

"Yes. You know, for a writer, you'd think you might be a little more creative in your tactics." I smiled so he knew I was teasing. He seemed relieved that I wasn't angry, but I could still see the distress on his face.

"Allie, it's just that you were such a water bug. You've always loved the water. To see you cut yourself off from it almost feels like you've given up a part of yourself."

"Dad, I—"

He cut me off with a raise of his index finger, silencing my efforts to tell him about Damien and swimming at the waterfall. "There's something else I want to say first." He sighed, rubbing his head. "I know since your mom and I divorced, I haven't been around much. I thought about what you said to me the other day.

No, don't feel bad. You're right. We haven't talked much and it got me thinking about the past few years.

"I know I messed up. I'm more ashamed than you know, and I wish that's all it took for your mom and me to resolve everything. But it was my fault. I let things between us slip too far. And after what I did that summer, there was no coming back from that—not when we weren't standing on solid ground to begin with. Then after you moved away, I became so caught up with work and meeting Clara and Nick that somewhere along the way, you got pushed to the side, and you grew up without me. I see that now. But for selfish reasons, that's also why I brought you up to the cabin for a longer visit. I've lost so much time with you."

An uncomfortable part of me cringed inside. This soft, emotional side of Dad was so unfamiliar that I was unsure how to react. Had I been able to run, I might have fled, but another part of me was curious, almost yearning for this lost interaction, and so I continued to listen.

"To be honest, the whole idea of trying to help you overcome your fears and how much you hurt from Maddie's death—it was a little bit for me, too. I haven't always made the right decisions. In fact, we both know I've made some irrevocable mistakes that hurt the whole family."

I squirmed, recalling my callous comments regarding his affair. Dad continued.

"I guess in part, that's why I wanted to be a part of helping you heal, to feel like I could contribute to your life again. And that's not fair to you. I know that now. So, if you want, I will call Aunt Heidi's therapist and decline his offer to come out."

I waited another minute to be sure he was finished. We exited the canyon, entering the small town of Twain Harte. I pulled over to the side of the road and parked, but neither of us made a move to get out. I spoke, feeling a spark of sincerity and affection for him that had dwindled over the years.

"Thanks for explaining. It makes a little more sense why you wanted me to come up here. Doesn't mean I agree with your methods, but I can see why you did it. And I am sorry for what I've said to you." I looked down at my hands, picking at old nail polish. My thoughts turned to the past four years, remembering the quiet, yet fierce, pain that echoed through the home—a home where a mother and her three daughters struggled to feel whole. Our family had been severed—disconnected from stability, turning our home into merely a place of shelter.

"What I said in my room the other day...I didn't even realize how angry I was about it until it came out. I shouldn't have said that about you leaving us. It must have been hard on you, too." I sighed, feeling the loss I had tucked away. The unraveling continued. I could feel it in my heart.

"What else are you feeling, Allie?" Dad asked. "You can be honest."

I fought to maintain composure, but I wanted to be truthful, to let him in. "It's been hard being back up here, Dad. All the emotions from Maddie drowning a year ago still feel so fresh. It's like picking at a wound that maybe never quite healed in the first place. She was so young. It just wasn't fair." A burning lump started to form in my throat. It seemed to have made a permanent residence there these days.

Dad put an arm around my shoulders, and I leaned into him, resting my head against his shoulder. "Honey, it's ok. Nobody blames you. You know that, right?"

I sniffled but didn't answer, letting the fresh tears soak a puddle into his shirt. I blew out a breath of air, trying to recover, but I didn't move. Instead, I enjoyed the comfort of my father's arms.

He kissed the top of my head, failing to hide a sniffle of his own.

I sat up in surprise, braving a smile as I caught sight of his watery eyes. "Dad, are you crying?"

He cleared his throat and looked out the window. "You're my little girl. When you're sad, it hurts me, too."

I smiled, my eyes brimming again, and buried my head against him once again. "Dad, I'm not that little."

He patted my head. "Doesn't matter how old you get. I'll always be your father. And I'm going to do a better job of being right here for you, ok?"

I nodded my head. "Ok."

We sat for another minute, both of us lost in thought. Dad cleared his throat.

"Uh, one other thing. About this guy you're seeing..."

I sat up in my seat. I could no longer ignore the anxiety building in my stomach. I waited for him to continue speaking.

"Except for the other night, I'm sure the last time we ever had a conversation about boys was about how they have cooties. In fact, I do remember trying my best to emphasize that point...."

"Dad—" I protested.

"Allie, I'm sorry. I know you're going to college and I can't control who you see or what you're going to do with your life, but I just want you to be careful. Just make good choices. You have the rest of your life ahead of you, and the way it turns out starts with the decisions you make right now." Dad paused before putting a hand on my shoulder. "That's all I wanted to say. All right?"

I didn't even know how to respond. I had too much confusing information in my head at the moment, and I just needed to get some real answers before I could make any decisions. I licked my lips, trying to restore the sudden dryness in my mouth.

"Dad, things are a little uncertain in that area. I need to sort some things out first. But I'll keep your advice in mind."

He looked at me with questions in his eyes, but gave a simple nod of his head. "Ok. I trust you."

I smiled in relief. "Thanks. So, should we get going? We don't want to get back too late if we want enough time on the boat."

Dad raised his eyebrows at my final comment,

looking pleased. "Ok then. Let's get this show on the road."

With a mere fifteen-minute drive down the canyon, Twain Harte was a convenient and busy little town. Its close proximity to the lake attracted a consistent stream of business. Overall, the local people were proactive and friendly, catering much of their work life towards the year-round visitors.

"Should we hit the bookstore first?" Dad asked. It was just a couple more blocks further from where we were.

I needed some time alone.

"You go ahead. I'm going to stop in a few stores along the way and do some window shopping."

Dad pulled out his wallet and extracted a few twenties. "Well, don't hesitate if you see something you like."

I accepted the money, feeling guilty while I slid it into my handbag. No time to argue. "Thanks. I'll meet you down there in a bit."

I stepped into a clothing store and ran my hands along the colorful racks of shirts. Ignoring the floor associate who offered her overly cheery assistance, I waited just a minute longer. Then I exited the store and looked down the street. I could see Dad's form a few blocks away. He was almost to the bookstore.

Good. Now, where to start...

I continued in the same direction, wandering with an outcome in mind, but no real plan.

"Something I can help you with, Miss?" The thin, older man to my right smiled at me, standing just outside the entrance to a small store. He was dressed in mustard-brown khakis with a striped white polo tucked into the high waistband of his pants. "Souvenir, perhaps?" He gestured inside.

I looked through the glass window he was in the midst of cleaning with a paper towel and spray bottle. He wasn't joking about the souvenirs. There were T-shirts hanging on circular racks throughout the store, though not to be outdone by the colorful layer of clothing plastering the walls. Even from the window, I could see the various Hidden Pines Lodge logos printed across the fronts of the shirts, cheesy and cliché with every statement. The shelves were littered with small porcelain figurines of wild animals, mountains, and other keepsake trinkets. Mugs, hats, postcards, sunglasses, swimwear... the room was packed full of vacation reminders.

"No, thank you. I have my fair share of Hidden Pines souvenirs at home."

"Oh, you come here often then?"

"Yep, every year. My family has a cabin up at the lodge. Are you from here?"

"Oh yes, I've been around a long while. Got myself many a memory 'round these parts. Dad used to take me up to the lake all the time when I was a young thing. Fun place to grow up, I'll tell you what." He scratched his balding, white hair.

"Well, maybe you could help me with something,"

I said.

"Oh sure, sure, Missy. I'll be glad to help if I can. So long as you buy something in return." He winked at me with a gruff chuckle. "Ah, I'm just joshin' with ya. What can I do for you?"

I took a chance. "Well, I heard a story...about a family who died up there in a fire just north of the lodge. But they had a son who survived. I guess, well, I wondered if you knew much about it."

The smile on his wrinkled face disappeared. He narrowed his eyes at me and did not answer. I waited, chewing on the inside of my cheek.

"What you want to do with an awful story like that?"

I hesitated at his reaction, but driven with a need to know, I persisted. "Just curious, I suppose. I mean, it didn't happen too far from the lodge. I heard about it during the festival, and read a couple of newspaper headlines. Most of the reports seemed to suggest the son was involved with the deaths. But you know the media these days." I gave a hopeful, lighthearted laugh. "It's hard to gauge what's factual. They tend to exaggerate events."

The man seemed distraught. He looked at me, then inside the empty store, and then back at me again. "Not in this case, darlin'. The media was dead on. No, uh, pun intended, of course..." he mumbled, walking into the store. He turned back around, where I still stood at the doorway. "Well, come along, then. If you want to hear more, there's one person you should talk to."

I followed him to the back of store. He pushed through two swinging doors and entered another smaller room. It was bare, uncarpeted, and appeared to be storage. The room was scattered with boxes of various sizes, some stacked on top of one another.

"Martha!" the man called out. "Martha, where you hidin' at?"

"Stop yer yellin'. I'm right here! What is it?" A woman's head popped up behind a stack of boxes. Her straggly black hair hung long beneath her shoulders. Thick, silver roots betrayed her age, as did the cranky wrinkles along her face and neck. She raised an eyebrow at me.

"If it ain't in the store, it's not available. I'm not digging inside these here boxes for nothin' and nobody." She looked at the man in front of me, accusation in her voice. "You already know that, Robert. What'dya bring her back here for?"

He turned around and rolled his eyes at me. Facing Martha, he explained, "This young lady—Oh, didn't catch your name—"

"Allie. Allie Collins."

He continued. "This is my lovely wife, Martha. Martha, Miss Collins here wants to know 'bout them Michaels, poor souls. Told her you're the one to talk to 'bout that. Or 'bout anything for that matter." Robert turned to me again and muttered, "Nosiest woman you'll ever meet. Knows everything about anyone and everything. Keep your own secrets to yourself," he warned.

Martha's face lit up, brightening with a cracked smile. Her haggard, nasally voice lifted a notch. "Oh? Oh now really?" She stepped out of the boxes and hurried towards me. She stuck out her hand. "Well, in that case, it's nice to meet you. Let's have a seat, shall we?"

She towed me over to a row of boxes lined up next to each other. "Here we are. Not fancy or nothin', but this will do for a nice chat."

"Martha will talk your ear off if you let her. Holler if you need any help gettin' away, darlin'." He winked at me again, and then turned to Martha. "I'll tend to the store."

He left me with the older woman at my side, who oddly reminded me of a little girl withholding many secrets herself. A wrinkled, decrepit little girl, that is. I contained a shudder.

"So, you want to know about them Michaels, hmm? Well, now, that *is* a story. I been around these parts for quite some time. Heard a lot of things about a lot of different people, but none as tragic as that one." She shook her head in pity.

"The Michaels were well-known and well-liked 'round here. They stayed at their cabin often throughout the year, skiing, boating...quite an active little family. And, 'course, they would make frequent trips into town for fancy dinners and needless shopping. Great supporters of this town, they were. Always willing to buy and donate if things were slow for local business."

"What do you know about their son, Damien?"

Martha's eyes narrowed and she raised her index finger. "That boy...yes, that boy was a bit of a monster around here, even before word got out 'bout what he'd most certainly done."

"What do you mean?"

"Oh, he was getting into all sorts of trouble during their last visit. Nothin' too major to begin with, of course. He pulled pranks on the locals, spray-painted a few walls, shoplifted here and there...Odd behavior for a kid who comes from that kinda wealth, if you want my opinion. He could've had anything he wanted, yet he still chose to sneak around and steal whatever would fit in his pockets or inside his jacket. Got caught a number of times here in town. His father had to come down and pick him up from the jailhouse. Had to pay the fine, too. Neighbors 'round here say it was never a pleasant sight, or a quiet one either. Mr. Michaels would come late in the evening, hollering at his boy for what a 'screw up' and embarrassment he was to the family."

I cringed, imagining the scene.

Martha looked at me in surprise and then chided, "Oh, don't feel sorry for him. The boy deserved it. Back in my day, he would have been given a whoopin' that would have left his hide raw. It's too bad his father wasn't harder on him to begin with. Perhaps it might'a prevented the worst that was to come."

"What else happened?" I asked. Martha smiled with enthusiasm, more than happy to share her wealth of gossip.

"There was talk he had started hanging out with a rough crowd of older boys from Oakland the same year his family died in that awful fire. Sometimes he'd come through town with a large group of hooligans and commit all sorts of mischief, those nasty little rogues. Well, they were quite large, truth be told. Frighteningly so. Most of them were thick as tree trunks with skin brown as milk chocolate. Not sure where to place them in the world. One of those islands, I suppose. Either way, Damien Michaels stuck out like a sore thumb. Perhaps that is why everyone around here remembers him so well."

"So, the fire...." I prompted.

"Ah, yes, the fire." She shook her head again, letting out a remorseful sigh. "That poor, poor family. Maybe it wouldna' happened had his father not threatened to send him away to military school.

"Trina, the waitress at Ramsey's Grill, just a ways down this street, says the family was over there for dinner. They had just done eatin' their meal, and Trina was about to see if they cared for dessert. She heard Mr. Michaels tell Damien that he might be going to military school. The boy made such a fuss, yelling to the whole restaurant that he wished his family were dead, that he wished he'd never been a part of their family. And within a week, the cabin burned down, killing all of them but Damien. You can imagine the talk that stirred the community 'round here."

Quiet, I sat there, ingesting this information. Could this spoiled, juvenile delinquent be the Damien

I knew? I paused, rolling the last part of the question in my mind.

I could not deny how powerfully I was drawn to him. Even the mere thought of his lips pressed against mine released the butterflies in my stomach. But did I know him? Did I know anything about him? Before now, that is...

Martha was watching me battle with my emotions, a look of curiosity in her eyes.

"Why so interested?" she asked me with sudden scrutiny.

I looked down at the ground, not trusting myself to speak. But it was impossible to hide the warm redness that flooded my face, betraying the deep connection I felt to Damien. Martha threw a shrewd smile at me.

"He's found you, hasn't he? Swept you right off your feet from the looks of it." Her voice was softer now, a hint of surprise and mockery touching her tone as she dissected my thoughts. "I've seen him now and again when he's driven through town on that reckless bike of his. Grown into his looks now, hasn't he? Dark haired, handsome young thing. I suspect you're not the first Hidden Pines visitor to fall for him. You're pretty, unsuspecting...and naïve." The last word was harsh, hurtful.

I lifted my face to look at her, perplexed at her intended slight.

"If you know what's good for you, Miss Collins, you best stay away from him. Dark pasts will always find a way to catch up with ya. You seem like a nice girl. It'd be a shame to read about you in the papers."

CHAPTER 16

"Did she say anything else?" Brooke asked me over the roar of the motor. We sat at the bow of the ski boat with Dad behind the wheel. Looking over the edge, I tightened my life jacket, watching the water split and bubble while we picked up speed. The wide lake sparkled in the blazing afternoon sun, expanding until it touched the rim of the mountains around us.

I shook my head at Brooke's question. "No, that was it." I looked back at Dad, who was driving with Clara sitting beside him. He waved, still happy that I was on the boat.

I lowered my voice, even though I knew the motor and the whipping air around us would drown it out. "My dad called me right then, wondering where I was. So I left the souvenir shop and met him at the grocery store. This reminds me, you need to help me figure out what to make with clams, quinoa, and olives."

"With *what*? What are you trying to make, vomit?"

"Hey, give me a break. I had to pick food items that I knew we wouldn't have in the kitchen."

"Or anyone's kitchen," Brooke added.

"Funny. But at least you see my dilemma. I told my dad I was planning on making dinner tonight and needed special ingredients we didn't already have. That's why he thinks we drove into town this morning."

"And that's what you came up with?" Brooke gagged. "Well, I'll help you figure out what to make. Just don't invite me over for dinner."

"You're a real pal." I gave her a light shove.

"I know. So anyway. Back to Damien." She hesitated, looking down at her feet for a moment. "Ok, I know this is opposite of what I was saying earlier, about giving him a chance and all. Please don't take this the wrong way, but if everything that Martha woman said is true, well, maybe you should keep your distance." She bit her lip, waiting for my reaction.

"Having a bad past doesn't make you a bad person, does it?"

"No, not necessarily. But it's not like he just had a bad habit of shoplifting and vandalism, though apparently he was into that as well...." She grabbed my hand with both of hers.

"Allie, he might have killed his entire family on purpose. And if he didn't, it's bad enough that so many people believe him capable of it. The fire happened only a year and a half ago. How much do you think a person can change in that amount of time? And do you really want to risk finding out?"

The boat slowed to a stop, not easing the queasiness that stirred my stomach.

"Who's up for a run?" Dad called out, looking towards the back of the boat at Nick and Aaron. "We have two boards today if you both want to go at the same time."

I took a deep breath. "I'll go." All eyes shot my direction, looking as astonished as I felt inside. Ignoring the raised eyebrows and open mouths, I moved to the stern, placing myself between Nick and Aaron.

Dad tried to hide the shock and excitement from his voice. "Ok, Allie's up." He handed me the board with a smile.

I was sure it was all he could do to contain himself. Had my nerves not been shooting up and down my spine, I might have laughed. I fastened one foot into the boot, sitting on the edge of the platform. I looked at the water and the small waves that popped up and down below me. Despite my success swimming in the small spring, there was something different about being pulled behind a speedboat.

"So are you any good?" Aaron asked, trying to maintain a casual conversation. He offered an encouraging smile.

I swallowed, looking up at him and then back at the water. "I do all right." My voice trailed off to a quiet mumble. "At least, I used to."

"Maybe if you sit there long enough, we'll have just enough time to watch the sun go down. Get in or get out." The impatience could only belong to one person.

"Nicholas, can I talk to you for a minute?" Clara's

stern voice spoke from beside the wheel, with her arms crossed. She waited for her son, her eyebrows creased. Nick rolled his eyes but complied. She tugged him to the very front of the boat, her voice full of harsh whispers.

"Never too old to be chastised by your mother, I guess." Aaron laughed, lightening the mood.

Dad put a hand on my shoulder. "You all set?"

"Yeah. I guess I'm ready." I paused a moment longer, before I scrunched my face and hopped into the water. I made a loud splash, sinking for an instant before the water buoyed me back up. The boat pulled away, tightening the slack in the rope. I wiped the water from my eyes.

"Ready, Allie?" Dad called. His voice sounded far away. Looking around, I felt very small, curled up and bobbing inside this mass of water. I was on my own. There was no Damien to lean on for support. Not today. Maybe not ever again.

I swallowed hard, fighting against the ball of fear in my stomach. I tried to calm my nerves, pocketing the image of Damien in my mind. His hand reaching out to me, guiding me into the water, but the image wavered and I let it go.

It's now or never, I thought, blowing out a breath of air.

I raised my arm in the air, and then clenched the handle with both hands. The rope tightened. I felt the pressure behind my board at the same time I felt the pull of the rope in my hands. The water split as the rope yanked me onto my feet, the water rocky beneath me.

My mind flooded with images:

Maddie's pale face. Terrified blue eyes. My own lungs choking, gasping for air.

The rope tore out of my hands. I plummeted face-first into the water. The images disappeared. Resurfacing, I spit out a mouthful of water and waited for the boat to pull around beside me.

Chagrined, I met Dad's concerned expression. "I'm sorry," I said. "I thought I could do it." Feeling miserable, I swam towards the ladder.

A large splash exploded in front of me, showering me with water. Aaron's body popped back up, the second board attached to one foot. He finished clasping his other foot into the boot.

"What are you doing?" I asked, once again wiping water out of my eyes. "I was just about to get out. You could have used my board if you waited just a minute." I started to unfasten my feet.

Aaron grabbed my wrist. "Hang on a second." He reeled in the rope and placed the handle in my hands. "Nick, throw on another rope, will you?"

Nick complied with a grudging expression. He tossed the second rope to Aaron.

"Ready to try again?" he asked me. His blue eyes glinted in the sun.

"Um, I—"

Aaron didn't wait for my answer. "We'll be ready to go in just a minute, Mr. Collins!" He gave him a thumbs-up. Dad hesitated, trying to read my expression.

Too stunned to argue, I watched Aaron line up his rope parallel to mine. I stared at my hands gripping the handle as I heard the motor kick on. The boat pulled away to tighten the slack in the rope. I shook my head in doubt.

"You're wasting our time. I can't do it right now."

"Sure you can. Didn't you tell me you already went swimming?" Aaron asked.

"Yes, but swimming in a small pool of water is one thing. Being pulled behind this boat—it feels like I'm not in control. Something else is in charge. Just like when I was in the river."

"You can do it. I know you can," Aaron said.

"It's too soon!"

"It will always feel too soon unless you keep trying." Aaron leaned back against the rope, resting a couple of feet behind me with his longer rope.

I looked back at him in frustration. "You don't know what this feels like. You can't understand."

"You're right, I don't. But can I offer a suggestion?" He took my silence as a yes because he continued. "You just need to let go a little. Not of the rope, of course, unless you want to face-plant again."

I didn't laugh at his joke.

"Sorry. What I mean is, whatever you're feeling, use it to your advantage. For instance, before my basketball games, everyone's adrenaline is pumping. Their blood is flowing, the team is excited, nervous...Sometimes players let it get out of control on the court. They're running all over the place, making sloppy passes, missing shots. They let the adrenaline control them. On the other hand, some players know how to channel that energy into good use. Their bodies are alert; their response is quick. The adrenaline becomes power rather than a hindrance. It's all just a matter of how you use it."

I raised my eyebrows in confusion. "What does this have to do with basketball?"

Aaron looked down, rubbing his lips together in thought. "Sorry. Basketball just makes sense to me." He tried again.

"Ok. I know you're scared and a little anxious. But those emotions are just energy. Put them to good use. Let go with your mind, and allow your body to put that energy to work."

Skeptical, I nodded my head.

Aaron looked across to the boat where all heads were turned our way. He raised his hand. "We're ready!"

Whatever I was feeling right now...I tried to empty my mind, letting my emotions flow through my torso, out to my limbs, my fingers. The handle was hard inside my grip, my feet planted against the board.

The rope pulled in my hands. I leaned back, my rapid heart sending shocks of blood and endorphins through my veins...and then I was standing on my board, coasting across the crisp water. I inhaled as the wind tackled my face. My ponytail whipped behind me.

But I was soaring. The sense of triumph was

exhilarating.

"There you go, Allie!" Aaron called from behind me.

I took a moment to glance over my shoulder, grinning. Aaron glided twenty feet away, sliding to the opposite wake. From the boat, I could see Dad waving and Brooke clapping her hands.

No longer anchored by fear, my body recalled the motions so ingrained from years of wakeboarding. As the boat turned and curved my path, I tilted my board. I bent down and dipped my hand in the water, my fingertips slicing along the surface. Straightening, I jumped as I caught air, grabbing the edge of my board before I landed a simple trick. The waves bounced beneath me when I came back down, attempting to knock me off my feet. Wobbling, my legs shook beneath me.

"Allie, hang in there!" Aaron called again.

My body flexed, tightening every muscle to regain control. I found my balance. I was in charge. My confidence returning, I beamed. I looked back to see Aaron zigzag back and forth, his board swooshing as it curved up against the waves. He flipped in the air, landing with a loud whoop.

I was not to be outdone. I popped up and twirled through the air, spinning a 360. Landing with ease, I cut across Aaron's path, meandering in front of him and laughing as I left a spray of water behind me.

"Is that the best you got?"

His taunting urged me on. Taking a deep breath,

I flipped, spinning my board over my head. It was a short moment but I felt weightless, rotating through the air without a care in the world. The long-awaited euphoria trilled through my spine.

And then I stuck the landing, not turning to look back at the turbulent wake I left behind me.

The sun was setting as I sat on the dock that evening. My legs draped over the edge, and I leaned back against the post with a sigh. The elation I had felt from this afternoon's wakeboarding had surpassed. With the darkness approaching, I had another matter weighing on my mind.

I looked down at the pages stacked in my hands, the edges now crinkled on every side. My eyes fell across the words, stirring up the relentless confusion in my mind. Despite having read them over and over again, I was still at a loss of what to do or how to feel about Damien. Everyone's words, including his own, echoed in my mind:

"I'm not a good person, Allie."

"He's manipulating you...dangerous and unstable."

"You're naïve...you best stay away from him."

I shook my head, fighting to clear my thoughts. Maybe I *was* being naïve. Maybe I was just like those stupid girls in the horror movies who never run when they are supposed to. They always just stand there like deer in the headlights, not making a move while they have the chance.

"I'm starting to sound like Brooke's dramatic headlines," I said aloud, remembering that first day of the festival. It was even back then that Brooke had warned me of a "homicidal maniac," the one she was so sure was following us. The one who turned out to be Damien after all.

A motor roared, increasing in volume as it drew nearer. I sat up, alert and searching the foreground. Before long, a silver dirt bike tore across the sand. My heart skipped a beat at the sight of Damien in his black leather jacket and jeans. He pulled up beside the dock, shaking the wind out of his rumpled hair.

My stomach twisted inside itself. Unable to decipher if it was nerves or excitement, I stood up and leaned on the rail for support. I questioned my ability to act nonchalant, to pretend I didn't know what I knew. The papers crunched in my right hand, reminding me of their presence. There was nowhere to hide them now. In effort to better conceal them, I rested my arm at my side. I forced my wary eyes to meet Damien's.

Walking towards me, he exchanged a small, dimpled smile. "Hey."

"Hi." My feet shuffled back and forth. My left hand gripped the rail.

Damien paused, a step away from me. He studied my face. "You ok?"

"Me? Yeah. Why wouldn't I be? I'm just uh—tired,

is all. It's been a long day." I pursed my lips, breaking eye contact for a moment.

He paused as he looked back at me. "I stopped by earlier and didn't see you around. What have you been doing?"

"Well, we had a late dinner for one thing. I made the mistake of offering to cook and that was a catastrophic. For future reference, clams and quinoa are not a good combo." I shook my head for emphasis.

Damien raised his eyebrows. I rattled on.

"Yeah, bad idea, right? So, we threw it out and settled for a box of macaroni and cheese. But then my mom called, I lost track of time, and it burned the bottom layer of the pot...." I paused to catch my breath.

Slow down, I had to tell myself. I was telling the truth, so I had no reason to allow my nerves to ramble.

Damien spoke. "Now you know why I stick to peanut butter and jelly." His expression changed to one of puzzlement. "Did something happen today?"

"Uh, yes. Believe it or not, this afternoon I was out on the boat. I went wakeboarding for the first time since, well, you know, since last summer."

He seemed a little surprised. "How'd it go?"

"Pretty well." I gave a genuine smile, reliving the exhilaration for a moment. "It was so surreal being pulled across the water like that again. I had forgotten how much I loved it. It all happened so fast...I never would have tried it had you not—"

I stopped. I had turned around to find Damien

staring at me. He took a step closer so that I had to crane my neck to look up at him. Out of instinct, my hand pushed against his chest, maintaining a small barrier between our bodies.

"You really have beautiful eyes," he said, putting a hand behind my neck. "I've been meaning to tell you that." My hazel eyes locked into his spellbinding gaze. His lips began to lower towards mine.

A part of me ached to respond. Yet the hand at my side tightened, crinkling the papers that I gripped—a reminder of the fears, the doubts, and the unanswered questions penetrating my mind. I took a small step backwards, feeling a tremor shoot through my spine.

Damien stopped inches from my face. He studied my expression, which I imagined was a combination of desire and trepidation visibly countering each other's presence. He pulled back, uncertainty touching the curves of his dark brows. His hands slid down my arms, down to my wrists.

"I'm sorry. I thought—"

The papers pinched together. Damien looked down, tugging them from my hand. "What is this?"

Staggering, I struggled to complete the racing thoughts in my head. "Nothing. It's, uh—" Panic ripped through my chest, and I reached for the papers. Damien stepped back from my straining grasp, flipping through the pages. His face tightened; his body suddenly rigid.

"Where did you get this?" His tone was hollow, low, and empty.

"Damien, I—" My desperate words were silenced by the alarming shadows in his face when he looked down at me. His eyes were dark, no longer emanating their piercing blue. Clenching his jaw, he took a menacing step towards me. His voice was gruff.

"Apparently, I've been your personal research project." He shook the papers at me.

I flinched, too stunned to answer, and too terrified to look away.

"Are you afraid of me now? Is that what this is about?" Damien threw the papers on the ground. They fluttered and scattered onto the dock. He grabbed my wrists, pulling me towards him.

"Ow! Damien, you're hurting me." I struggled to free myself, wrenching in vain against his strength. He tightened his grip.

"You know what? Great. I'm glad you know. Now you can just go on your merry way and enjoy the rest of your summer!"

"Damien, stop it!" I squirmed in anger.

It was then that I glimpsed a familiar figure sprinting towards us.

"Get your hands off her!"

Aaron body checked into Damien's side. Damien grunted, plummeting to the ground and dragging me with him. I tumbled at his feet, skinning my knees on the dirt.

Aaron stood beside me, breathing hard. Both fists were clenched and ready. Damien looked up at him in surprise, and then glared at him as he jumped to his feet.

Aaron held his ground. "You want to try something, tough guy?"

Damien stood almost level to Aaron's height, but assessed his opponent's lean build with a mocking expression. However, he didn't make a move.

Keeping a steady eye on him, Aaron reached out a hand. I put my hand in his and allowed him to pull me to my feet. I dusted off my cut-off shorts and my knees, grimacing as my fingers brushed against the fresh abrasions.

Damien sighed and took a step towards me. "Allie—"

"Don't even think about it," Aaron threatened, stepping between us and pulling me behind his back.

Damien gritted his teeth, staring hard at Aaron. He worked his jaw, struggling for composure. "Fine. It's better this way anyway." He trudged through the dirt and jumped onto his bike, revving the motor.

Aaron watched him with wary eyes, pulling me into his side with one arm. Still shaking, I held onto him, watching Damien glance our way just once more. The expression on his face made my heart ache.

"Damien!" I called out. He paused, his eyes connecting with mine. I broke free from Aaron's protective grasp and ran to him, ignoring Aaron's voice of warning.

"Just answer this one question." My voice softened, quieting my inquiry for our ears alone. "Did you do it?" I searched his eyes imploringly as they bore into mine.

"Does it matter to you?" He waited while I wrestled with my thoughts.

"I just need to know."

He, too, softened his voice, but his words were threaded with pain and anger.

"Yes. I killed them." His bike roared as he sped away. I stood alone and watched him leave, with tears stinging my eyes.

CHAPTER 17

I lay in bed the next morning and stared up at the ceiling, unwilling to remove myself from the comforts of my bed. I was unsure of what time it was, but the sick feeling in my stomach had awakened me long before the sun was shining outside my window.

I rubbed my eyes and massaged my forehead with both hands. Did last night really happen? It was hours before I could fall asleep last night, remembering the look on Damien's face before he drove off. I replayed the evening in my mind, over and over again.

I rubbed my wrist, remembering Damien's firm grip and the anger that hardened his face. What if Aaron hadn't jumped in when he did? Would that unfamiliar side of Damien have escalated further?

I tried to shut my mind off. I knew better than to dwell on "what ifs". I had driven down that path for a long time before I realized it led to nowhere. No matter how many times thoughts and ideas revolved around them, they never changed the past.

Three short knocks on the door interrupted my thoughts. I sighed, not bothering to move from my position.

"Allie?"

"Yeah, come in."

Dad entered the room, dressed in his usual casual attire of khaki shorts and a T-shirt. He looked refreshed this morning, which was more than I could say for myself.

"Still in bed, huh?"

"Yep."

He pulled the chair from the desk and sat down across from me. I could smell the sweet scent of banana pancakes and maple wafting through my bedroom door.

My stomach turned. I was in no position to entertain the thought of food.

"So...I hear you're having some trouble with that boy."

My head shot back to face Dad. He sat back against his chair, attempting to appear at ease. His eyes roamed around the room, as he twiddled his fingers. In truth, his efforts were somewhat comical.

Catching me eyeing him, he admitted, "Brooke stopped by. I heard her and Aaron saying something about it."

I rolled my eyes. *That figures.*

"I didn't quite catch the details of their whispered conversation, but I just wondered if you wanted to talk about it."

I looked back up at Dad in confusion.

Huh?

"I'm sorry, what?" I cocked my head to the side.

Dad adjusted his position on the chair, clearing

his throat. "Well, seeing Brooke and Aaron talking in hushed tones and you not coming out of your room this late into the morning, I'm assuming this has to do with whatever you needed to sort out, and I wanted to see if you are ok. That is, if you want to talk about it."

Oh, boy...

I hopped out of bed, sidestepping Dad, and fleeing to the bathroom. I turned on the faucet and threw cool water on my face. Pumping out a handful of face wash, I massaged it into my skin, taking extra care and more time than usual.

"Allie?" He was at the doorway.

I loaded my toothbrush with mint toothpaste and stuck it in my mouth. I ran it over my teeth, lathering up the foam. "Saurry, Daud," I murmured through my brushing. I spit once. "I haven't even brushed my teeth. Thanks for getting me out of bed though." I stuck the toothbrush back between my teeth and faced the mirror. My uncouth avoidance reflected back at me. I could feel Dad watching me while I rolled the bristles over my molars in haste.

Entering the bathroom, he placed his hands gently on my shoulders. "I didn't mean to intrude on your privacy. I just wanted you to know I'm here if you want to talk."

I paused for a minute, my teeth clamped against the bristles. Rinsing out my mouth, I grabbed the hand towel, wiping it across my face. I turned to face him, still hiding behind the towel. He continued.

"I don't blame you for not feeling comfortable talking to me about whatever happened with this boy you've met. In fact, I'd be lying if I tried to say *I'm* comfortable with it. But you know that already."

I put down the towel, revealing a humored smile. Oddly enough, his honesty was reassuring.

"Now, I may not be the best person for advice when it comes to relationships," he said. "But I do know one thing. You deserve to be treated with the utmost respect, so don't let anyone say or do anything to treat you otherwise." He put a hand to the back of my head and kissed my forehead.

"Thanks, Dad." I smiled in appreciation as he turned to leave.

"I'll just be up in the loft working on my laptop if you need me."

"Ok."

As he exited my bedroom, I thought about his words and felt the knot in my stomach return. Or maybe it had never gone away in the first place.

I pulled on a tank top and grabbed a pair of jeans, grimacing as I pulled them up my legs. The tough material rubbed against the developing scabs on my knees. It was a fresh reminder of last night's altercation between Damien and Aaron, and how I had been knocked to the ground in the process. Disgruntled, I tossed the jeans in a corner, settling for a pair of shorts instead.

Stepping outside, I breathed in the fresh air, hoping to clear my head. My eyes roamed eastwards, skimming through the thicket of trees beyond the lodge. I willed my eyes to see what I wanted to find—the tall, thick outline of his body, dark hair tossed across his forehead. Shadowy eyebrows emphasizing the sharp hue of his eyes, yet softened by the gentle dimples he was unable to hide—not even when he tried to mask a smile.

But no one was there.

I battled the desire to see him, a part of me hoping he'd come and take me away with him. Perhaps we'd pretend last night didn't happen, that I had never heard about the troubled boy who killed his family, had never read the accounts reporting the mysterious and fatal fire. Then I could savor the memory of our time together at the spring, when it was just the two of us shutting out the rest of the world.

But the image was shattered, recalling the menacing anger in his face as he gripped my wrists. My heart rate increased, remembering the fear he had seized me with. I struggled to understand the root of his emotions.

Was he upset with me because I had discovered the truth, or because I believed him capable of doing so?

Casting my eyes at the ground, I started walking. When I looked up, I found myself approaching the basketball court. Brooke and Aaron were seated on the ground, their faces close together as they spoke. Brooke jumped to her feet when she saw me.

"Allie! How are you feeling? Are you ok?"

I met Aaron's gaze before answering. "Guess

you've been filled in already."

"Yeah. I'm so glad Aaron showed up when he did. Who knows what else might have happened?"

I frowned. "He only grabbed my wrists. It's not that big of a deal. I mean, Damien was upset, but I think he had good reason to be."

"Look," Aaron started. "It's not my business, but don't downplay what happened. It doesn't matter why he was mad. No decent guy should ever put his hands on you like that."

I shook my head. "I still could have handled it differently."

"No, Allie. Don't put this on you."

"I wasn't being fair. I should have just talked to him about it!"

Brooke looked concerned. "Allie, you don't have to defend him. He could have reacted differently, too, but he didn't."

I looked down at the ground. "Maybe it doesn't matter," I said with a soft voice.

"What do you mean?" she asked.

"Damien asked me if it mattered—if it mattered whether he did kill his family or not. I told him I needed to know. But people can change. Maybe his past shouldn't make a difference in how I feel about him."

"Are you listening to yourself?" Brooke asked, her sapphire eyes wide and alarmed. "He said *yes*, that he killed them. That's not an insignificant part of someone's past to overlook!" The expression on Aaron's face testified his total agreement.

My head was beginning to spin as my emotions caught up with me. "No. This is being blown way out of proportion." Turning, I stalked towards the cabins. "I'm just going to grab the car, drive over there, and talk this out with him."

My footsteps didn't get me far. Aaron put a hand on my shoulder and held me back, stepping in front of me to block my path. "I don't think that's such a good idea."

I glared at him, peeling his fingers off my shoulder. "Aaron, I appreciate you stepping in last night, I do. I know you were trying to help. But you're right; it's not your business. I need to do what I think is best for the situation. Follow my instincts, right?" My mind set, I pushed past him at a steady pace.

"Allie—Allie, wait!" Brooke called. "Let me come with you, at least."

I turned around. "No, Brooke. I don't think that's going to help. He's kind of a private person. I don't think he'd appreciate me bringing you along."

Aaron lost it, throwing his hands up in the air. "A private person? Who cares what he appreciates! A person doesn't get to act like *that* and have his concerns met. You are falling right back into his trap, Allie. He's luring you in by manipulating your emotions, making you feel bad for him. Do you think I'm going to stand by and let something happen to you?"

My level of exasperation reached its peak. "I don't

understand! What exactly do you think he's going to do to me??"

I had never seen so much frustration displayed on Aaron's face until that moment, as he struggled to organize his thoughts. It was unusual to see his natural charm and charisma fractured with distress. Brooke looked back and forth between us helplessly.

Aaron's eyes fell to the ground before he lifted his head to look at me. His voice was calmer, quieter, but still lingering with a hint of desperation. "He's a guy who's angry with you for discovering a past he admits to committing, who seemed to have no intention of being honest with you otherwise. He's also a single, older guy living alone in an isolated cabin. And you want to go off on your own and be with him."

Aaron shook his head with a soft, sardonic laugh. "Even a guy without that kind of history is capable of taking advantage of a situation like that." He paused before adding softly, "Unless...that's what you're going for...."

I clamped my mouth shut, fearful for what might escape. Fuming inside, my cheeks glowed with more than just anger. I gritted my teeth. "That also, is none of your business."

"I'm sorry. I shouldn't have said that. I just worry—"

"Well, stop worrying, then. I know you're used to taking care of your sisters, but I'm not one of them. I don't need to be protected, not by you or anyone." I turned to leave.

"Allie, please don't go!" It was Brooke calling after me again. "We're all a little high strung right now. Why don't you just wait a couple days, let things cool off? If you're going to talk to Damien, it's probably a good idea to let him calm down, too."

This was going nowhere. Although, maybe Brooke had a point. I sighed in resignation. "Ok. Fine."

"Good." Brooke linked arms with both Aaron and me, pushing a smile. "Besides, it's a beautiful day today. Let's go get some sun."

It was early evening the next day that I found myself salt-and-peppering ground beef patties. Brooke stood next to me chopping potatoes, followed by a teary-eyed Clara.

"Whew! These are so strong!" She turned her head away from the onions to give her eyes a breather.

"And they'll be that much more delicious," Dad said, sneaking in a kiss. "How's our little assembly line?"

Clara smiled at him with a sniffle. "Very efficient. We're just about done."

"Lacking some help from the Y-chromosomes, if you ask me," I said. "Does anyone else think it's fair that the only people in the kitchen are the women?"

Dad ruffled my head. "Oh, Allie, don't you worry. The boys are rounding up the tents and filling the packs. Besides, you're doing a fabulous job preparing the tinfoil dinners."

The front door swung open. Nick and Aaron merged through the entrance with boisterous laughter. Nick socked Aaron in the arm.

"Bags are packed and ready to go," Nick said, dodging Aaron's retaliating punch. He threw a bear hug around Aaron's arms, pinning them at his side. Maneuvering them into the living room, Aaron slammed Nick onto the couch, landing on top of him. Nick hollered in pain before rolling off the couch and crashing Aaron into the ground.

"Hey, hey, watch the coffee table!" Clara warned. "Can you girls finish up in here? I still need to finish getting ready." She washed her hands and went to her bedroom, shaking her head once more at the brawl.

Brooke turned to me. "I don't understand boys. Why are they always wrestling like that?"

I shrugged. "Don't look at *me*. I didn't grow up with brothers either." I watched them with envy, wishing I could feel that lighthearted. I had still avoided Aaron thus far, not eager for more lectures. He seemed to be doing likewise, as he had not cornered me about Damien, or even spoken much to me about anything since then.

Today Dad insisted we go hiking and camp out under the stars. In the past, I would have jumped all over the idea. My family and I shared some of my favorite memories out there, burning s'mores, telling ghost stories, and playing tricks on one another in the dark.

But this time, I had other matters on my mind

and had tried to get out of it. I worried that Damien might stop by. What if I wasn't here? Would he think I didn't care? Or maybe Damien didn't care about me as much as I thought he did.

The tormenting cycle in my head continued to spin in tireless circles, accomplishing nothing. Either way, there was no evading our "family event," as Dad put it. I wondered if Dad still hoped Nick and I would build any sort of friendship through all this.

I ducked as a carrot flew at my face. "Hey!"

Nick laughed from across the room, munching on a carrot stick. "What are you all zoned out about?"

I returned my attention to folding our evening meal in sheets of aluminum, feeling Nick's eyes boring into me.

Not today. I wouldn't allow him to goad me into another argument.

"You can't stop thinking about him, can you?"

I continued to ignore him, though I managed to smash a couple patties more than was necessary. I made a mental note to label that one for him.

"Lay off, Nick," I heard Aaron murmur. "Come on, we need to find a flashlight and the first-aid kit." I met Aaron's eyes. He seemed to understand what had been occupying my previous thoughts. He pressed his lips together into a hard, thin line and turned away, pulling Nick with him towards the bedrooms.

"Just forget about Nick," Brooke whispered, misinterpreting the cause of my gloom. "I don't know what his problem is, but he's not worth your time or energy."

"Yeah. I know." She helped me throw the dinners into a backpack, followed by snacks and drinks.

"Ok, gang, I think we're all set," Dad called from the doorway. "Let's get moving!"

I muffled a sigh, throwing the pack onto my back, and followed everyone out the door.

CHAPTER 18

"Nobody told me...we were climbing...Everest." Brooke collapsed on a fallen log, her pale face flushed and splotchy. "Go on without me. I just need...to catch my breath."

Aaron handed Nick his pack, pausing to pull out a water bottle. "Here, it's your turn to carry this. I'll help Brooke." He hopped down the steep trail, careful not to bowl us over.

Nick accepted the pack, mocking Brooke's defeated form. "Yeah, sure. Good luck with that. See you at the top, man."

I continued to walk behind Nick, Dad and Clara but, after a minute, I stopped to watch Aaron attend to Brooke, noting the gentle way he helped her to her feet. She smiled with gratitude, looking very small and fragile next to his towering height. He spoke softly to her and I watched her laugh as she sipped the water, and then nodded her head. He turned his back to her, leaning over while she hopped onto his back. Wrapping her arms around his neck, she swung her legs around his waist. I looked away before they caught me watching them, and trudged up the hill on my own.

At last, the trail leveled out, exposing a flat area of land. I dropped my pack by the fire pit, looking down from the mountain we stood on. The breathtaking view never ceased to amaze me. It overlooked the entire lake and the rows of cabins throughout the lodge, bordered by tall pine trees wafting their distinctive scent through the wind. I could just make out where the river should be, far off in the distance.

Clara and Brooke murmured in awe of the view. Dad put his arm around Clara.

"All right, James, you were right," she said to him, nuzzling into his side. "It was worth it."

Brooke hopped off Aaron's back. She nodded, her cheeks still pink, but her mouth open in wonderment. "I had thought about turning around, but now I'm glad I stuck it out."

Nick laughed from where he was squatting by the fire pit, poking a stick at the old coals. "Stuck it out, huh? Yeah, if I could have been carried up the hardest part of the climb, I wouldn't complain either—especially by *this* guy." He reached out and squeezed Aaron's bicep, who reacted by pushing Nick over into the dirt.

Dad pulled away from Clara. "Nick, how 'bout you and I get a nice, big fire going. The lighter fluid is in here somewhere. We're going to need some dry wood," he instructed all of us. "We should be able to eat by sundown if we hurry."

"I'll help unpack the food," Brooke offered, walking beside Clara. I watched everyone move in different directions, each set with a task to complete. I had something else in mind.

The falling sun reminded me of one more view I wanted to see. Just a hundred feet behind our campsite was another hill. I hurried to the base of it, eyeing the sharp incline. I had forgotten how steep it became near the top.

Even so, desire won over laziness. I dug into the crumbling dirt with my sneakers, leaning forward to stabilize my balance. The last five feet were almost all vertical. I grabbed hold of protruding roots and thick brush to help pull me upwards. By the time I reached the top, I was puffing against the elevation.

Despite my weariness, I smiled in satisfaction. The hill opened westward, offering a clear view of the glowing sunset. The sky melted into a pink blur, the ball of orange radiating just above the distant mountains.

A shuffling sound of falling dirt and pebbles made me spin around. I took a step backwards, eyeing the far side of the mound I had ascended. A soft grumbling accompanied the tumbling soil. I gasped when Aaron's head popped up. He crawled up over the edge and grinned at my surprise.

"What are you doing here?" I asked, unable to refrain from glowering at him. This was *my* space, my time.

"What?" he breathed, scrambling to his feet and dusting off his clothes. He leaned on his thighs, his chest heaving. "You think you're the only one that can enjoy the sunset?"

"Well, I—no..." I folded my arms across my chest. "How did you know I was up here?"

Aaron shrugged, commenting offhandedly, "Ok, so I followed you. You've been to this campsite before. I knew you must know something good around here to disappear like that."

"I was getting firewood."

He eyed my dirty, empty hands. "Really? All the way up here?"

I turned my back on him. Never being very good at lying, I settled for the truth. "I just needed some time alone."

I could feel Aaron's indecision dangling in the air. I listened, waiting to hear his retracting footsteps.

Silence.

"Do you want me to go?" his voice asked from behind me.

I stood there with wavering uncertainty, biting my lower lip. The calm wind was shifting to a cool breeze. I shivered and wrapped my arms around myself. "Do whatever you want. You always do anyway. And apparently, you're the only one that can do that," I added with a sullen tone. I dropped onto the ground, curling my knees to my chest. Hugging them, I returned my attention to the dimming sky, appreciating the lit backdrop in the distance.

It was another minute before Aaron sat down beside me, resting his forearms on his knees. We didn't look at each other, but I could feel warm heat emanating from his body, his arms almost touching mine. Neither of us said anything as we watched the sun falling from the sky, preparing to sleep behind the mountain.

My peripheral caught Aaron watching me, his face angled in my direction. Uncomfortable, I swallowed, my eyes wandering anywhere but his.

"So what's the deal?" he suddenly asked.

I jumped at the unexpected sound of his voice, noticing his slight irritation. I feigned incomprehension. "What do you mean?" I couldn't maintain his gaze, so I watched my fingers intertwine with each other instead.

Aaron disapproved of my contrived efforts to be clueless. "You know what I mean. What's going on with you?" He watched my face for a reaction, reading my thoughts. "I know you're mad at me, and I can only assume it's for trying to protect you."

He put his hands up as I gave him a stern look, and he added, "Because apparently you don't need me to do that. I get that. I just wonder...Allie, explain something to me. Why are you so drawn to someone like him?"

I juggled with my thoughts, struggling to put my feelings into words. My eyebrows pulled together in concentration. "'Someone like him?' Aaron, all you see from Damien are pieces of paper condemning him for mistakes from his past. There's a whole other side to him, a portion that I can't explain. I feel connected to him somehow. And that's rare for me." My fingertips found each other again, playing with the cuticle of my nails, my thoughts uncertain as how to continue.

Aaron waited with patience, prodding me on with his quiet attentiveness. My jumbled mind struggled to articulate my thoughts.

"I was thirteen when my parents split. My dad wasn't around and my mom was preoccupied with pulling double duty as a working mom. Over the next few years, all my friends were dating each other, and I was baffled as to how or why. I didn't know a thing about how to maintain a relationship. I still don't. How could I, when the most important examples in my life offered me nothing but promises of a broken heart and instability?"

I shook my head, reliving the confusion in my mind. I had never divulged my reasoning out loud before. I spoke quietly, continuing to unravel.

"I guess I've just developed the mentality that, if two married people with a family can't make it work, there was no point in trying to make anything out of high school relationships. What's the purpose in putting your heart into something that's going to end anyway?"

The bottled emotions felt like a shaken soda can inside me. I fought for control—afraid that any minute now, they were going to erupt all at once. Aaron took my hand, which I hadn't realized was trembling. He held it with both his hands, calming my nerves. His warmth seeped into my chilled skin. Our eyes connected for a long moment as he absorbed my emotions.

"Sounds awfully pessimistic," he commented.

I withdrew my hand from his. I could feel Aaron's

eyes on my face again, trying so desperately to read my thoughts. I could feel him breathing deeply beside me.

"It's realistic, that's what it is," I corrected, reeling in my emotions.

"So are you saying you've never been in a successful relationship before?"

"Depends on your definition of successful, I suppose. Sure, I've had a couple "boyfriends," if you want to call it that—each of whom declared their love for me after a month or something ridiculous like that. Naturally, I broke up with them because anyone who thinks you can fall in love that fast is absurd."

Aaron raised his eyebrows at me and laughed softly. "Is that really what you think?"

"Well, yeah. Why wouldn't I? Love is so overused these days. It doesn't even mean anything anymore." I gave a critical shake of my head.

"I know what's going on," Aaron commented.

"Oh yeah? What's that?"

"You sabotage yourself."

I looked back at Aaron in surprise and tilted my head back. With a slight edge to my voice, I asked, "What did you say?"

"You sabotage yourself," he repeated. "No wonder you've never been in a serious relationship. You destroy it before it even stands a chance."

My angry hazel eyes glinted at him, but I was unable to find the words to defend myself. He continued without waver.

"You're afraid. You don't let anyone get close to you because you're afraid of getting hurt." He stared back at me, confident with his conclusion.

I opened my mouth to argue but, as much as I wanted to fight his argument, I felt the truthfulness of his words. *As long as no one loved me, no one would reject me.* I would not suffer the broken heart and loss that I witnessed with my mother—the muffled sobs seeping from her bedroom at night, audible through the walls and locked door. The pain and sorrow etching lines in her face and bags under her eyes, and the strained, cheery disposition she put on for her daughters, though we could see right through her.

Just like Aaron could see right through me.

"Must get lonely once in a while."

His words weighed down my heart. And then I remembered the question that began this conversation, discovering the answer. "You understand, then, why I hold onto Damien."

Aaron's expression transformed from surprise to frustration, realizing his words had backfired. I continued before he could interrupt me.

"You asked me earlier what I see in him. At first, it was his mystery that was so intriguing. I was frustrated not knowing anything about him, but also excited to figure him out. Still, I've always wanted to trust him, to depend on him. And despite all my questions about who he is...there's a bond there. I don't know how or why, but I've never experienced that with anyone before. I know it sounds ridiculous, and it's hard to explain, but—do you know what I mean?"

Aaron watched me, running his blue eyes slowly along my face. I held my breath, waiting for his reaction, feeling an air of uncertainty between us. He turned away, hiding his face from my vision. "Yeah. I know what you mean."

I had no more words to say. I was afraid to venture any further into this discussion or touch on the emotions it aroused. And so, we sat in silence.

Darkness folded around us, all except for the west sky before us. The sky was a watercolor wash of pinks and deep hues of orange, bleeding together. The sun blazed gingery red, its light painting the mountains into a darkened silhouette. The moon glowed awake with each passing minute, iridescent as it replaced the sun.

Standing up, Aaron offered me a hand. "Well, we better get back. Dinner is probably ready, no thanks to us." I joined him on my feet, my hand clasped in his.

"We'll make it up to them. How about we cook breakfast together?"

Aaron nodded. "Sure. We can do that."

The brilliance of the moon lit our path as we descended down the hill. We returned to the campsite, following the smell of beef and potatoes, and the carefree laughter in the air.

CHAPTER 19

"Allie, you awake?" Aaron called from down the row of sleeping bags.

Rolling over, I turned my head towards him and rubbed my eyes. "Sort of."

"Good." He rustled around as he unzipped his sleeping bag. He hovered over me, dressed in his athletic pants and a long-sleeved thermal.

"What are you doing?"

He smiled at me. "What do you think? Breakfast, remember?"

I groaned, burying my head under my pillow. I had forgotten about that.

"Come on," he encouraged. Grabbing my arm, he pulled me into a sitting position. "Don't think you're getting out of it."

I shook him off and watched him move to the cooking supplies.

"You going to make the fire or what?" Aaron said, pulling out a bag of easy-make pancake mix and a frying pan.

"I'm coming, I'm coming," I grumbled. After taking a minute to freshen up, I noticed Nick by the fire pit. He was restacking the wood into a clumsy pile, with the bottle of lighter fluid sitting a couple feet away.

"You don't have to make the fire," I said to him. "That was going to be my contribution to breakfast."

"I like making fires," Nick responded, piling the wood into a ridiculous stack. He opened the lighter fluid.

A thought popped into my head. "What do you think about starting over and making the fire the right way?"

Nick glowered at me. "What do you mean 'the right way'? You seem to think I don't know how to make a fire. There's not much to it." He made a move to pour the fluid.

"Wait a second," I said. He paused and watched me jog over to one of the backpacks. I pulled out a small cloth bag with a drawstring. The package fit in my palm as I returned.

"What's that?" Nick asked, peering with suspicion at my closed fist.

"It's a flint and steel kit." I opened my palm and pulled out the flat piece of flint and the accompanying steel. I handed them to Nick.

"What am I supposed to do with this?"

I was unable to contain my surprise. I thought every guy knew how to make a fire with these tools. "You don't know how to use them?"

I didn't mean to sound condescending, but the look on Nick's face told me that's exactly what I had done. He shoved them back into my hands.

"Why don't you go make your own fire then, and I'll handle this one the way I know how."

Something inside me encouraged me to try again. "Well, I can show you how to do it."

Nick glanced at me over his shoulder.

Interpreting that as a minor peak of interest, I continued, "It's not the easiest way." I nudged the bottle of lighter fluid with my foot to indicate the more obvious, straightforward method. "But it's more satisfying."

Nick still eyed me warily. "You got my attention."

I breathed a quiet sigh of relief. One fight this morning evaded.

"So, to start with, we need better tender." I took a couple steps towards the wooded area. I paused to look over my shoulder, catching Nick watching me. "You coming?"

He hesitated, looking around at the campsite to see what everyone else was engaged in.

"What are you waiting for?" I asked Nick. "It will just take a minute. Nobody's going think we've run off together or anything." The words slipped out of my mouth before I caught myself.

We cringed simultaneously.

"Don't ever say that again," Nick warned, marching behind me.

"Never," I agreed. We walked quickly, striving to leave the awkward comment behind us.

It took a couple minutes to gather up the tender. Nick followed my lead, collecting dry pine needles, weeds, and dry moss from tree trunks. We put our small piles together into one, placing it inside the pit.

"Here's what we do," I explained, pulling out the flint and steel once again. I held the flint in my left hand, with the sharp, thin edge pointing up, and the steel handle in my right. "You strike it a few times—"

I cracked the steel against the flint, watching the sparks ignite. "And ideally, you want to be as close to the tender as possible so it catches the sparks. Here, you try it."

Nick accepted them, unable to veil his eagerness. I smiled to myself as he practiced striking the flint and steel just right. Tiny flickers of yellow light jumped off and away from his hands.

"That's pretty cool," he commented, still concentrating on the task.

"Ok, now just get lower to the ground."

Nick crouched low. After a few cracks of the steel, the sparks ignited the tender, causing a thin layer of smoke to rise. I dropped to my knees and blew against the tiny flame. The tender crackled and glowed a dim orange.

Nick helped me create a teepee with the twigs, hiding our kindling in its center. He blew on the flame once more, slow and steady. His broad smile widened as the flame grew, blazing when it caught the twigs.

"How did you know how to do that?" Nick asked, still kneeling beside me.

I shrugged, realizing I took my knowledge for

granted. "My dad showed me when I was young. He bought me this flint and steel set when I was ten, and I've been using it ever since."

I caught a faint shadow slide across Nick's face. He was quick to look to the ground. I paused, watching him contain his thoughts.

"You haven't camped much, huh?" My obvious statement sounded stupid exiting my mouth. Why couldn't I ever think of the correct thing to say in the moment?

Nick expression turned scornful.

I winced and prepared myself for the usual barrage of insults. However, his expression softened, and he shook his head. He sat back on the log behind us. I joined him, reducing the distance between us.

"Might know a little more about camping if my dad was around," he muttered. His focus remained on the dancing flame.

"I'm sorry," I said, following his gaze. "That must have been hard." I held my breath, unsure of the ground we were treading on. "Do you miss him?"

Nick grimaced. "Can't miss what you don't know." He tossed a stray twig into the fire. It hissed in response.

"I guess that's something I've taken for granted," I voiced aloud. Despite Dad not being around as a teenager, I valued my memories with him as a little kid.

"What was it like?" I asked, not daring to look at him in the eyes.

He snapped his head around. "Let's get one thing

straight—I don't need you feeling sorry for me. It's over—it's done. Just forget about it." He looked at his feet, his jaw clenching.

My cheeks reddened. What did I think was going to happen? That he would pour out his heart and soul to me? I mean, this was Nick we were talking about. He was just a—

"Sorry." The single word was subdued, escaping as a quiet mumble.

I tried not to let my jaw drop. That one word coming from his mouth was more shocking than any rude comment he'd ever said to me.

"Oh no, it's fine. It's not my business, anyway." My hands fidgeted. Nick glanced my way, his light brown eyes meeting mine for just a moment.

"It was hard on my mom. I don't know. I just don't like to think about it, let alone talk about it." His words were so soft that I almost had to lean into him to hear what he was saying.

"It's ok. I know what that's like." I offered a small, uncomfortable smile. I was surprised when he returned it. Perhaps that encouraged me to risk my next question.

"And hard on you, too?"

Nick was silent while the question seemed to bring about painful childhood memories. His voice was gruff in response. "Yeah. Hard on me, too."

It took another minute, but he continued.

"There never seemed to be enough money. Even with the monthly check coming in from my so-called dad, my mom couldn't keep up with rent. We kept moving around, staying with my mom's parents for a while, then maybe my uncle's place a few months later in a different city, then back to some crummy apartment. I was enrolled in too many elementary schools to count."

"How did you end up in Danville?"

"My mom finished school and received her CNA license—you know, nursing stuff. There was a job opening in Danville and I was just about to start junior high. She figured it was the best time to make yet another move—but she promised she'd do her best to keep it permanent. And she kept her promise. We've been in Danville ever since."

I nodded my head in thought, piecing his story together. "Aaron told me you two hit it off as friends right away." I waited to see what else he might divulge.

"Pretty much," Nick said, letting out a small chuckle. "During the first week of school, I got into some fights with some guys who thought they were real tough. Problem was, I believed I was tougher—even two against one. In reality, it turns out I was wrong. I was taking quite a beating when Aaron walked by. He jumped right in, no questions asked. That evened things out. I'd like to remember us as winning that fight—though we were all suspended, of course—but that just allowed Aaron and me time to hang out and get to know each other. And his mom liked my mom, so it all worked out in the end."

"Danville was a good choice for you and Clara, then," I concluded.

Nick hesitated. "Well, at first, I got into a little trouble. Aaron tried getting me to hang out with his jock friends, but it didn't work out right away. Instead, I got sucked in to this other crowd and experimented with some stuff...it's not important. But Aaron didn't quit on me. He kept insisting I join some of the sports clubs with him after school, even though I'd never done much of that before. Turns out I could play ok—not like Aaron—but it was fun, and it was a better alternative than what I was using before."

"Can I ask you one more question?"

Nick looked at me with a hint of caution, but he didn't say no. So, I pressed on.

"What's the hardest part about your mom marrying my dad?"

He shrugged, but he was quiet as he took the time to think about it. "I guess, well, having to share my mom. Growing up, we only had each other, you know? It's not easy to see her so happy with your dad. And she liked you right away, too. She always wanted a daughter. I never liked that."

His honesty surprised me, but that explained some of his animosity towards me. That and the fact that I grew up with money, and he didn't.

"How about you?" he asked, returning the question.

"Mmm..." I pressed my lips together, my head tilted towards the sky. "*You*, probably."

I met his eyes. We both felt the blunt impact of my words, recalling the embedded hostility between us.

Curt laughter escaped our lips.

"Well. That's straightforward enough," he pointed out. "And true, I guess. I haven't gone out of my way to make it easy."

"No," I said, shaking my head. "And I don't deal well with change."

"Me either," he agreed. He scratched his head. "Huh. What do you know? We do have something in common." He grinned. "Who would have thought?"

I laughed, amazed and baffled at our ability to hold a conversation. It was then that I felt a beam of curiosity boring into my head. I turned, catching four pairs of eyes watching us, each with raised eyebrows. Brooke and Aaron held a sleeping bag in each hand, gawking at us. Clara leaned into Dad, her mouth close to his ear in a whisper. The corners of her mouth twitched into a smile.

I cleared my throat. "Can we...help you?"

That seemed to snap everyone out of their obnoxious stares. The air filled with stuttered comments and sheepish expressions.

"No, no," Dad said, smiling as he busied himself with one of the packs. "Just wondering what you're up to." Everyone seemed to be awaiting our answer, their feigned nonchalance failing miserably.

It took everything I had not to roll my eyes. I stood up, dusting off my pants. "Nick was just showing me how to make a better fire." I ignored Nick, who whipped his head around to look up at me. Dad observed me with a doubtful expression, though he remained silent.

Clara's voice was full of surprise. "Really? Nick, I had no you idea you knew—"

"Yep," I continued, drowning out her comment. "He's a natural."

The hardening expression on Nick's face backed down. He looked at me curiously, with a hint of appreciation.

I smiled back at him. I wasn't about to rat him out that he knew nothing about building fires, or worse, that I had discovered a soft side to him. Those were two very sure ways to destroy any man's ego.

Dad's smile outweighed my own as he watched the two of us standing side by side. "Well, now, it's certainly nice to see—"

"Nice to see the fire up and running," Aaron interrupted, striding over to us with a griddle and a bowl of pancake mix. "Who else wants breakfast?" He placed the cast-iron grill on top of the fire and then laid the griddle on top of it.

I exchanged a grateful smile with him as the attention diverted to everyone's empty, growling stomachs. Aaron paused long enough to wink at me, and then he poured four circles of batter onto the griddle. We all watched them bake with hungry anticipation.

CHAPTER 20

$\mathcal{A}$aron jumped and spiked the ball. It shot down like a bullet, nailing the sand between our front-row opponents.

"Nice, one, Aaron!" Brooke called out, rubbing sunblock on her legs. She was sitting on her towel, fifteen feet outside of our makeshift volleyball court. Having been hit in the head with the ball, she opted to play cheerleader on the sidelines instead.

Nick, Aaron, and I were teamed up against the three guys standing opposite the net. It was our serve. Randy, the guy in red board shorts, tossed me the ball.

"Fourteen serving twelve. Game point," I informed, lobbing the ball in the air. I hit it with my right palm, watching it sail over the net. The two other guys, Ben and Grant, bumped and set the ball, positioning it for a perfect spike. Randy jumped and smacked the ball, sending it hurtling between Aaron and me.

"Got it!" Nick called as he dove. He fell to his knees and hit the ball high into the air with his outstretched hands.

"Nice!" I set the ball for Aaron. He slammed it down again. The kid named Grant scrambled to get

ERICA KIEFFER

under it but failed. The ball sunk into the sand. That was game.

"That was a sweet dive there, Nick," I complimented, wiping sweaty sand from my forehead.

"Yeah, I know," Nick agreed in playful arrogance, making a show of brushing sand off his shoulders. "Nothing a little skill can't handle."

"Like it was all you," Aaron interjected. "Did you even see the spikes I laid out there?"

I pushed past the two of them towards Brooke. "So much for teamwork," I mumbled.

"How's the head?" I asked Brooke.

She scoffed at me. "Don't even start. I don't know why anyone likes volleyball, anyway. It's practically a broken nose waiting to happen." She tossed her hair. "Besides, it took two showers this morning to get the campfire smell out of my hair and every pore of my body. Why would I want to break a sweat and have to get ready all over again?"

I was pretty certain breaking a sweat would not be the case in any game she played, but I kept my opinion to myself.

Aaron jogged over to us. "Allie, you ready? They have two more friends that want to play, so we'll go four on four."

I noticed the boredom on Brooke's face. "Why don't you go ahead without me?"

Aaron appeared bummed and about to complain.

"Besides," I continued, "you and Nick both know

225

who the real star of the game is. So I just thought I'd sit this one out and give the other team a fighting chance."

He laughed. "All right, all right. How about you, Brooke? Ready for one more shot?"

She sparkled at him. "No, I'm good. It's more fun to watch you play."

Despite the competitive game in front of me, my attention drifted along the shore of the lake. I continued skimming beyond my favorite climbing tree, and through the line of trees that hid the river.

"You're not going to find him," Brooke's voice informed.

"What are you talking about?"

"Damien. I'm talking about Damien." Brooke pressed her lips together into thin line of concern. "Look, I'm not trying to be mean, but it's been three days. Don't you think if he really cared about you, he would have shown up to talk to you about it?"

I fumbled with the drawstring of my board shorts. Her words hurt, but I couldn't be mad at her for voicing my own conclusions. Why hadn't he come to see me? Was what we had not worth saving?

I recalled last night's conversation with Aaron up on the hill. My confessed feelings about Damien were real—I was connected to him. He did fit differently into my skewed view of relationships. He broke the mold. But perhaps it was one sided. I pinched my eyebrows together, confused all the more.

"Allie, I'm sorry. I hate seeing you miserable. I just

worry that maybe you've put too much of your heart on the line for this guy."

My eyes flew to her face, flawlessly made up as usual. "I'm not like you, Brooke. I can't just fall for any guy that walks across my path." I winced the instant the words left my mouth, putting my head in my hands and apologizing.

Brooke shook off my insult. "I'm not trying to squash how you feel about him. But there are so many other guys out there. Why settle for one that already has a huge black mark against him?"

I thought about what she was saying. In a way, perhaps she was right. Damien wouldn't be the last guy I was going to meet. Anything I developed with him would be all for naught, right? I was going to college in the fall and could forget all about my summer.

I swallowed a sigh, reality kicking in once again. Damien didn't interfere with my theory of ever-failing relationships after all. How could I have made the mistake of believing otherwise? I turned my head when I heard Brooke sigh, noting the closed smile on her face. Her eyes were glued to Aaron.

"Allie, he is so adorable, isn't he?"

"Um, yeah, I guess. How's—how's that going, anyway?"

"Well, he hasn't kissed me yet, if that's what you mean. But he's so sweet and attentive to me. Did you see how he carried me up that awful hill yesterday?" Her thoughts drifted into silence for a moment. "I don't know.

I'm thinking about going for it." She turned to look at me. Her words caught me by surprise.

"What did you say?"

"Maybe I need to make the first move. Maybe even tonight." Her mischievous smile twisted.

"Are you sure that's a good idea?" I asked.

"Yeah, why wouldn't it be?"

"I don't know. It's just more, uh, traditional to let it happen the other way around." I wrestled with the thoughts flying around in my head. Why did I care if she kissed him?

She crossed her arms across her chest. "What's wrong with you? I thought you'd be excited for me."

"No, I am. Sorry. I don't know what's going on with me."

"Well, it feels like you don't want things to work out just because you and Damien aren't working out."

"Brooke, no. That's not...What I mean is, I'm sorry. My head is just a little fuzzy right now." I forced an encouraging smile. "If that's what you want to do, then yeah, definitely."

Her lips still pushed out in a tiny frown, but she said no more.

My attention was drawn to three guys sauntering over to us. Two were Caucasian, while the shortest of the three stood out with his darker skin—perhaps a mix of ethnicities. They appeared around the same age as Nick and Aaron, and were all wearing board shorts and T-shirts. Looking at us, they whispered and laughed as they approached. Somebody whistled.

The one with the black, backwards hat on his head sidled up next to Brooke. He leaned down on his knees, his face turned towards her.

"Hey, there, gorgeous. You got plans tonight?"

Brooke smiled back at him, not shying away from his approach. "Well, I guess that all depends. What do you have in mind?"

I dug my elbow into her side, scowling at her. She flinched, but otherwise ignored me.

"And what about you?" A long arm was thrown across my shoulders to accompany the mild whiff of alcohol on his breath. I faced the ethnic culprit, whose buzzed head rested right next to my face. "I must say, you have a fine pair of legs."

I grimaced and shrugged him off. Grabbing Brooke's arm, I stood up. "We were just leaving."

The third guy stepped in my way. He was the thickest of the three, his black, sleeveless top showing off his bulk. "Going so soon?"

"Come on, now," the guy with the hat said. "You at least got to come with us to the party tonight."

"Yeah," ethnic guy said. "Big gathering downtown. We're hanging around here and driving down this evening if you want to come with us." He shoved a small, yellow flier in our hands.

"No thanks." I let the flier fall to the ground.

"Hey!" Aaron called from the volleyball pit. "Is there a problem?" He turned so he was facing us, his arms crossed along his chest.

The guys beside us looked him up and down with taunting smiles.

"If there was, what you gonna do about it, huh?" the one in the black shirt asked, puffing out his chest. Hat guy put his arm around his friend's shoulders with a casual smile.

"No, no. There's no problem. Isn't that right, Rob?" He exchanged a meaningful look with him as he started to guide his friend away. "Don't waste our time," he said quietly to his friend. Then louder, he called out, "We'll see you ladies tonight, yeah?" He smirked at us.

Brooke gave a small wave of her fingers and a teasing smile.

"Brooke, what are you doing?" I chastised, yanking her arm down. Aaron was oblivious to her behavior, still guardedly watching the guys walk away.

Brooke hushed her voice. "Relax, Allie. I was just having some fun. I had no intention whatsoever of going with them. It's just fun to be in control and let them *think* I'm interested."

"Yeah, until you're not in control," I said. "Besides, what was all that talk about Aaron?"

"Oh, please!" she whispered back, her eyes returning to Aaron. "I was just playing around. My interests and plans for Aaron still stand."

Trying to ignore the grating feeling inside my chest, I returned my attention to the volleyball game, watching the ball rally back and forth.

I lay on the couch, propped up with pillows behind my back. My eyes wandered outside the window, observing the post-dinner crowds still hanging around outside. The day had not been that eventful for me, other than playing a little volleyball. Now the evening was dragging on, feeling too quiet and empty in the cabin since Dad and Clara left that morning for a two-day excursion to Palm Springs. I yawned, feeling the effects of their early morning departure.

One of Dad's best friends owned a private plane and agreed to fly them from Columbia to the resort, as long as they could leave first thing in the morning. Dad and Clara were thrilled at the chance to get away on their own to celebrate their first anniversary. I was less than eager, seeing as how I was elected to drive the forty-minute stretch to the airport at five AM.

But then again, I was the one that encouraged them to leave in the first place. Dad, in particular, was hesitant to leave Nick, Aaron, and me alone for two days, but after pointing out that I was about to be in college and didn't need to be babysat anymore, they both agreed to go off and enjoy themselves. Besides, I, for one, didn't like the idea of being in the same cabin during their first anniversary.

"You must have picked a real winner." Aaron's voice disrupted my thoughts. He was coming from his room, where I assumed he and Nick had been shooting aliens and other villains of war. He pointed at my lap. "The book, I mean. You don't seem too interested in it."

I pushed myself up to a better sitting position, *Jane Eyre* lying closed on my lap. Remembering the last time someone had doubted the intrigue of Charlotte Bronte's writing, I could almost feel the sunburn from that day when I fell asleep on the sand.

"What are you thinking about?" Aaron sat down on the couch next to mine, facing my direction.

Damien. I'm always thinking about Damien.

"Nothing," I murmured. "I'm just feeling a little out of it today."

"Well, you know what always helps make my day?" Aaron leaned behind the couch and picked up a hidden basketball. He grinned. "What do you say to a little game of one-on-one?" He palmed the orange ball with one hand, holding it in the air.

"Is basketball the solution to everything for you?" I asked, taking the ball from his hands.

He put a hand to his chin, mockingly pausing in thought. "Mmm, let me think. It's fun, great for your health, develops friendships, and makes great analogies... Yep, just about everything."

I scoffed. "I don't know. I'm not in the mood, Aaron."

"Sure you are. You just don't know it yet. Come on—just ten minutes and, if you're not having fun losing to me, we can move onto something else."

I couldn't help but smile. "Ok, you win." Wearing jean shorts and a purple tank top, I didn't bother changing, except to throw on socks and sneakers.

Reaching the dimly lit court, we checked the ball to each other, with Aaron taking the ball first. He was quick, dribbling around me before he jumped, scoring an easy two-pointer.

My turn. His towering height over me was going to be tricky. I dribbled forward, crouched low, looking for an opportunity to go around him. Backing up, I drew him in. He swiped, attempting to steal the ball. I spun around, taking advantage of the widened gap behind him. I beat him to the hoop, landing a layup.

Aaron gave me a high five. "Not bad. See, less than five minutes, and you're already having a good time. I'm telling you, basketball is life's new remedy."

"Yeah, well, you better not throw the game just to make me feel better," I warned, checking the ball.

"I wouldn't think of it," Aaron said. "We're even now, four-four. Game on."

We played for the next forty minutes, battling good-naturedly. Despite some proud moments on my part, it wasn't a contest. Aaron crushed me in every game, no matter how many times we reset the points.

During the last play of the game, I tried to block a shot. I spread my arms wide, stepping into his path. Aaron's momentum charged into me, knocking me over. On impulse, I grabbed his white shirt to brace my fall but, instead, pulled him down on top of me. I groaned as his body weight crushed me into the cement court.

I burst into an exhausted fit of laughter, sprawled on my back, my legs tangled with his. We laid there for a moment, sweaty and both too tired to move. I looked up at Aaron.

He wasn't laughing. He was staring down at me, his face positioned just above mine. Without warning, he lowered his head, his lips enclosing around my own. His movements were slow and deliberate, his mouth opening to wrap around mine. For a surprised second, I tried to pull back my head, but Aaron's persistence squashed my resistance. Instead, my body responded, moving my mouth with his.

It took another moment before my mind caught up with my body. When it did, I shoved my hands against his chest with a gasp, pulling my face free from his.

Mortified, I squirmed out from under him on my hands and knees. It wasn't until I turned back around that my heart stopped. Brooke stared at us from behind Aaron, her mouth gaping.

Aaron, still breathing heavily, said nothing, though his guilty features said as much. I tried to speak, to soften her heartbreak.

"Brooke, I—"

Her countenance changed, twisting into fury with clenched fists. "How *could* you?"

Her eyes flitted back and forth, making it unclear whether she was speaking to me or Aaron, but I knew it didn't matter. The damage was done. Her eyes were brim-full with anger. It was the last thing I saw in her face before she took off, running back towards the cabins.

"Brooke!" I made a sound of frustration, hurrying after her. Standing to his feet, Aaron grabbed my wrist.

"Allie, wait—"

I yanked my hand out of his grip.

"Let go of me! Don't you realize what we've just done?"

Running after Brooke, I left Aaron behind. I didn't have time to tell him that I was more disappointed in myself than anybody—disappointed that I allowed impulse to hurt my friend, and disappointed because a weaker, subliminal part of myself welcomed Aaron's subtle advances, gave in to the bold sensation of his lips against mine.

Stupid, stupid, stupid!

Darkness was falling. Still, I caught the shadowy outline of Brooke a good hundred feet ahead of me. She was in the parking lot next to a sedan. I could hear the running motor as the driver revved the engine. Who was she talking to?

I nearly tripped. Brooke was flanked by two of the guys who had disrupted the volleyball game and gave us the party flier. The one with the black hat put a hand on her shoulder, talking with his face close to hers. She shrugged and nodded her head, allowing him to escort her inside the car.

What is she doing?

Brooke!" I called out again, as her head

disappeared inside the car. The sedan began to pull away just as I reached it. I banged on the trunk. "Wait!"

The car stopped. The driver's window and rear-seat window slid down.

The guy with the darker skin sat in front passenger seat. He flashed a wide smile at me. "You comin' with us, baby?"

Gritting my teeth, I ignored him. Brooke was in the back row on the far side. She wasn't looking at me, but I could see the glistening in her eyes.

"Brooke. What are you doing?" I kept my voice calm.

"What does it look like I'm doing?" she asked in a cool tone, refusing to look my direction. "I'm going to go have some fun."

"Yeah, you got that right." Hat guy smirked, sitting beside her. He wrapped an arm around her shoulders. I tried to hide my disgust at the way he looked her up and down.

"Come on, Brooke," I pleaded, trying to conceal the desperation in my voice. "You can't go with them. We need to talk about this."

"Quit telling me what to do. You're nothing but a lying, back-stabbing hypocrite!"

Jeering laughter filled the car.

"Look out for the catfight," someone mumbled under his breath. More laughter and quiet taunting followed.

The guy behind the wheel addressed me. "Look.

Either get in or move along. The party's not going to wait on us."

I hesitated, fuming and distraught as I waited for Brooke to get out of the car. Noting the hard lines around her eyes and her set jawline, I knew that would not be the case. I didn't have a choice. "Move over, then."

I slipped into the car as all three guys smiled and hooted. The stereo system thumped with rap music.

I didn't know what we were getting ourselves into, but I wasn't about to let Brooke face it alone.

"Hey, so listen," the guy next to Brooke said as the car pulled away. "Now that we have all night together, we got time for proper introductions. I'm Jordon. This here is my buddy, Rob," he said, putting a hand on the driver's shoulder. "And, of course, Joel."

Joel raised his hand. "Welcome to the party." He turned up the base, bumping to the music. "We're going to have some fun tonight. Aren't we, boys?"

CHAPTER 21

"This is it, ladies," Jordan said, stretching his arms into the air and puffing out his chest. "It's time to get your party on!" He grinned at Brooke, putting an arm around her once again. "Let's go."

She didn't even look back at me once. Concern and irritation flared inside of me as I watched her leave with him.

What is she thinking? Of all the naïve, immature things to do...

"You comin' or what?" Joel called from ahead of me, but he didn't pause to wait for an answer. He hurried to catch up with his friends—and Brooke, of course—all of whom were striding into the narrow, unlit street.

I hesitated a moment longer, my eyes searching up and down the street for—for what? Who was I looking for? No one knew where we were. I kicked myself. Why hadn't I at least stopped to tell Aaron where we were going?

Because Brooke would have taken off without me.

Answering my own question didn't solve my problems, but it did remind me I was on my own. I needed to find Brooke, knock some sense into that thick blond head of hers, and get us both to a phone.

I hurried after them, pushing past a young couple in front of me. I ignored the sparsely clothed female who threw me a dirty look, her heels clicking behind me. I felt her look me up and down, no doubt criticizing my odd choice of clothing for a party. Picking up the pace, my tennis shoes thumped against the cracked asphalt.

It felt even darker inside the street than it looked from outside. The buildings seemed to close in around me, most of which appeared rundown and abandoned. Despite the shadows, I caught sight of a curtain of highlighted hair disappearing inside a doorway.

I hurried past the shattered windows of the building, stepping with caution around the shards of glass littering the ground. Reaching the entrance, I attempted to follow a group of people through the open doorway.

A firm hand gripped my shoulder, holding me in place.

"Hey—" I protested.

"Cash first." A thickset man stood in my path, his tight shirt emphasizing his bulging biceps. His gruff features loomed over me as he held out an open palm.

My hands slipped into my empty pockets, coming up with a mere shrug of my shoulders. "I'm sorry—I don't have any money. I just need to find my friend and then we're leaving."

"Yeah, I've heard that one." He pushed me out the door.

"No, you don't understand—"

"Next!" he called.

"Wait. She's with us." I turned around in surprise. Joel grabbed my forearm, thrusting a five-dollar bill into the bouncer's hand. Someone stamped my hand with little care as I was pulled inside the club. I allowed Joel to hold onto me while I stumbled inside, my eyes struggling to adjust to the large room with poor lighting.

Techno music blared in my ears with every beat pulsing through my body. Twirling, florescent glow sticks helped illuminate the dancing crowd. To the side was a small stage seating a DJ and a table of audio equipment and other gear. Colorful, flashing lights projected from the ceiling, circling the crowd with spinning lights that made me dizzy.

"I was wondering where you disappeared to," Joel said—or yelled, rather, over the deafening music.

Distracted, I looked around. "Yeah, thanks. I guess." Joel pulled me against him.

"No problem. Now you owe me one," he sneered, laughing as I pushed him away. I glared at him, daring him to put his hands on me again.

"Where's Brooke?" I demanded through my teeth, scanning the swarm before me with frantic eyes. It was impossible to distinguish any one person from the crazed, bouncing crowd. Towards the edge of the stage, they were smashing into each other and knocking each other over. How was I supposed to find her in this madhouse?

"Where is she?" I asked again.

Joel smirked at me. He pointed towards the back

of the room. Brooke was leaning against the wall next to that guy, Jordan.

I pushed past the crowd, disgusted as sweaty arms slid against my own. The air tasted staler by the minute. Reaching Brooke, I put my hand on her arm and said, "Come on, we have to get out of here."

She jutted out her chin and threw my hand off.

"What do you think you're doing?" I asked.

"How do you have the nerve to ask me that? I don't suppose you asked yourself the same question when you were stabbing me in the back!"

I let out exasperated air. She had every right to be furious with me.

"I just need to talk to you. Please," I begged her. She hesitated with indecision.

"Why don't you lighten up a little and let your friend be?" Jordan motioned to the beer on the table, taking a sip from his own can. "You're in and it's paid for. Grab a can and relax."

Ignoring him, I waited for Brooke's response.

"Fine," she said. "Five minutes." She followed me back through the crowds, passed another bouncer, and exited the back doors. I inhaled the cool air. While I wouldn't describe the hint of mildew in the air as fresh, it was easier to take in than the smoke-filled room.

"Ok. So what do you want?" Brooke snapped. She crossed her arms.

I sighed. "Look, I know I don't have any business telling you what to do, considering what happened at the basketball court tonight. But if you stay here with these guys, you're just going to get yourself in trouble."

She rolled her eyes at me.

"Brooke, I am so sorry," I said. "What happened between Aaron and me shouldn't have happened."

"Then why *did* it happen?" she spat out. "All this time, I've been excited and happy for you and Damien—at least before he turned out to be a criminal. And you knew how much I like Aaron. Why would you do that?"

I shook my head, looking at the ground. "I don't know. I've just been confused! Everything feels so screwed up with Damien—"

"So what—you had to take second best?"

"No! Brooke, I just want to fix it. If I could go back and change it, I would. You've been a good friend to me and you don't deserve any of this." I took a breath, watching her with a hopeful expression.

The fury seemed to be dying in her eyes. She pulled away, sniffling. "I shouldn't have made such a big deal about it. It's just a crush, you know? I mean, let's be honest. We both knew he wasn't that into me. It was always you."

Raising my eyebrows, I started to shake my head.

"Don't look so surprised," she continued. "I wasn't entirely blind. I've seen the way he looks at you when he thinks nobody's looking. I just hoped he'd change his mind and look at me like that, too. I guess I tried to force something that wasn't there."

I jumped as the door behind us burst open. Jordan

and Joel ambled towards us with an unsteady stance.

"Hey ladies," Joel said, stepping close to my side. "Time to get back to the party, don't you think?" The smell from his warm breath made me gag.

I took Brooke's arm. "You know what, guys? We're about done. We'll find our own way home. Thanks anyway." Brooke walked by my side, keeping up with my pace. I could feel them watching us.

"Quickly," I murmured. Brooke's breathing increased in tempo, sensing my urgency.

Hurried footsteps echoed behind us.

"I don't think so." Joel's menacing voice accompanied the grip around my bicep, swinging me around. Jordan yanked Brooke from my side.

"Ow!" she cried out. "Allie—"

Joel pushed my back against the wall. "You still owe me a favor," he said, stepping into me. I turned my head, pushing both hands against his chest.

"Get away from me!" The fear in Brooke's voice seemed to fuel their intent. Their low laughter resonated through the hollow street.

From my peripheral, I could see Brooke squirming.

"Come on," Jordan coaxed. "You wanted to have some fun, right?" His jeering laughter was cut off when he cried out in pain. "She just clawed my face! You're gonna regret that."

"Leave her alone!" I wrestled against Joel's weight. He had my arms pinned against the wall above my head, using his body weight as leverage. I dodged a sloppy kiss and spit in his face. He growled, releasing one arm to wipe it off.

I twisted around in time to see Jordan throw Brooke to the ground. Her body collided into the dumpster, slamming her head against the wall.

Pulse racing, I jerked my knee upwards. Joel grunted as it made contact. He doubled over, cursing at me. I stepped around him, running to Brooke's sprawled body, and crouched beside her. She whimpered as she lifted her smudged cheek off the ground.

Strong arms grabbed me from behind and spun me around. Falling back onto my rear, I kicked my right leg out, aiming for Jordan's face, but he grabbed my foot and yanked me towards him. With one swift movement, he struck my cheek.

I cried out in protest, my eyes brimming with tears.

"You shouldn't have done that," a deep voice informed from behind him.

Identifying the familiar voice, my mouth fell open with a quick intake of breath. Jordan didn't even have time to turn around before two hands wrenched him off me. I sat up, my breaths heaving in my chest, as Jordan was hurled against the asphalt.

In his place stood Damien, three feet from me, towering over Jordan's body.

"Maybe you shouldn't have done *that*," Joel said, having recovered from my retaliation. Striding towards Damien, he called to Jordan, who was rising to his feet.

"Come on, man. We got this."

Damien eyed the duo. Reaching into the dumpster, he pulled out a broken two-by-four jutting over the edge. "Look, the two of you together can probably take me." He paused, gripping the wooden plank with both hands. "But whoever comes at me first will be going to the hospital."

Wrapping my arms around Brooke, I pulled her as close to the wall as possible, distancing ourselves from the imminent fight.

With a cocky laugh, Joel made eye contact with Jordan and gestured towards Damien. They approached him simultaneously, each strategically choosing a side. Joel swung first. With a swift movement, Damien sidestepped him and cracked the plank into Joel's rib. He hollered, curling over.

"Behind you!" I yelled, but my warning came too late.

Jordan charged and clocked Damien in the head, knocking him off his feet. Rolling, Damien evaded Jordan's kick. Lunging off the ground, Damien tackled Jordan, landing his weight on top of him. Their arms locked around each other as they wrestled, jockeying for the upper hand. Damien won the advantage, locking Jordan down with his legs before striking one side of Jordan's face and then the other. Jordan moaned, grabbing his bleeding nose.

I cringed at the sight, watching Damien rise to his feet. He picked up the board.

"Are you done?" Damien asked gruffly, surveying the two guys struggling nearby. Neither made a move except to tend to their wounds. "Now get out of here," Damien finished.

Joel limped over to Jordan, still gripping his injured rib, and helped his friend to his feet. Damien tossed the two-by-four against the wall, breathing deeply.

My attention returned to my Brooke. I slid my arm under her shoulders, hoisting her up against the wall.

"Brooke!" I tried to swallow my nerves, ignoring the blood pulsing in my veins.

"Is she ok?" He met my gaze, his mouth drawn together.

I wanted to throw my arms around Damien and hold onto him, preventing him from disappearing again, but I didn't move from my position.

Damien knelt down beside me to inspect Brooke, who held a hand at the back of her head. She winced in pain.

"Ow, that hurts."

I tilted her head forward to check for blood. "Well, you've got a huge goose egg, but at least it's not bleeding."

"Come on," Damien said, scooping her up into his arms. "We need to get out of here."

Main Street was still packed with cars parked along the curb. In haste, I walked beside Damien. I didn't know where we were going, but I felt confident following his footsteps. He surprised me by stopping beside a black Dodge Ram truck. He set Brooke on her feet with care, while he fumbled for keys in his pocket.

"This is yours?" I asked, observing the body of the full-size truck. I raised my eyebrows in surprise.

Damien opened the back door. "You didn't think I just drove my dirt bike everywhere, did you?" He lifted Brooke into the cab, which was fortunate, considering I wasn't sure how she'd step into it otherwise. The seat rested a good two-and-a-half feet off the ground.

I pulled myself into the front passenger seat with effort. Damien already had his keys in the engine and revved the motor. It roared, reverberating through the still night air. I looked over my shoulder at Brooke.

"Feeling ok?"

Groggy, she blinked and leaned her head against the window. "Just tired," she mumbled, closing her eyes.

"She might have a concussion," I whispered to Damien.

"We'll take a look at her when we get back to the cabins," he responded.

It was quiet inside the truck as it pulled into the street and sped towards the canyon. Before long, the only sound was Brooke's breathing, slowed to a steady rhythm.

I looked at the clock on the dashboard. It was almost ten. It was a good thing Dad and Clara were out of town, saving me from creating a clever explanation for my disappearance. I chanced a look at Damien, whose eyes remained focused on the clear road. Other cars were few and far between through the canyon. I doubted it required as much attention as Damien was giving. I squinted at him.

"What were you doing in that part of town tonight?"

"I might ask you the same question." He turned to look at me. "And with dirt bags like that?"

I glanced at Brooke, making sure she was asleep. She seemed to be.

"Just keeping someone out of trouble." I looked back at Damien. "How about you?"

Damien let out a short laugh, flexing his right hand with a grimace. "Guess you can say I was doing the same thing as you."

"Yeah, about that. Thanks, by the way. I'm not sure how well that would have panned out without you." I touched my right cheek, sensing a bruise.

"Well, I know exactly how that would have gone down." Damien's tone angered. His brows pulled together. "They're lucky that's all I did to them. What were you doing with them anyway?"

Memories of the evening raced through my mind, starting with the incident at the basketball court. My face felt hot as I looked out my window. I could feel Damien watching me. Was it dark enough that he wouldn't be able to see the warmth on my cheeks? I cleared my throat.

"Brooke and I kind of got in a fight. She was upset with, uh, something I did. She ran off with those guys on impulse. Needless to say, I didn't trust them so I went with her. Thought it'd be a better idea than letting her go alone."

"What'd you do to upset her?"

I wanted to tell him that it was none of his business, but I realized that maybe it was. Or was it? I struggled to put my thoughts into words, rearranging them back and forth in my head. There was no other way to say it.

"Aaron kissed me." I let the three simple words linger in the air. "And I kissed him back." I didn't dare look him in the eyes.

His response was silence. It dragged on for another minute or two before I spoke.

"Are you going to say something?"

Damien continued to stare out the windshield. He did well maintaining a neutral expression. "I guess that's what I get for leaving you alone."

His words brought to remembrance the hurt and confusion over the past three days—the questions and concerns mulling in my mind, the what-if scenarios that never amounted to anything useful, and even the vulnerable gap of confusion that allowed something to pass between Aaron and me.

"What is going on with you?" I knew the usual moments of silence following my questions would, without fail, lead to an evasive answer. A spark of anger touched my voice. "And stop playing games with me. Tell me the truth."

Damien released a breath of air, scratching the top of his head. He lowered his hand to massage the back of his neck but said nothing more.

I sat back in my seat, staring at my hands. I lowered my voice, pleading. "Why won't you just talk to me?"

At last, Damien spoke. "I knew where you were today because I followed you." He paused, and I didn't say a word, hoping he would continue without further prodding.

"I was in my truck sitting in the parking lot, which I assume is why you didn't see me. I was waiting for you to show up at your cabin so I could talk to you. Then you and Brooke ran up and left with that carload of punks." Irritation touched his features. "I couldn't hear what you were saying, but something didn't look right about it. So I kept my distance but followed you downtown and into that party. I lost track of you inside that whole mess, or I would have stopped those guys sooner."

"What were you going to talk to me about?"

Again, the hesitation—the galling pause.

"I was coming to say good-bye."

I must have heard him wrong. That couldn't have been what he said.

But the guilt in his expression confirmed his words. My words caught in my throat.

"What—what do you mean good-bye?"

"I'm leaving town. Heading out tomorrow." His words were so casual.

I shook my head, disbelief heavy in my voice. How could he be leaving?

"Why? Is this because I read those news reports?

Damien, I don't care about your past! It's not who you are. I—"

He put a hand to my lips, interrupting my panic. It was then that I realized we were pulling into the lodge parking lot. The gravel crunched beneath the tires. Pulling into an empty spot, Damien cut the engine. I stared at him, a million questions reflecting from my eyes.

"You can't understand," Damien said.

"Can't? That's because you won't explain anything to me. Everything with you is a mystery! Secrets and half-truths...every time I search for an answer, you leave me with more questions! Please, just talk to me—tell me what's going on."

"I've hurt people, Allie. I'll hurt you, too."

The expression in his face told me he believed his words.

Brooke's movements from the backseat caught my attention. She sat up and looked around, momentarily confused. "Where are we?" She rubbed her eyes, and then gingerly touched the sore spot on her head. She seemed to remember the events of the evening. "Oh."

Damien hopped out of the truck and opened Brooke's door, helping her to the ground. I let myself out and met them at the rear of the truck bed. I confronted Damien once again.

"So that's it. You're leaving."

"Yes."

Brooke looked back and forth between us, dumbfounded.

"Um—I'm just gonna go home. My parents might be worried." She started walking towards her cabin.

"Wait, Brooke," I said. "I better walk you home. You might have a concussion."

"No, I'm good. I'll have my dad take a look. I'll tell him I fell out of a tree. If it can happen to you, it could certainly happen to me." She almost smiled.

I hesitated. "Are you sure you're ok?"

She shrugged. "Nothing a little sleep won't take care of." She gave me a hug and whispered in my ear, "I'm sorry I got you into this. Let's talk tomorrow. Good luck." She turned to Damien. "Thanks for being there tonight."

Damien nodded with a solemn expression. Brooke waved at us with a flick of her wrists, then turned and left, leaving Damien and me standing across from each other.

I stared at him with wide, hurt eyes. "Was it all just a lie?" I asked, my voice just above a whisper. I put an arm out, gesturing between the two of us. "This sort of thing, whatever this is, doesn't happen to me. Ever. It has to mean *something*."

Damien took my arm and pulled me into him. He held my head against his chest and squeezed me. I felt his lips touch the top of my head ever so softly.

"That's why I have to go."

Tears stung my eyes. "That doesn't make any sense."

He lowered his face and brushed his lips against mine. I closed my eyes. An involuntary tear fell down my cheek. I felt Damien's soft mouth move leisurely along my face, my chin, my cheek, my forehead. His lips slid down and matched mine once again. He opened his mouth just enough to close with tenderness around my lips. My body seemed to melt inside his kiss, weakening my senses.

Without warning, he pulled away. Hurrying to the side of his truck, he yanked open the door and jumped inside. I stepped out of the way as he backed up, my woozy head struggling to function.

Damien didn't even pause to look back at me. The truck tore out of the parking lot and sped away, leaving me feeling very much confused and, once again, alone.

CHAPTER 22

"I've hurt people, Allie. I'll hurt you, too."

My brain ran over and over last night's brief conversation with Damien. What was he talking about? In fact, why couldn't he ever just talk to me, straightforward, without any roundabout comments that were misleading and confusing in so many ways? It was so frustrating!

And now, here I sat, staring at my bowl of cereal, with random thoughts still racing through my mind. If only there was a reset button to make it all go away. Except I didn't want it to go away. I wanted to figure it out—to understand what Damien was hiding from me, and why he was disappearing from my life.

"Will you walk with me?" Aaron's voice right beside my ear made me jump. My hand knocked the spoon, and it clattered against the porcelain dish. I fumbled for my utensil and placed it on the table. Aaron stood behind me with both hands resting on either side of me on the table. He leaned over with his face next to mine. I squirmed.

"What for?" I asked, failing nonchalance. My fingertips played with the crinkled edges of the tablecloth.

I tried to ignore Aaron's proximity to my body.

"You know what for. Come talk with me."

I cleared my throat, wishing it were that easy to clear my head. Memories of our kiss breached my thoughts, amplified by Aaron's cologne permeating through the air.

"I don't know, Aaron."

"Please," he whispered, putting his right hand on my arm. The warmth of his hand seemed to burn into my skin.

"Ok," I agreed, agitated as I pulled my arm away. Subconsciously, I rubbed my skin, trying to rid the guilt that formed from his lingering touch. We walked to the amphitheater, and I sat down on a bench. Aaron sat beside me, straddling the bench so he was facing me.

"So, listen," he began. "About last night. I'm not going to apologize for what happened."

His words took me by surprise. I hadn't known what he was going to say, but I assumed he would apologize for kissing me, realizing it had all been a mistake—an impulsive action that never should have happened.

Aaron seemed to read my thoughts, or perhaps just the expression on my confused face. "I don't think it was a mistake. I like you, Allie. I've felt something between us and I know you have, too. I don't think it's fair to pretend those feelings don't exist. And it's not wrong to act on them."

My jaw slipped open, as I struggled with a

response. Aaron's hand came up to my chin, and he leaned in close to me. I put my hand up and pushed against his chest, keeping him a fair distance away. He stared at me, his intentions clear.

"Aaron, this can't happen, for a lot of reasons. First of all, Brooke—"

"I know," Aaron interrupted. "Like I said, I'm not going to apologize that it happened. But I do feel bad for the way it happened, with hurting Brooke's feelings and all. It's my fault. I knew she liked me, and I led her on, not intending for anything to happen—with either of you, actually. But it did. And we can't change that."

"No, you're right. We can't change it. But that's as far as it goes, Aaron." I swallowed, watching Aaron's features twist with disappointment. He removed his hand from my face, leaning back a little.

After a few moments of silence, he asked, "So, what happened last night, anyway?"

I was quiet for a minute while my mind wrapped around last night's events. "We got into some trouble," I started. Then I filled him in on what happened at the party, ending with Damien showing up and driving us back to the cabins. Aaron listened, though I could see he wasn't happy at the mention of Damien's name, despite his heroic act.

"So, you still don't know what is behind his behavior?" Aaron commented.

I shook my head. "No. That's what I need to figure out. I care about him, Aaron. I can't just let it go.

Something else is going on with him, and I don't know what. But there's more to his story than he's telling me."

Aaron looked skeptical. "Listen, Allie. I know he's the competition here, but I'm not just saying this because I wish you'd forget about him. It's great you're giving him the benefit of the doubt and all, but what if he really is "the bad guy" and he's giving you this one chance to let you off the hook, to stay away from him and be safe? Maybe you should just listen to him and let him go wherever he's going."

I stood up, frustrated with Aaron's cynicism. "You don't know him, Aaron."

"Oh, and you do? Because if you did, you wouldn't have to play this guessing game with him."

Dusting off my jeans, I glared at Aaron. "I'm going to check on Brooke—and it'd be nice if you'd do the same. Just do me a favor and wait until I'm not there." I stalked off towards the boardwalk.

"Aw, Allie—Come on!" Aaron called after me, but I ignored him. I had to. He only added to my confusion.

When I cooled off, I knocked on the door and waited on the doorstep. Moments later, Brooke appeared. I waited, not sure how she was feeling about me today. I also wondered if Aaron had stopped by to see her first. After my poorly ended conversation with him, I ended up going for a long walk along the trails. Not that it helped any.

Within seconds, Brooke embraced me in a bear hug.

"Allie, I'm sorry about last night. I was being so stupid and something worse could have happened."

Surprised—and relieved—I returned the gesture. "Please don't be the one apologizing, Brooke. I feel like the biggest jerk as it is. How's your head?"

Brooke looked behind her towards one of the bedrooms. Other than the murmur of the TV, it was quiet inside her cabin. She stepped out the front door, and closed it behind her.

"It's ok," she said, touching the back of her head. "It's a little sensitive but not bad."

"What'd you tell your dad?"

"Oh, just that we were playing hide 'n seek and I fell out of a tree."

I couldn't help but laugh a little, and Brooke shrugged her shoulders.

"So," I continued, "Did, uh, Aaron stop by?"

"Yeah, he came by," she admitted with a sullen expression.

"I'm guessing it didn't go so well?" The guilt was back, gnawing at my insides, as I watched the disappointment etch across her face.

"No, it was ok," she said, playing with her bracelet. "I mean, it's not the ending I was hoping for, but it's what I expected. Still, it was nice of him to stop by and talk to me about it."

"So what'd he say?"

"Are you going to make me repeat the rejection?" she asked. I felt worse, but she offered a half-smile. "He apologized for hurting my feelings, and said he still wants to hang out with me, but just as friends, of course." She laughed. "That line had to be in there, right?"

"Anyway," she continued. "It was fine. We both knew nothing serious was going to develop between us. Anything that happened would have just been one of those summer flings, you know? Nothing like you and Damien."

At the mention of his name, my stomach flipped, worried and intrigued all over again. "What do you mean?" I managed to ask through my dry mouth.

Brooke sighed. "Allie, I've been worried about Damien since we found out about his past. But then Damien showed up last night at just at the right moment and saved the day. He followed you because he cares, and the way he looks at you...I wasn't that out of it last night not to notice. It's obvious you mean a whole lot to him."

I pictured Damien's dark features looking back at me, mesmerizing, enticing, and so puzzling at the same time. Could he care about me that much if he was ditching me?

"What was he saying last night, anyway?" Brooke asked, catching the bewilderment gathering on my face. "About leaving?"

With effort, I relived the conversation I had with him, ending with how he had driven away and left me alone again.

"But that doesn't make sense," Brooke stated, her furrowed eyebrows suggesting she was as puzzled as I was. "I think you're right, Allie. There's something else he's not telling you—something that is missing. What are you going to do?"

"I don't know." I sighed in discouragement, but it was in that moment that I was tired of questioning what I was going to do—tired of puzzling over what Damien and I meant to each other. Something had to be done.

"I'm going to find him," I said, rising to my feet. "Right now. I'm going to drive over there and get some answers."

Brooke bit her lower lip as though afraid she had encouraged something regretful, but she joined me on her feet and nodded her head. "Ok, Allie. But just be careful."

Jumping into our suburban, I turned the key in the motor, pausing only momentarily to pull the seatbelt across my chest. Locking it into place, I threw the car into drive and sped out of the parking lot.

I needed to find Damien, but what if he was already gone? What if, for once, he was true to his word and had left first thing this morning? Then I would never find him.

While I wasn't entirely sure how to drive to his cabin from the main road, I took a chance and pulled onto a road that seemed to be leading in the right direction. I floored the gas. It was only a couple miles before I could see the bridge in the distance. Luck seemed to be on my side.

Minutes later, I pulled up in front of his cabin

and hopped out of the car. I hurried to the front door and
placed my hand on the doorknob.

Do I knock? His behavior didn't deserve a knock.

I twisted the handle and marched inside. I stopped
mid-step as I caught sight of Damien. He stood at the
entrance of his bedroom, bending over a large duffle bag.
His head jerked up, and he stared at me. Our eyes locked
into each other's.

The shock on his face was outdone by the anger
that altered his expression. He threw the handful of
clothes in his arms with great force against the duffle
bag. Stepping over it, he stalked over to me. I stood still,
waiting for the reaction I knew was coming.

"What are you doing here?" He didn't wait for an
answer. His eyes flickered to the window, and he gave a
strong shake of his head. "You have to go." He pushed
my shoulder and turned me around, steering me towards
the open door.

I resisted, digging my feet into the floorboards.
Spinning around, I grabbed his arm. "I deserve an
explanation. A truthful and thorough explanation," I
emphasized.

Damien expelled an air of frustration. "Allie,
listen to me—"

"No, you listen!" I pushed past him towards the
leather couch. Turning around, I ignored the hard lines
by his eyes. "You've gone on and on about how I can trust
you—so much in fact that I risked sharing my darkest
emotions with you. I trusted you, just like you asked. It

wasn't some easy joyride!"

I sighed and lowered my voice. "All I'm asking is that you do the same."

He took a tentative step towards me, his hands resting at his side. "I told you the truth about what I did to my family. And I saw the look on your face. You were horrified. What more do you want me to say?"

I bit my lip. "Ok, you're right. That *was* my initial reaction. I was unsure how it all made me feel, but I haven't been able to stop thinking about you while we've been apart. No matter what you've done, you're still a good person. I can feel it every time I'm with you." I took a deep breath. "And I know there's more to your story. You haven't told me everything, and there's no way I can understand unless you do."

Damien heaved another sigh, looking across the room before he met my eyes again. "Allie, there are bigger things going on here—bigger than both of us. It's just better if you don't know."

I stood my ground. "I deserve the truth—the truth in its entirety."

Neither of us moved. I dreaded the thoughts behind his reticent eyes. But he seemed to be considering my words.

"The police stopped by two days ago." Damien's low voice broke the silence. I was bursting with questions but managed to contain myself. Damien shut the door behind him.

"They needed information—information that I

could give them, but I chose not to. I didn't tell them because I've spent years putting that past behind me. And I didn't tell them because it puts me in danger, and risks the lives of anyone I love. And the truth is, Allie...I'm in love with you."

My breath caught in my throat, and my eyes ran across his face. He stared right back at me, cupping my face with his hands.

"I love you," he said again. He tried to suppress it, but I detected the fear in his eyes. "And you will be their number-one target."

I furrowed my brow, overwhelmed by my emotions.

"Who are they?" I asked, my hands reaching up to hold onto his wrists. I didn't want to let him go—couldn't allow him to leave me, especially not now. "Please tell me—talk to me."

"It's a long story," he warned.

"I'll listen."

Damien took my hand and led me to the couch. I sank into the leather. Sitting down beside me, he looked down at his hands. He wrung them together, over and over, as he prepared for what he was going to reveal.

I waited.

"It started about two years ago."

DAMIEN'S STORY

When I was seventeen, my senior year began at a new school. My father received a promotion that summer, so we moved to Oakland Hills, just twenty minutes from our hometown in Hayward. My family always had money, as did our new neighbors, and all the spoiled rich kids I had to associate with. Of course, I was one of them in that sense, but I was new, and that put me on a whole new playing field.

High school was a joke. It wasn't about gaining an education. It was about how far you could raise your social status. Anyone who was anyone aspired to be among the top tier of the social tower.

Me—I was somewhere in the middle. I was nobody special—just another countless number in the mix of judgmental teenagers. I sat in class, did my work when I was supposed to, and when the bell rang, I'd throw my bag over my shoulder and walk up the hill to my house.

Jenna was always at my side, talking my ear off.

"Meet anybody interesting today?" she asked one day. It was a couple weeks into the new school year. "I did. I made a friend with a girl just around the corner from us. Her brother is your age, you know. His name's Kevin Ramsey. Do you know him?"

Ten year olds. They never shut up, but I happened to like this one.

"I don't know. Probably not."

She peered at me. "Why don't you like people?

"I never said that."

"Well, you don't have to say it. But that's how it seems to me. Do you even have any friends?"

I threw my arm around her shoulder and rubbed my knuckles against the top of her head. "Anyone ever tell you that you talk too much?"

She grinned at me, exposing the dimples in her cheek that marked us as siblings. "Someone's got to do the talking around here." She waited for me to respond. When thirty seconds passed, she was at it again.

"You didn't answer my question. Do you have friends yet?"

There was no stopping her inquisitiveness.

"I talk to a couple people. Why do you care?"

"Well," Jenna said, pulling on my backpack to slow me down. She leaned on her knees to catch her breath. The steepness of the hill always required a short break. "You never invite anyone over to play. Don't you get lonely?"

"Lonely?" I let out a laugh, tugging her along. "No one could ever get lonely with you around." That was the truth. At ten, Jenna was outgoing and kind to everyone. She was also like a puppy dog that never left you alone.

She smiled at me, leaning on my arm for support. "Well, I'll always be here for you when you get bored. That's what sisters are for, right?"

I chuckled again. "Right. I can't wait to play with your Barbie dolls again."

"As if I still play with those baby toys!" she huffed. She spun her head around to see if anyone had heard my ludicrous accusation.

I continued to laugh in surprise. Since when did she get too old for Barbies? I watched Jenna rake her fingers through her long, dark hair. Stringy strands fell across her face, and she brushed them away with the back of her hand.

When we reached our home, Jenna pushed through the double-wide doors, announcing our return.

"Mom! I made a new friend today!" She ran off down the hall on her way to the kitchen.

I, on the other hand, retreated to my bedroom. Throwing my backpack on the ground, I grabbed my headphones and iPod from off my desk. Then I lay down on my queen-size bed and sank into the thick mattress, content to keep to myself.

Halfway into the semester is when the trouble began. My old friend, Conner Hamilton, from my previous neighborhood, was throwing a party at his house. His parents were away for the weekend, and we had big plans for Friday night. By the time I arrived, the music was blaring and the house was full of friends and acquaintances from my old high school.

"Damien! How you doin', man?" Conner threw an arm over my shoulder, careful not to spill the beer in his other hand. "Good to see you! Yo, everybody!" he hollered over the stereo system. "Look who it is!"

I nodded my head at the crowd of teenagers, some who turned around and waved, and others who were too absorbed with being the center of attention themselves to even notice. A couple of buddies yelled from their corner, signaling me to come over. I didn't recognize everybody, and I was sure Conner didn't either. But that's just how he rolled. He was hosting, and he didn't care how many people showed up, so long as they didn't bring the cops.

But late into the night, some unexpected visitors showed up at his door, barging their way in. They were large, and they were loud. Three massive figures pushed their way through the door.

"Hey, hey. WASSUP!" one of them called out in a deep voice.

All eyes turned their way and stared. Their dark brown skin stood out among the sea of comparatively skinny, white flesh. You'd almost have to tape two of us together, standing side by side, to stand a chance against their broad build. Their legs were walking tree trunks, covered in jeans and hanging chains. A couple of them wore cut-off white shirts, exposing their biceps. From shoulder to elbow, they were decorated in tattoos—pictures and words inked into their skin. One of them wore his afro long, pulled back into a ponytail, while the others sported cornrows. I knew enough about ethnic

California to gather they were Polynesian of some sort.

"Somebody mention a party?" another said. Their boisterous laughter filled the room, and their bass voices rumbled above the music.

"Hey, Afano! Grab us a few beers, yeah?" One guy led the rest of the group into the living room. He sunk into the couch, followed by his buddies. He looked around the quiet room. Somebody had turned down the music, creating an uncomfortable pocket of silence in the air.

"What's everyone looking at?" the Polynesian growled, throwing up his large arms. "Haven't you ever seen a brown man before? Turn that music back up!"

Heads turned away, whispering to each other and edging away from them. Anxious girls clung to their boyfriends, their eyes looking the Polynesians up and down. The music returned to its booming volume, but not loud enough to deafen the tension in the room.

The two on the couch started talking to each other in a choppy, tonal language. They looked around at their audience, all of whom tried their best to appear at ease. Everyone was failing miserably. One of them caught me looking at them.

"Hey, *Palagi*—come here." He motioned with his fingers.

Ignoring the girl who pulled on my shirt, I sat on the edge of the coffee table in the center of the room. I leaned my elbows onto my knees, watching them carefully. If they were trying to intimidate me, it wasn't working. I was not going to be toyed with for their party entertainment.

"So, what's your name?" one of them asked. The gold chains around his neck gleamed under the ceiling bulb.

"Damien."

"Dam-i-en." He tested the sound of my name on his tongue. "You afraid of us, Damien?"

I made eye contact with each of them, including the other one who joined us with the beers in his massive hands.

I was never small growing up. At seventeen, I had already reached six feet, and was thick across my chest and arms. I could thank my father for those genes. Despite my dislike for the man, he allowed me to inherit his build, as well as his temper. I could hold my own. I had proved it on more than a few occasions.

"No," I answered.

The Polynesian in front of me leaned forward, placing his face close to mine. His breath smelled of alcohol and cigarettes. He paused, not moving for a moment. "Why not?"

I opened my hands and sat back against the table. "I'm just here for a good time, man."

Nobody spoke while they continued to scrutinize me.

"Good," he said. He broke into a wide smile, exposing a missing molar. "That's good, bro. Afano! Toss him a beer." He turned to look at me again. "The name's

Fanua. You got Afano right there, and Iona." Fanua nodded at me. "If you want a good time, you can hang with us tonight."

That was the first night I hung out with the Samoans. We went from party to party, drinking and growing louder with each party we crashed. I was sure they brought me along just for their own amusement, but once I was with them, they seemed to enjoy my laidback nature. Soaking up the excitement of something new, I felt grateful to be away from the trimmed lawns and the flawless neighbors of Oakland Hills.

"Yeah, this guy knows how to chill," the group of Samoans kept saying. Their threatening size diminished in effect as I spent time with them. Constantly messing with each other, they often broke into heavy laughter, slapping each other on the back good-naturedly.

I continued to meet up with them every weekend, following them wherever they suggested we party. Before long, I slipped out of the house on school nights, too. With the amount of time I spent in my room, it was more than easy to sneak out my window. Nobody noticed because nobody cared.

My mother and father had dismissed all the brooding I had offered when we first moved to Oakland Hills. My father didn't care that I had to spend my senior year away from the friends I had grown up with. He didn't care that I escaped to my room every night, making my brief appearance during dinner to appease them. They accused me of playing the martyr for a dying cause.

"It's all about taking advantage of your opportunities in life," my father said one night, as he chomped on a pork chop. "My job offers a great opportunity. Son, someday, when you've graduated from Stanford and have a family and a real job, you'll understand. You have to do what's best for your whole family, not just for one individual and his high school social life."

I hated him for not understanding. He was too caught up in excelling at work to realize he wasn't winning any awards as a father. Sure, he maintained his strict enforcement of dinner together every night as a family. Curfews were always in place, and he made sure his kids were dressed presentably at all times. Michaels were not sloppy dressers, but that's as far as his fatherly role extended—with me, anyway.

Jenna was a different story. She could win over an angry bull without even trying—which, at times, was the precise metaphor for describing my father. When that man was upset, which generally was my fault as of late, it was difficult to rein him in, but Jenna's uncanny ability to calm heated situations saved a brawl between us more than once.

As for my mother, she was good at playing her part, too—the dutiful and beautiful wife of Jonathon Michaels. Primping throughout the day, her makeup and hair remained flawless from sunup to sundown. She didn't have a life of her own. She was manipulated into anything he wanted to do, and she didn't even know it.

So I hung out with my new friends who accepted

me, despite our differences. Sometimes we drove around listening to music, or played ball in the city parks at night. Every so often, we set up harmless pranks inside ritzy neighborhoods, tossing fireworks and cherry bombs inside windows or unlocked doors. We'd hide and watch the reactions of the irate residents storming outside and threatening to call the police. That further egged us on to decorate their gated walls with spray-paint when we thought we could get away with it. And we did.

The Samoans introduced me to a whole new night life. Sometimes they asked for money to fund the evening, and I did so without complaint. I was happy to contribute. I found ways to swindle the money from home, stealing small amounts from my father's wallet, or telling my mother pitiful stories of the things I needed to buy. No one knew the difference. Everyone was so caught up in their own lives that they didn't bother paying attention to mine.

Except for one.

"Damien," Jenna said to me one day, standing in the doorway of my bedroom.

Throwing on a hoodie, I prepared to head out for the night. I was meeting the guys in the city. They said they had a surprise for me. Their only clue was to bring a bottle of pain pills. That didn't sound very promising, but I wasn't about to say no.

"What is it, Jenna?" I asked, looking through my closet for shoes. When she didn't answer, I looked back over at her. Her lower lip trembled, despite her obvious efforts to contain the tears.

I stopped what I was doing and crouched in front of her. "What is it?" I asked again. I put my hands on her shoulders. "What's the matter? Did someone hurt you?" I looked into her honey-brown eyes, searching for the answer.

She threw her arms around my neck. "Damien, you're not a bad person, right?"

"What?" I held onto her, allowing her to cling against my chest. Her small-framed body shook, releasing wet drops onto my neck.

I pulled her away after a minute, still kneeling in front of her. "Why would you say that?"

She sniffled and wiped her runny nose with the back of her hand. "Katie Ramsey said her brother told her you hang out with bad people."

Kevin Ramsey. I recalled his name. He was my neighbor, and also in my gym class. I'd had a few words with him the other day. He had wanted to bring to my attention to the gossip that was flying around.

"Rumor has it you've joined a Samoan gang," he'd said.

I laughed right in his face. "That's absurd. I'm not part of a gang." But he seemed to detect the discomfort in my expression. He had warned me to be careful, to get out while I still could. I brushed his comments aside.

I hadn't thought any more of that conversation until this moment.

"Jenna, I don't hang out with bad people," I told

her.

"Katie heard Kevin on the phone. He said you are getting yourself into trouble—doing bad things with bad people. He didn't say what. But maybe that's why Dad gets mad at you all the time."

I sighed, glancing at the clock on my dresser. It was time to go.

"Listen, Jenna. I made some new friends, just like you hoped I would. And they're not bad. People are afraid of them because they look different, that's all."

Jenna seemed skeptical.

"Really," I assured her. "They're more like brothers than friends. They look out for me, and I'm safe with them."

That was one thing I knew for sure. Each of them carried a gun "just in case", they had said, but I'd never seen the Samoans use them. They carried them discretely in the back of their pants or inside their oversized jackets. The only time they pulled them out was to let me admire them— holding the identical nine-millimeters in my hand. It was empowering. And it was just for protection.

I kissed the top of Jenna's head and stepped past her, looking over my shoulder. "Sorry, I need to go. Just remember, you have nothing to worry about, ok?"

She watched me leave, though I didn't see her usual dimpled grin on her face, but I couldn't worry about it right then. I had somewhere to be.

Hurrying down an alley in downtown Oakland, I glanced over my shoulder as I walked. The door jingled as I opened the glass door to a room that was the size of a small studio apartment. The walls were covered from corner to corner in artistic drawings and posters. To my right was a long, flat table with a sheet pulled across it. Next to it was a reclining chair with armrests. Behind both of those were my Samoan brothers.

"Hey, Palagi! My man, you made it." Fanua stuck out his large hand and shook mine.

It was then that I noticed the gangly white man beside him, his stringy hair dyed black and hanging long across his face. One ear was pierced multiple times from his earlobe all the way up his curved cartilage, as was his lip and nose. His arms were covered in tattooed sleeves. He showed his yellow teeth in what appeared to be a smile.

"Hey, what's up?" I said, still eying his artwork. "So what's going on, guys?" I asked, sticking my hands in my pockets. They all gave knowing smiles.

"Damien, it's time," Iona said, putting an arm around me. He guided me to the chair and sat me down. "You're one of us, brotha."

I eyed the needled contraption on the table.

"You got those pills?" Fanua asked. I nodded. "And the cash?"

Pulling out the wad from my wallet, I handed it to him. "Is this what it's paying for?" I asked.

"In part. And for the after party," Afona laughed deeply.

"Your tattoo is already picked out," Iona said. He

held up the carbon paper that revealed three letters on it.

USO.

"What's that stand for?" I asked, studying the paper in my hand.

Fanua put a hand on my shoulder. "It's pronounced 'ooh-so'. Means 'brother' in Samoan."

Afona chimed in. "Nothing is more important in Samoan culture than family. Brotherhood means the same as loyalty. You always got each other's back, no matter what."

I could feel the magnitude of what they were saying. To be a "brother" was not to be taken lightly, nor the significance behind accepting the branding.

"You'll really be one of us," Iona said again.

I looked at each of them and nodded my head. "Ok. Let's do it." I shook the pain killers in my hand. "Am I going to need these?"

"That's up to you," Fanua said, folding his arms across his burly chest, but I knew it was another test—a test of bravery and manhood.

I forced a tight-lipped smile and tossed the bottle to Iona. He grinned in response, rattling the pills as he watched me try to relax my arm.

USO.

The constant pinching of the needles irked the nerves of my bicep as the word was etched into my skin. I grimaced but tried to ignore it. It was worth it to officially be a part of the Samoan brotherhood. I'd have their back, and they'd have mine.

I would never have to worry about anything again.

A week before Christmas, we packed up and made the two-hour drive to our vacation home. It resided in the most northeast corner of Hidden Pines and sat on top of a hill, overlooking both the lake and neighboring lodge. We stayed there two or three times out of the year for short trips. My father ran a ski resort called Eastridge, not far from our house. Sometimes that was why we were "vacationing" at our house in the first place—so Dad could check in on one of his many business venues.

This trip, I had plenty of other places I'd rather be. I didn't feel like playing "happy family," especially with how unhappy my father was with me on a daily basis. I had overheard him discussing my "ill-mannered behaviors" with my mother and questioning what to do about me and my alarming group of friends. It was some mumbo-jumbo about them being a bad influence on me and tainting the Michaels' name.

My mother was sure we just needed more time together as a family—to get away from work and school and be together. It was her solution that elicited this extended trip. Rather than our usual five days, we were going to be stuck together for the next two weeks, long enough to absorb my entire Christmas break from school.

I found ways around my mother's proposed torment. It wasn't hard to convince Fanua, Iona, and

Afona to make the drive and meet up with me during the first week. Once they arrived, all expenses were paid for, including three nights at our lodge. My father might own the lodge and run the business, but I had connections of my own that got me what I wanted. It paid off to be the son of an overly busy, thriving businessman.

It was the trips into town that got us into trouble. We ran out on quite a few meals, when I had been unsuccessful in pilfering extra money from home. Getting caught vandalizing on the restaurant property didn't help either, but they deserved it for ratting me out to my father.

I guess ditching on the bill wasn't the smartest decision. All the locals knew my father. He was the "big man in town"—one of the wealthiest and most generous visitors that returned throughout the year. Of course, they would give him anything he wanted. And, of course, they knew very well who his wife and kids were, and that made things difficult on my part. It was tricky to slip by unnoticed.

One night, I got caught shoplifting for the second time that week. It had been a dare. Iona said they made bets on how many items I could walk away with. Unfortunately, I wasn't quick enough. Before I knew it, an employee had grabbed me and pinned me against the counter.

When the cops finally showed up, my Samoan friends were nowhere in sight. I ended up spending the next few hours in the local jail, waiting for my father to come and pay the fine for the second time that week. When he did, it wasn't pleasant.

He grabbed me by my shirt and yanked me out of the building. Livid, he turned me around. "All I wanted was a son to make me proud." He shoved a finger hard into the center of my chest. I grunted but settled for scowling at the angry man before me.

"You," he said, "are nothing but a screw up. Look at me when I'm talking to you!" He didn't seem to care about drawing more attention. Heads turned our way, curious voices whispering.

Resentful, I lifted my head to look my father in the eyes. Having inherited the silvery-grey color, it was like looking into an aged version of my own.

"I don't know what's gotten into you this year. Your grades have slipped, you're falling asleep in class, and you sneak out at night and come home smelling like cigarettes, alcohol, and who knows what other garbage you've gotten yourself into. But I'll tell you this much," he said, shoving his face close to mine. "I meant what I said last week. If you don't shape up this next month, I swear I will send you to military school where you can be someone else's problem."

I ground my teeth together, but maintained the apathetic expression on my face. "I meant what I said, too."

My father paused his march to our Audi. "Which part, exactly?"

I swaggered past him and pulled open the

backdoor of the car. I looked over my shoulder and spoke. "The part where I said I wished you all were dead."

The next evening, Jenna answered the unexpected knock on our front door. We heard her let out a frightened cry as she came running back into the dining room.

"Daddy, there are some giant men at the door!"

My father and I jumped up at the same time. Neither of us moved far. Fanua, Iona, and Afona strutted through the hallway.

"Yo, yo! Damien, my man! You ready or what, bro?"

My father turned to me and grabbed my arm. "What are they doing inside the house?" He looked at the three of them. "None of you thugs are welcome here. Leave now, before I call the cops."

Iona took a step towards my father, glaring at him. "What did you call us? You want to start something here, old man?" He touched the inside of his jacket, where I knew the nine-millimeter lay hidden.

I jumped between them, putting my hands on Iona's shoulder. Pushing him back towards the door, I said, "No—we don't need to go there. Come on, I'm with you. Let's go."

"Your old man better watch himself," Iona said, throwing another intimidating glace towards Dad.

"Damien, you are not to go anywhere with them. Do you hear me?"

I kept walking and didn't turn around. "I'm out. See you later."

I jumped in the car with my buddies, surprised to see a thin, white kid in the back. His blond hair was short and spiked with gel. He was slouched in his seat, leaning against the side window.

"Uh, hey," I said. I turned to Afona on my right and whispered, "Who's this?"

Afona spoke up. "This here is Tom."

"Um, actually, it's Tommy. Tommy Miller." The feeble voice came from the pale figure to my left. He stuck out his hand.

I shook it. "I'm Damien Michaels." I looked at my Samoan brothers for an explanation.

"Tommy's been hangin' with the crew in the city this last week while you been away on vacation," Fanua explained from behind the wheel. He smiled into the rearview mirror. "He's from your part of town." He nudged Iona, who was sitting in the passenger seat. Iona laughed.

"We go to the same school," Tommy said to me. "We're in English together."

"We are?" I asked, somewhat baffled. I'd never seen this kid before in my life.

"Yeah. Front row, in fact. You always sit in the very back, right corner. But I don't suppose you would see me because your head is always down."

I looked Tommy up and down, eyeing his striped polo shirt that hung around his thin frame, tucked into his white slacks. I whispered to Afona, "Where did you find this kid? And why?"

"Yo, Iona. Bump the music!" Afona lowered his voice as the music boomed. "He was hanging around outside a party we crashed up by your neighborhood. Seemed like he was working up the nerve to go in. He paid us some straight-up cash to walk in with him and act like his friend. Trying to boost his social life or somethin', I don't know. But hey—he got money and doesn't mind spending it. So we're keeping him around."

Something about his statement started to click in my head.

"Yo, Damien. Your dad is whacked, man," Iona said, shaking his head.

"Yeah, that guy's got some problems. What's wrong with *us*? Nothin'," Afona said. "You gotta get yourself out of there, bro."

"I'm working on it," I muttered, still looking out the window. As we headed into the city, I was grateful to get away from my father for the night, but looking around at my Samoan buddies, I was becoming wary. Something seemed increasingly not right with them.

They kept talking about Tau—someone I knew they both feared and respected at the same time. I was with them when their cells rang and they had "assignments" to complete. They either ditched out early or made me stay in the car until they were finished. They never explained what was going on. And they didn't always tell me where all my money went.

"No worries, bro," they would always say. "No worries." So I didn't push the issue by asking too many questions, but I felt there was something much bigger going on with these guys than I realized, or dared to figure out.

While we were in the car, Fanua pulled into the empty parking lot of a convenience store.

"What are we doing here?" Tommy asked.

"Just making a routine stop, my friend," Fanua said. "You got it, Iona?"

"Fanua," Afona interrupted. "Right now? You sure about this, man?"

"Yeah, sure," Fanua said. "Just grabbing a snack."

Iona and Fanua both were getting out of the car. Iona had a bag slung over his shoulder. "Yeah. Be right back."

They both stepped into the store. Through the windows we could see them browsing along the left side, looking at the wall of sodas. Grabbing an item or two, they headed over to the cashier.

Tommy opened his door and stepped out. "I need to grab some food, too," he said.

"Hey, kid. Wait!" Afona said, but Tommy hustled into the store. Afona maneuvered out of the car to follow him.

The moment Tommy stepped through the doors, he looked to his right and stopped. His jaw fell open. Afona threw open the store door, and I heard Tommy cry out, "What are you doing?"

A gunshot sounded through the air, followed by a second. Iona and Fanua, both wearing black masks, ran into view. They grabbed Tommy as they dashed through the door. Afona followed behind.

"Let's go, let's go!" he shouted. They all jumped into the car, shoving Tommy on top of me. Afona was in the driver's seat now. He threw the car into gear and took off, peeling out as he tore across the parking lot.

Iona tossed the bag at his feet and removed his mask, as did Fanua, who was sitting beside me. They looked behind them with frantic eyes, scanning the streets. Already police sirens were sounding through the air.

"What just happened back there?" I asked, looking from face to face, afraid to believe what logic explained. My eyes rested on Tommy's, the full whites of his eyes exposed. He trembled beside me, staring with disbelief at all the Samoans.

"Someone tell me what just happened. Now!" I demanded.

"I told you to wait," Afona said to Tommy, his deep voice breaking the stunned silence. The car continued to race down the street, running a couple red lights.

"Slow down, Afona," Iona hissed. "You want the cops to pull us over like this?"

"They're already going to be on us with the sloppy job you just pulled."

"It was the kid," Fanua inserted. "He distracted us. The clerk hit the alarm and pulled out a shotgun when we turned our heads. We had to fire first or we'd be the ones lying dead on the floor."

"I heard two shots," I said.

"Yeah, well, he's dead for sure." Iona sighed, tapping the dashboard. "Tau ain't gonna like this. Bag's only half-full. And this is gonna draw some attention."

"You think? Of course it will! You shouldn't have pulled the job with these two in the back." Afona slammed his hands against the steering wheel. "Tau told you we can't trust anyone who's not a part of the brotherhood."

Fanua turned to Tommy and me. He shoved a hand against my shoulder, pinning it against my seat. "Now, you listen here," he said through his teeth. His brows doubled over as he studied us. "You two better shut your mouths if you don't want a hole through your head."

"Nu-no problem," Tommy stammered. "I won't say a word, I swear." He fiddled with the edge of his shirt, which was no longer tucked inside his pants.

"What about you?" Fanua asked. I stared back at him, unwilling to fall prey to his intimidation. I didn't know yet what I was going to do, but I knew what he wanted to hear.

I pulled up my left sleeve, exposing my tattoo. USO. "You said this means brother. You know you can trust me."

Iona laughed, looking back at me. "That doesn't mean nothin', man. That's just wasted ink. It takes more than that to be one of us. You can't be a brotha! You ain't got what it takes, and I'm not just talkin' about color. You're just a spoiled rich kid who's good at sharing his money."

My lips hardened into a thin line. My jaw clenched together. "Well, I guess that's it then. We'll go our separate ways from here. Stop the car."

Afona pulled over, chuckling with the rest of his gang. "Fine. Have it your way."

"Get out," I ordered Tommy, following after him. Fanua stuck his head out the window.

"Just remember what I said," he warned, staring hard at Tommy. Tommy swallowed beside me and nodded his head.

"Say a word and you'll regret it, for the rest of your short life." The car pulled away and sped down the street.

Tommy looked over at me. "What are we doing to do?" he asked. "Should we tell the cops?"

I started walking down the street. Tommy followed after me, catching up with my strides.

"I don't know," I mumbled, looking for a cab.

"They killed him," Tommy continued. "A man is dead because of them. I walked into the store, and they had masks over their faces, pointing guns at the clerk. The man looked so scared and was throwing cash into the bag." He paused. "Is...is it my fault? Would they not have killed him if I hadn't distracted them, like they said? Because then maybe he wouldn't have pulled out his shotgun in the first place."

I stopped in my tracks. "Ok, listen here, Miller. This is not your fault. We both were just in the wrong place at the wrong time."

A wave of anxiety rushed through me.

"We got to get back home. I think we better just lay low for a while. We both know they're serious about what they will do if we say anything. Maybe...maybe we should just wait a while and see if the cops can figure it out on their own. Then we'll still be safe."

Tommy looked skeptical. "But isn't it our duty to tell?"

I let out a frustrated breath. "Man, I don't know! I mean, probably. But I don't want to end up splattered on the sidewalk like that clerk, do you? Taxi!"

We both hopped into the same cab. Same dilemma, same ritzy neighborhood.

"Oakland Hills," I informed the driver. Too absorbed with our own thoughts, Tommy and I both sat in silence, staring out the window the entire ride home.

I awoke the next morning with grogginess, all alone in my empty house. My family would still be up in the cabin for another week. I needed to find a way up there.

Kicking off the thick layer of blankets and sheets, I sat up with a shake of my head. The events of last night had played over and over in my mind until I fell asleep into a hazy swirl of dark, confusing dreams. Tommy Miller's face came to mind, his wide, scared eyes, no longer innocent and pure. I sensed he still wanted to talk to the police, but I also feared the reality of what would happen if he did. Or if I did.

A twinge of guilt pried at my heart as I thought about the man at the store, and the family he left behind. Whether he had a wife and children or not, he was still someone's son, brother, or uncle. People out there were grieving and deserved to know the truth behind his murder.

But a feeling stronger than guilt overcame me, one I was ashamed to recognize.

Fear.

I looked at the tattoo on my arm, which seemed to be burning alive on my skin.

Brotherhood. Loyalty.

They had no stronger devotion than in protecting their gang, their family. If I said one word, I would be a targeted dead man for the rest of my life. They would hunt me down until they found me. They might even hurt Jenna.

No. I would follow my initial plan and just lay low. Give the police time to figure it out on their own. Then I would reconsider my plan.

Stepping off the bus, I pulled my phone out of my jacket and flipped it open. I dialed the cabin's landline, dreading the voice that answered.

"What is it?" my father's voice asked, gruff and

serious as usual. But it was particularly gruff today.

"I'm in Twain Harte. Can you pick me up?"

Silence.

"Or...I can find my own way up there. It's not a big deal. I guess I'll—"

Dad interrupted. "Just what makes you think we want you back up here after that disrespectful stunt you pulled last night?"

The stubbornness inside of me wanted to retaliate and tell him I didn't need any of his help, anyway, but I refrained.

"Look, about that. I'm sorry I took off like that. I've, uh, been doing some thinking. You won't be seeing those guys around anymore. And neither will I, for that matter. I swear."

I could hear my father murmuring on the other line. I waited until he spoke.

"Fine. I'll pick you up by the post office in twenty-five minutes." He hung up the phone before I could respond.

With Christmas approaching, my mother insisted we all go into town and do some shopping as a family. Jenna and I were both handed a generous wad of cash and set loose.

I followed two steps behind Jenna, barely acknowledging her stories and comments. After half an hour, she stopped asking my opinion on shirt options for Dad or perfume scents for mom. She even stopped making jokes about what I could get her for Christmas.

Her steps came to a sudden halt and she turned around, putting her hands on her narrow hips. I almost bumped right into her.

"Hey, what's going on with you?" she asked, frowning at me. She tapped her foot, waiting for my response.

"Nothin', Jen. Just not much in the Christmas shopping mood."

"You're not being yourself," she said, glaring at me. "Well, you haven't been yourself for months. But now you just seem nervous and weird. What happened yesterday?"

I started walking and grabbed her arm, guiding her into the store.

"You want to shop. Let's shop." I held a couple ties in her face. "Here. Which one do you think Dad would like? Red or blue?"

Jenna scowled at me, folding her arms across her chest.

"Not into the ties, huh?" I turned my back and snatched a silver frame from off a shelf. "Beautiful, isn't it? Toss a picture of you and me in there and we're all set for Mom. What do you say?"

It wasn't possible for her to glare any harder at me. Her honey-hued eyes filled with tears.

"Stop treating me like I don't know what's going on. I'm not a baby!" She slid the back of her hand across her eyes, destroying the glistening evidence.

I returned the frame to its dusty shelf. Turning around, I kneeled down to Jenna's level and hugged her.

She wrapped her arms around me, squeezing my neck in a vise. "You're not the same," she choked out. "I miss you, Damien."

My wall crumbled for the time being. I held Jenna at arm's length, looking into her innocence. "I'm sorry I haven't been nice to you. Something did happen yesterday."

"With your bad friends?" she sniffled.

I nodded. "Yes, with my bad friends. They're not my friends anymore."

Jenna continued to wipe the tears from her face. "What happened?" she asked. Her long lashes emphasized the purity in her eyes.

I shook my head. "I can't tell you about it—not right now. Just know I won't be hanging out with them anymore, ok? Can that be enough for now?"

She paused, studying my face. She almost seemed ready to argue but the expression washed away. "Yeah, ok," she agreed. She smiled, revealing her dimples. I smiled back in relief.

"Now, what do you say we take a break for some hot chocolate?"

Hand in hand, we walked across the street, prepared to indulge in twenty-ounces of steaming, mint-truffle cocoa.

For a moment, I seemed to forget my troubles. There was no gang. No robbery or murder. Just Jenna and me, Christmas shopping together like we did every year.

Two days later on December 23, Tommy Miller was found shot to death with a nine-millimeter bullet in the back of his head. I watched the breaking news from inside my home, unable to tear myself away.

"Sixteen-year-old Tommy Miller was found in Oakland Hills Park at eleven PM in what appears to be a homicide. A resident and fellow classmate of Miller found him dead at the scene with a bullet wound to the back of his head. It is believed to be a drive-by shooting.

"Local police report Miller was seen inside their station just a day before the shooting. Miller requested to fill out a police report. However, he abandoned the papers and disappeared from the station before an officer met with him. The police suspected gang involvement but have no suspects or witnesses at this time."

"Damien, honey, doesn't that boy go to your school?" my mom asked, placing a hand on my shoulder, as she listened to the breaking news with wide eyes.

"He did." My face was expressionless, somehow able to hide the terror and grief in my chest. The Samoans must have been keeping tabs on Tommy and seen him walk into the police station. Poor kid didn't stand a chance—not even when he apparently got cold feet and kept his mouth shut after all.

And neither would I if I followed suit. Now I was the sole person who knew what happened to the store clerk. And now to Tommy.

They had meant what they said, and their warning was clear. The police could not protect me.

I tossed and turned all night, tormented by troubling dreams...

I was suffocating. The air was warm and too heavy to breathe. I felt as though someone was squeezing my neck and blocking my trachea. A familiar voice called my name, again and again...

"Damien! Damien!"

I looked around in the darkness, searching for the source.

"Damien!"

I sat up, my head spinning around the room. I coughed as my lungs inhaled the smothering smoke. My eyes adjusted to the darkness, while my brain struggled to awaken.

The voice from my dream was calling my name again.

Jenna!

Reality yanked me out of my dreaming state. I jumped out of bed. A thin layer of smoke was seeping through the crack under my door.

I twisted and pulled on the doorknob, fanning the hazy air as I looked down the hall.

Jenna's door was open. Her bedroom light lit the hallway.

I ran to her room. "Jenna! Jenna, where are you?"

Panicked, I threw her quilt aside. Nothing but

the warm shape of her body indented into the mattress. She couldn't have been gone long. I opened her walk-in closet. Besides her hangers of clothing, it was dark and empty.

A muffled cry alerted my attention to the north wing of the house, where my parents slept. I ran out of the bedroom and down the hall, where the smoke thickened. I heard the crackling flames before I saw them. My eyes widened.

The brilliant inferno engulfed the side of the home where my parents' bedroom resided. It roared in my ears, blocking my path. I couldn't get to them. And they were nowhere in sight.

"Mom! Dad!" I listened for their voices, coughing as I inhaled black smoke.

Nothing. Nothing but the sound of the walls and ceiling burning around me.

"Jenna, where *are* you?" I spun in a circle, dizzy and disoriented. Covering my face with my hands, I fended off the fumes. Where could she have gone?

Running to the front door, I threw it open. I inhaled the cold, crisp air from outside, relief and clean oxygen filling my lungs.

I looked around, hoping to find my family huddled in safety outside our burning home.

But my family was nowhere in sight.

In the distance, I could hear the faint sounds of sirens approaching.

Hurry! Get here NOW, I wanted to scream. But

the rescue teams were too far away to hear me. They would never make it in time.

And my family was still in there.

The warm heat wave behind me made me spin around. Stepping back inside the home, I cringed against the contrasting temperature that sheathed me. I sprinted to the east end of the house towards Jenna's playroom, following the path of the growing flames. I hurdled over scorched pieces of furniture that lay broken and blazing before me, holding my arms in front of me.

"Jenna! Jenna, where are you?"

She might be in there. Despite her insistence that she was too old for her playroom now, I knew she still played in secret with her favorite dolls, and colored on the chalkboard. More than once, I had found her in there when she was hiding from the loud arguments between my father and me. Or when she was scared from a show on TV she had seen.

Maybe just when she was scared.

The fire had beaten me there. The ceiling was charred, with pieces of wood falling around me. I put my hands up, dodging the debris. My face stung red, and my eyes watered, blinking the smoke out of my eyes.

The playroom door was ajar. I kicked it open, coughing and gagging. Smoke filled my lungs, suffocating my breaths. I lifted the bottom of my shirt up to my nose and mouth, my throat burning.

My eyes rummaged among the toys and dolls lit up in flames, their fake doll hair singed bald. The air smelled of burnt plastic.

From there, it all became a little hazy. The next moments seemed to move in slow motion, like being caught in a bad dream and desperate to wake up. The fire seemed to be chasing behind me, reaching out its long, blazing fingers.

I don't recall when the back of my shirt caught fire. I don't remember the searing pain that melted off a layer of skin.

But I do remember the small, limp body huddled in the corner, surrounded by her childish dolls, and almost hidden behind the smolder. Her tiny hand was clasped around one of her Barbies, tucked into her chin.

I'm sure I called out her name as I scooped her up. I'm sure it hurt when I broke through the glass windows with Jenna curled protectively in my arms.

But nothing mattered in that moment. Nothing but reviving my little sister.

I laid her onto the cold ground, vaguely aware that I was tearing off my burning shirt and hurling it to the side. Piercing, cold air shrouded my bare torso.

Sirens blared nearby, but I didn't see them. My eyes focused on the pale face beneath me, her cheeks and forehead stained with soot. In vain, I breathed air into her lungs and pumped her chest, over and over again.

My tears cascaded against her unresponsive body.

An unfamiliar hand touched my arm, pulling me back.

"Come on, kid. You gotta move!"

"No! No!" The raspy, hysterical sobs resonated from my throat. I watched them wheel Jenna's small body into the ambulance as they continued CPR.

Someone pulled me off my knees, and I staggered with them. Leaning on their arms was the only reason I hadn't collapsed. My head swung around, catching glimpses of my home lit up in orange flames and shadowed by plumes of black smoke. Water blasted from two separate hoses, bathing the overgrown flames. Lights flashed all around me, swirling in reds, blues, and yellows. They seemed to blend together into a dim halo of color.

"My parents..."

A million thoughts raced inside my foggy head, but coherent words would not form. I relinquished control to the uniformed stranger beside me.

Someone laid me facedown on a white-sheeted table inside the ambulance. A mask was thrown over my own face while someone examined my back.

I observed my little sister lying beside me. Her eyes were shut, her face peacefully still. She looked like one of the dolls from her playroom—the ones whose eyes always closed shut when lying on their backs.

I wanted to reach over and pull Jenna into a sitting position—to watch her eyes flutter open like her porcelain dolls.

I wanted to put my arm around her, hold her close, and read her favorite fairy tale to her like when she was little. Back when we all believed in happy endings. Back before reality destroyed "Happily Ever After".

"1-2-3 CLEAR." Her body arched in response to the electric shocks to her chest.

Again. And again.

A single, drawn-out beeping from the machine beside her rang in my ears. Frantic movements flurried beside me, surrounding her body.

But the piercing, flat tone continued to resonate inside the ambulance.

"That's it. There's nothing more we can do."

Gone.

My Jenna was gone.

That's the moment when I felt it—the searing, fiery sensation along my shoulder blade causing me to cry out. I was inside the flames all over again, fire engulfing my entire body. I writhed, hollering wildly.

Gloved hands struggled to hold me down, to prevent me from further tearing the damaged, raw surface of my back.

The roaring beneath my skin was intolerable—second only to the serrated knife that twisted and wrenched unmercifully inside my heart.

CHAPTER 23

I couldn't hold back the tears as I listened and watched Damien relive the memories of his past. His eyes were dark and hollow, yielding to the painful images in his mind. The tortured expression lingered on his face as he stared across the room.

I'd seen that vivid look hundreds of times, reflected in my own eyes. The times when I allowed myself to think about Maddie, and the unbearable pain I had caused her family. Sometimes there seemed no escape from the torment.

As I watched Damien struggle with the very same demons, my heart ached with understanding. I reached my hand out to his. My fingers touched the skin of his knuckles, but he didn't seem aware of my touch. His mind was trapped elsewhere. His eyes still cast across the room, his dark hair falling across his right eye. His skin was warm—perhaps burning with the intensity of his memories. I couldn't bear to see him suffer.

On impulse, I threw my arms around him, pulling my body into his. I squeezed him, burying my head into the crook of his neck. I was desperate to absorb his pain, to break him free from the unchangeable past that plagued him.

"Damien, I'm so sorry," I said. His body was solid, his muscles stiff and immovable, but I didn't let go.

Returning the embrace, his hands pressed against my lean back.

"The fire wasn't your fault," I said. I felt his jaw tighten against the side of my face. Gently, he pushed me away, looking back at me.

"It *was* my fault," he corrected.

Perplexed, I squinted at him, waiting for an explanation.

"The police waited three days before they approached me for a statement. I was, of course, still bedridden in the hospital with third-degree burns on my back. I wasn't in danger of not surviving my injuries, even though I knew that's what I deserved. I hated lying there day after day, recovering. The process was slow and excruciatingly painful, but I was recovering nonetheless, while my parents' bodies were charred beyond recognition, and my little sister was being prepared for a coffin that should never have to be made for a body that small.

"The police couldn't wait to get the dirty details from me—how I planned and carried out my family's death, and happened to be the sole survivor. They asked if I was aware of the millions of dollars in life insurance that was coming my way in a few months. From the way they asked it, I knew they believed that was my intent, and of course, my motive." His laugh was bitter. "Every suspect needs a motive, right? Well, they seemed to have mine. Cops always think they know the answers."

"What did you say?" I asked. "Did you tell them about the Samoan gang?"

"No."

"What? Why not?"

Damien turned away from me, not daring to look me in the eyes.

"I was afraid," he confessed. I had to lean in to be sure I could hear him, but I could see the shame in his face—a shame that resembled a recognizable self-loathing.

"When the police told me they found evidence of an accelerant used to start the fire out on the back deck, I knew it was *them*. I don't know if the fire was intended to scare or to kill, but it accomplished both. It killed my family and scared me enough to keep my mouth shut. I knew if I said a word about them, I was as good as dead. Even if the police arrested those guys, there are always more of them. I hung out with Fanua, Afona, and Iona, but there were a lot of guys who were a part of that gang—a bunch of different factions branching down from Tau, the ring leader. I would never be able to run from them all. Brotherhood and loyalty—they all had each other's backs. A white kid like me didn't stand a chance.

"Of course, I told the police I didn't do it. But you read some of the reports. They were able to find more than enough disapproving people to create a case against me. All the locals knew I hated my dad and hung out with a rough crowd. They had heard the rumors and seen some of it firsthand, with the shoplifting and dinner-ditching...Even my neighbors in Oakland Hills didn't have much good to say about me, not from my behavior over the previous few months before the fire. As you read, there wasn't enough evidence to even arrest me, but I was socially convicted from the start. No one needed to see me behind bars to believe I was capable of it."

"But Damien, why, until now, have you insisted to me that you did kill your family?"

"I may not have started the fire," he answered, "but their deaths were my fault. If I hadn't gotten involved with that crowd—if I hadn't witnessed the murder and robbery at that convenience store—my family would still be alive. It was my choices and my behavior that led to their deaths. No one is going to convince me otherwise."

I wanted to argue with him—to shake him and make him see how it wasn't his fault. You can't control what other people do! Sometimes, that was the hardest part about life. You can control a fraction of it that is your own, but even then, people find ways to influence it all the time, both for the good and the bad. How could he hold himself responsible?

But I would be a hypocrite for trying to convince him otherwise. Did I not feel the same way about Maddie's death? Did I not hold myself accountable when I lost her in the river, for failing to save her?

I put a hand on Damien's shoulder. He turned his head to look over at me.

"I understand," I stated. I shrugged and offered a small smile. He studied my face and seemed to grasp what I was thinking. His body relaxed.

"I think we're more alike than we realize," Damien said. He wrapped his warm hand around mine. "I'm glad you're here. I didn't think you'd understand. But it seems I was wrong."

"Well, I hope you don't think I believe it's your fault. What I mean is that I understand why you feel that way. I've been stuck there, too, as you know." I paused in thought, comparing our situations. "It seems easier to take out the irrational blame when it's someone else's life and not your own."

I leaned my head against his shoulder, sighing with contentment to be with him again. Taking advantage of his unusual candor, I asked another question.

"So after your burns healed, where did you go? I mean, you were still seventeen right? Who took care of you?"

"I have an uncle who lives in San Jose. I lived with him when I wasn't recovering at the burn center. He and my dad had some big falling out years ago, so I didn't know him too well. Yeah, it was kinda awkward. But he made some phone calls, and I was allowed to finish up my senior year online. Not quite the memorable graduation a kid anticipates, but at least I finished."

"That was just last year," I said. "When did you move to this cabin?"

Damien looked around the room at his simple,

yet tasteful, furnishing. I only now noticed the lack of pictures or décor on the wall, remembering the distinction he once made about the cabin being merely a place of residence, rather than his home. Damien continued answering my questions.

"As much as I appreciated my uncle's help while I recovered, we were strangers to each other, and I felt more like an obligation to him than anything. Needless to say, I was eager to get out of there. I was already eighteen by the time I finished high school, since my birthday is in March. That allowed me to inherit the life insurance money, as well as my father's business at the lodge."

My jaw dropped, and I interrupted with, "You own Eastridge?"

"Yep."

I sat up and pushed hair out of my face. "You told me you worked there doing 'managerial stuff.' Yeah, no kidding! I suppose *owning* the business falls under that category."

Damien gave a light laugh at my surprise. "I didn't feel like going back home to live in our oversized, empty house. So I bought this cabin and moved in last May." He looked at his open hands. "I don't know. I guess it makes me feel closer to my family, even though they're gone. Hidden Pines is familiar."

My attention returned to Damien's features. I wanted to memorize his face, not sure when I would see him again, once he remembered he had been trying to leave. That moment came as if on cue.

Damien looked towards the door. "Allie, I need to go."

I could feel the desperation building in my chest, my mind racing for any and all excuses for him to stay. This was the part of the story I didn't want to hear.

"Why?" was the only word I managed to force from my throat.

"I told you the Oakland PD stopped by two days ago. Some new information has surfaced, regarding the Samoans."

"What is it?"

"Tommy Miller's journal." Damien's face tightened back up again, his lips pressed together into a firm line.

"He kept a journal?"

"I guess. His mom was going through his boxes, and she came across a notebook. The last entry to date was the night he witnessed the shooting at the convenience store. He wrote down everything—hanging out with the Samoans, bribing them with money, and then their threats to kill him if he said anything about the robbery. He also wrote my name in there."

I gasped. "But that's good, isn't it? That clears your name! His journal is evidence of—"

"—of the gang I was involved with and the trouble I was mixed up in," Damien finished for me. "That's not going to matter to anyone. People are still going to associate me with them, and I will still be at fault for my family's death in their eyes." He shook his head. "But that doesn't matter. I'm not talking to the police to clear my name. The Miller's deserve to know what happened to their son, and hopefully get some justice if the police can bring those guys in. I can't live as a coward any longer. I'm ashamed I've gone this long."

"So the police want you to testify to help build their case against the Samoan gang?" I said.

Damien nodded. "If the least I can do is help the Miller's earn retribution for their son's death, that's what I'm going to do. But I can't stick around here and wait for the Samoans to come find me. Word's going to get out soon enough that the police have a

Lead—if it hasn't already." Damien stood up and walked to his room. He finished throwing some final articles of clothing into his duffle bag, and then stepped into his bathroom. I could hear him knocking bottles and containers over in his haste.

He was really leaving.

Panic crammed its way into my chest. I hurried to his room, stepping inside for the first time. The lighting was dim, emanating natural light from the bathroom window, as well as the square windows on the east wall of his room. I hovered outside the doorframe of his bathroom, watching him throw small items into a gray hygiene bag. He stepped past me to throw the final items into his duffle bag.

With his back towards me, I swallowed hard, begging, "Don't go."

Damien stood up and turned around. "Allie, you know I have to."

I shook my head. "Not yet. Please." My eyes searched the room. I pointed to the clock above his bed. I was amazed how much time had passed since I had arrived, but it supported my argument. "It's already after six. The police station in town is closed anyway. There's no point in leaving tonight. Can I … just stay here until the morning? And then I promise I won't put up a fight."

A part of me wanted to shake the desperation from my voice, barely aware enough that I should be embarrassed for allowing my emotions to take hold of me like this.

Damien seemed to struggle as he stood before me, weighing the situation in his mind. My knees tempted to buckle as I watched him run his eyes across my face. I knew he wanted to stay, too.

"Your dad—"

"—is on a two-day excursion with my stepmom. He won't be worried," I reassured him. "I'll sleep on the couch tonight. I just want to be with you while I can."

Damien stepped towards me and wrapped his arms around me. "All right. You win." He sighed, allowing me to bury my face against his chest. "You sure are persistent," he accused. "But I happen to like that."

Now that I had solidified a few more hours with him, there was something else I was curious about.

"Damien, I wanted to ask you something."

"What is it?"

"Can I see your back?"

That wasn't the question he was expecting. I

waited while his silence grew. I found myself chewing on my lip again. At last, Damien pulled away from me, his decision made.

He turned around. Slowly, he tugged his T-shirt up and over his torso. He pulled the shirt over his head, dropping it on the floor, waiting for my reaction.

I inhaled, swallowing my surprise. The scars webbed from the bottom of his shoulder blades and crept to the top of his shoulders. I noted the ashy, purple hue that cascaded across his back, thickened with scar tissue. Tracing his scars with my fingers, I glided them across the stretched, destroyed skin. Damien didn't move while I explored his bare back.

How painful it must have been, not only the actual moments when he felt the searing, burning pain from the fire, but to lose his entire family all at once, to face the accusations and accept the undue responsibility. He had to bear that burden all alone.

Sighing, I wrapped my arms around him and placed my cheek against his skin. I closed my eyes, wishing I could absorb all his pain, as he'd already been doing for me. My thoughts turned to Maddie and the day I survived when she didn't. Someone had rescued me that day from her same fate. How I wished someone could have been a hero to Damien—to rescue him from suffering the loss of his family.

I felt Damien take my hands in his, squeezing them in understanding. He turned around to face me, lifting my chin with his fingers. He kissed me on the lips, sending a delicate shiver down my spine. My eyes connected with his, my breaths sharpening. Damien scooped me up into his arms and carried me over to his bed, lowering me onto the mattress. I scooted over, making room for him beside me.

He sank into the mattress and sat with his back propped against his pillows. I curled up beside him, laying my head in his lap. He caressed my face along my temple to my jawline. My face nestled into the palm of his hand, enjoying the comforts of his touch.

Hearing Damien's emotional account of his life seemed to drain me as much as it must have drained him. I could feel him relaxing into the pillows, his head resting against the headboard.

My breaths slowed. Within minutes, sleep tugged on the corners of my mind. I tried to resist, my last night with Damien disappearing too soon.

"It's ok," Damien's voice soothed. "You can sleep."

"I don't want to," I argued. But my thoughts began to wander...

Somewhere between awareness and dreaming, I found myself beside the river, cold and shivering against the damp soil. The rushing river roared in my ears as I coughed up a lungful of water. Someone lifted my head, holding my face in his hands. I shook my head, my eyes fluttering open, blinking out the river and rain. It was all a blur...coming into focus in small spurts—leaves waving in the wind, with slashing rain knocking them from their branches, and a dim, gray sky with dark clouds hovering overhead...

And someone looking down at me, while my head rested in his lap. His hands cradled my face with such gentleness that for one moment, I felt safe from the turbulent river beside me.

"You're going to be ok," his low voice informed me over the falling rain—a comforting sound that begged me to believe him, but it was his eyes that caught my attention—piercing, blue-gray eyes, covered ever so slightly by a wisp of damp, jet-black hair falling across his forehead...

My eyes flew open, no longer captured in memory. Memory.

I bolted upright, startling Damien, who looked at me in surprise.

"What's the matter?" he asked. "Are you ok?"

It was dark outside now—the window letting in the dim moonlight—but as my eyes adjusted, I could see concern fill his eyes as he examined my bewildered expression.

My breaths heaved in and out of my chest as understanding came.

"It was you," I whispered.

"Allie, what are you talking about?" Damien seemed confused.

"I remember now. By the river. I saw it so clearly." I touched my lips with my fingertips, remembering his mouth over mine, breathing life back into my lungs. My heart pounded awake and alert in my chest, keeping in time with my breaths.

I looked back at Damien. He was watching me, with that dark hair I recalled so vividly draping over one eye as it often did. I reached over and brushed his hair above his eyebrow.

There was no mistaking it. His unique, bluish-silver eyes reflected back at me, glowing against the moonlight. The very same eyes of my rescuer that day.

My eyes glistened as I choked back a sob, flooded with emotions. "Why didn't you tell me?"

Damien leaned back against the pillows. He blew out a breath of air. "It was the summer right after my parents and Jenna died. I didn't need anyone thinking I was trying to be a hero." He cast his eyes across the room, remembering that day. "The important thing was making sure you were safe."

I scrunched my eyebrows, my memory still imperfect. "I couldn't remember your face or anything about what you looked like. My nightmares never focused on that part. When I awoke in the hospital, no one could tell me how I got there, except that a young man dropped me off and didn't leave his name." I looked at him curiously. "You mind filling in the gaps?"

"It was just by chance that I found you that day," Damien said. "I was in my truck, driving into town for some supplies. I had only been in this cabin for a month or so. I drove across the bridge and heard you crying out. I saw you flailing around in the river, and your cousin just ahead of you. My truck wouldn't make it through the trees, so I jumped out and ran." He shook his head, looking down at his hands. He lowered his voice in remorse.

"By the time I got there, I had lost sight of the little girl. But I saw you, clinging onto the embankment. Your head kept dipping below the water. I reached you just as you let go of the brush. I grabbed hold of your wrists and yanked you out of the water. You weren't breathing. But it didn't take a lot of breaths from me before you choked up the water and were breathing on your own."

"You held my head in your lap," I interrupted, recalling my memories of that day. "And touched my face. That's what I remembered just now—looking up and seeing your face watching over me."

Damien nodded. The gentle hue of red that touched his face further highlighted his handsome features, even in the dim lighting.

"Half-drowned, I still thought you were beautiful."

This time I was the one reddening as I looked away, the insides of my stomach dancing around. "So you took me to the hospital..." I prompted, glancing back at him. Damien's dimple deepened at my expression before he continued.

"There was no sight of Maddie. I looked for her when I carried you to my truck. You were mumbling all the way to the hospital. As soon as my phone had service, I left an anonymous call with the police about your missing cousin, and they sent out a search and rescue team. At the hospital, you were swept up so fast that it

was easy for me to disappear without being interrogated."
Damien paused. "I'm sorry about your cousin. I wish I
could have helped her, too."

I took a deep breath, meeting his eyes once again.
"You did everything you could. Thank you," I said. "I
wouldn't be here either if it weren't for you." I threw my
arms around Damien's neck and clung onto him. "Thank
you," I murmured again. "You don't know how much I've
wanted to say that to the right person."

He hugged me back, stroking my hair against my
T-shirt. "After that day, I couldn't stop thinking about
you. I felt...connected to you. Not just because I had
pulled you from the river, but...." He hesitated before
continuing. "I heard what some of the locals were saying
about the accident."

Somber, I nodded, recalling the blame that was
placed on my shoulders for not looking out for my
younger cousin. "I know. They held me responsible as
much as I did. 'Negligent' and 'careless' are some of the
words that come to mind." I grimaced, remembering how
hurtful that was to hear, despite the fact that I believed
it myself.

Damien clenched his fists with a firm shake of his
head. "It made me so angry that they were putting you
through the same torment that I went through—that I
was *still* going through. It seemed deserved when it was
me. It was harder to see the same thing happen to you.

"Over the past year, I wondered where you were
and how you were doing. We'd met for just a few moments,

but you entered my thoughts all the time, even slipping into my dreams. The day I found out you were back at the lodge, I couldn't get you out of my head," Damien admitted in embarrassment.

"The way you walked around, smiling now and then like everything was ok, but I could see the hurt you tried to hide. It's much easier to recognize when you've felt the very same thing yourself. I wanted to protect you from everything. And I wanted to get to know you, to know more about you."

I looked at him in mock annoyance. "So you decided to scare me and make me fall out of that tree?" I laughed in remembrance. "Your tactics could have been a little more subtle."

"True. And like I said, I didn't mean to scare you. I was just...observing from the bushes—"

I laughed out loud at his choice of words. "Oh, is that what all the stalkers are calling it these days?"

He ignored my comments, placing a hand over my mouth. "Observing," he continued, "and working up the nerve to talk to you. I had no idea I would scare you so much. But I'm kind of glad I did."

I made a face. "What? Why?"

"Well, otherwise, I may not have discovered you were so feisty," Damien said impishly.

I grabbed a pillow and slammed it into his face. Grabbing my wrists, he wrestled the pillow from my hands, tossing it over the edge. He flipped over and pinned me against the bed, sitting on my legs to prevent me from further kicking at him.

Still fighting him, I shrieked, "That's not fair! You're so much bigger than me!"

He shrugged and smiled in satisfaction, but he didn't let me up. His grip on me was firm enough that my struggles were useless against him. I conceded my loss. I relaxed under his weight, pausing to catch my breath.

My laughter subsided as I looked up at him. He was watching me with such adoration in his expression that my heart skipped a beat. My stomach twisted inside itself all over again.

Here I was with my hero, at last.

His striking features watched me, absorbed in his own thoughts. Words came to my mind that I never dared believe in before, let alone voiced aloud, but our connection, however impossibly it had developed, begged recognition.

"Damien...I love you." The words felt so foreign on my tongue. But the words escaped from my lips, raw and unrehearsed. I was sure he could hear the penetrable thudding inside my chest. Or maybe it was his pulse I was hearing against my own.

Damien lowered his face in response, embracing his lips with mine. His movements were slow and tender. I placed my hand on the back of his neck, pulling him against me. He didn't resist.

My fingers slid along his back until I found his scars—the scars that represented all the pain Damien had been through, and the loss and torment that strangely allowed us to connect with each other. Swathed by an overwhelming emotion, our bodies pulled closer together.

It was then that we heard the slamming of car doors from the front of the cabin. Damien leaped up with astounding speed, hurling himself off the bed. I gasped in surprise as he grabbed my arm and pulled me to my feet.

"Come on!" his hushed voice urged.

Flustered and disoriented, my bare feet followed his. He hurried me out of his bedroom, towards a door that stood between his room and the kitchen. He pulled it open.

What I once thought must be a closet or a pantry, did in fact, open to a stairwell.

"Go. Hide. Don't say a word. And no matter what happens, don't come upstairs."

CHAPTER 24

My eyes widened as I detected the fear in Damien's eyes, and the taut line of his jaw. I had just enough time to nod before he shut the door, leaving me in the dark.

I heard his feet shuffle away, just as the front door burst open with a bang.

"Damien, my man!" a deep voice bellowed. "Long time, no see. Long time, no see..." An eerie chuckle filled the room.

I held my breath, trying to quiet the air that was exploding in and out of my lungs. I tiptoed down the stairs, my hands stretched out to the walls, as I descended into the basement. It was difficult to find my way in the dark. One hand was stretched out in front of me, while the other slid across the wall. My fingers found a light switch, but I didn't dare turn it on.

The low voices upstairs caught my attention again, their words seeping through the floorboards. I listened hard to decipher the rumble of voices.

"Look at you. You're all grown up now!"

"We've always liked you, Damien," a different voice was saying. "We tried to give you a break last time—"

"A break?" Damien's angry voice interrupted. "You think killing my entire family was giving me a 'break?'"

"Hey now, don't be so ungrateful. The fire wasn't meant to kill. They could have made it. But they didn't make it, did they? Natural selection, we like to call it."

Quick footsteps thudded against the floor and heavy bodies fell to the ground. Something like a wrestling match had ensued.

"Easy now, Damien!" A third voice interrupted them.

More sounds of struggle and grunting. There were at least three of them, then.

Three against Damien.

The dominant voice continued. "We could have killed you like we did that Miller kid—one shot to the head would have solved all our problems years ago. But we liked you. And see now, we leave you alive out of the goodness of our hearts, and look what happens. Cops show up with a lead, and you look like you're packed and ready to go rat us out. That's no way to treat old friends."

"*We* are not friends." Damien's voice was filled with such menace that it was almost unrecognizable.

"Well, that should make this easy then," came the second voice.

A gunshot echoed through the cabin.

"No!" I screamed. I threw my hands over my mouth, but it was too late. I could hear footsteps hurrying to the stairwell door.

I bolted across the room, stepping inside a small

bedroom. Cardboard boxes were scattered throughout the room, disheveled and disorganized.

There was nowhere to go. I tripped my way to the corner of the room, stubbing my toe and ignoring the throbbing pain.

I could hear the heavy footsteps descending the stairs. Falling against the corner wall, I buried my head behind a large, unopened box. I crouched low, too afraid to even peek around the corner.

A set of footsteps entered the room, pausing by the entryway.

My hand clamped back over my mouth, muffling my breaths and the scream that threatened to escape. I wished I could quiet the pounding in my chest that was sure to give me away.

"Hey, Damien's friend! We know you're here. Don't worry. We were coming for you anyway. We saw your car out front. Come on out now, and maybe we won't kill you."

I didn't move an inch, despite the painful cramping in my thighs. I closed my eyes, leaning my sweaty forehead against the cardboard.

A swift click flooded the room with light.

"There you are!"

I tumbled backwards, jumping against the wall as a very large man stalked towards me. At the sight of me, he lowered his gun, smiling in amusement.

"Stay away from me!" I managed to squeeze out from my dry throat. My voice sounded weak and small.

I barricaded myself in the corner, my eyes jumping from side to side, searching in vain for an exit.

There was nowhere to go.

I watched the tall, thick-statured man step towards me, smirking as he closed the gap. He held up his gun with his fingers, waving it loosely in the air. "Come on, now. We already shot one person tonight." He shoved the box to the side in one swift movement. Bending down, his left hand wrapped around my bicep, he tugged me upwards. He dragged me across the room, stumbling after him.

As we stepped into the living room, I gasped.

Damien was kneeling on the ground, his right hand covering a bloodied wound to his left shoulder. Profusely bleeding, his face was twisted in pain.

But he was alive.

The two other Samoans stood nearby, looking down at him. One of them held their gun ready, pointed at his head.

"Damien!" I tore free from my captor, dashing towards him.

"Hey!" a voice called out. I saw a flash of silver pointed my way as I fell next to Damien.

Damien leaned in front of me, wincing as he did so. "Stop! You don't have to do that!"

My eyes looked up to see the second gunman pointing his weapon at me. His build was similar to the one I met downstairs, but his eyes were dark and not amused.

Damien was livid, still gripping his injured shoulder. "What do you think she's going to do, huh? Yeah, takes a real tough guy to aim a gun at an unarmed girl."

The gunman knocked his nine-millimeter across Damien's jaw, whipping his head to the side with an agonizing crack. My hands formed around Damien's face, as if that would ease his pain.

"We'll do the talking from now on," the man informed. The Samoan next to him put a hand on his friend's shoulder.

"Easy now, Afona. We already have this mess to clean up." He kicked at Damien's foot, where the blood was trickling around him. "We'll take care of her elsewhere."

"She doesn't know anything," Damien insisted. He muffled a groan as he tried to reposition himself. "Just let her go."

"You need to stop the bleeding," I interrupted, my eyes still following the oozing liquid. I wished, now, that Damien still had his shirt on to soak up the blood.

Leaving my tank top, I tore off my shirt. Moving Damien's hand, I tied the cloth around his shoulder. I ignored the chuckling behind me, and the way his voice mocked mine.

"We need to stop the bleeding." More laughter followed. "Ha! That's a good one!"

I turned around to glare at the man, who sauntered over to join his two friends.

"You shouldn't bother," he said, tapping his gun with his index finger. "It's not going to make much difference in a few minutes."

"Iona," Damien said. "Please. Do whatever you're going to do with me. But leave Allie out of this." His eyes moved to the dominating Samoan. "Fanua. Please."

Fanua smiled. "Listen to the Palangi begging. Found love at last, Damien?" He laughed. "You know we can't do that. You think she's not going to say anything about what she's seen tonight?" His eyes moved to my face, studying my expression. "And you know, I don't think she knows as little as you are claiming, brotha."

My hands clung to Damien's bicep, feeling the warmth of his skin seep into my cold hands. I tried to hide how they trembled. I lifted my chin, staring hard at each one of them.

"Fanua," the one named Afona said. He pointed to the clock on the wall. "We need to get moving. Don't want any more unexpected visitors."

Fanua nodded. "Iona, take the girl."

I struggled against the firm grip that yanked me to my feet.

"Give him your keys," Fanua ordered.

"Where are you taking me?" I asked.

"The keys," Iona emphasized.

My eyes scanned the living room in defeat. "They're—they're on the coffee table." Fanua tossed Iona the keys. He lugged me towards the front door. I struggled, throwing my head towards Damien in desperation.

"Allie!" Damien jumped to his feet and lunged at Afona.

Afona struck his face with a solid fist and kicked his ribs. Damien grunted, falling back onto the floor. Afona cocked the gun, aiming it once again at his head. He stepped on Damien's injured shoulder, slowly adding pressure.

Damien hollered in pain, writhing on the floor.

"No!" I shrieked. "Please—don't do this!"

"For that, maybe we'll even have some fun with your girl before we're through with her. Each and every one of us," Afona emphasized. Damien cursed at the man, his voice full of rage.

Iona continued to hustle me out the door.

"Finish him off," Fanua ordered. "Come pick us up when you're done."

"Damien!" I turned my head, searching for Damien's eyes.

His eyes—those piercing, blue-gray eyes—looked back at me. The love and adoration from minutes before were now replaced by remorse and anger, which flooded his dark features. He watched helplessly while I stumbled out the door.

I was shoved into the passenger seat of my suburban with my hands bound behind my back. I grimaced. But I didn't expect my captor to notice or show any sign of mercy. He slammed my door shut and moved to the driver's seat.

I looked out my window. Fanua seemed to be

leaving Afona some final instructions. I saw them nod at each other. Fanua cast one last glance at Damien's tortured expression, leaving him with one more broad smile. Then he shut the door. Fanua jumped into the backseat of the suburban.

"All right, let's roll." Iona pulled the car into gear and took off, heading north towards the mountains. Nobody bothered to look back. Outside, the moon shone, lighting our rugged path and glinting off the lake.

Thoughts of Damien raced through my mind. I wanted to plead and beg these men to turn around, to stop this madness. But I knew my words would be wasted.

*Don't take Damien away from me...*Torturous thoughts of our last moments played through my memory: his soft lips around mine, our bodies holding each other close, and my first confession of love to the one man who would remain a hero in my heart.

Outside my head, there was heavy silence.

And then, two consecutive shots rang out, disrupting the quiet nature of the night.

The only sounds that followed were the inconsolable sobs emanating from deep within my throat.

CHAPTER 25

Nothing else seemed to matter. They had taken Damien's life, and now they were going to take mine. It was odd how apathy could replace my fear in such short time—to make me forget the pain in my chest and dry the tears in my eyes. Even the shaky, shuddering breaths after a hard cry were beginning to subside as I relinquished to my fate. All I felt now were the ropes cutting into my wrists. I had given up trying to wriggle out of them, but they were going numb.

Pressing my cheek against the cool window, I released a defeated sigh. I didn't know how they were going to end my life, but I knew it would be soon.

"Don't worry, now," Iona's voice interrupted in mock sincerity. "You'll be reunited with Damien soon enough." I didn't have to look over to know he was smiling maliciously at me from behind the wheel.

A wave of disgust rushed through my body. The sound of him saying Damien's name ignited a spark. "You are a cruel, despicable excuse for a man," I spat out.

Laughter erupted from the seat behind me. "Hear that, Iona?" Fanua said. "She thinks you're 'despicable'. We got to write that one down, eh?"

"I'm flattered," Iona commented. "From the way you look at us, Damien must have told you all about us. I hope we're living up to our name."

I stared straight ahead, glaring through the windshield. The dirt road was leading us northeast of the lake. We were just starting a gradual ascent through the mountain.

"It doesn't matter what you do with me. You'll be caught," I continued, not bothering to look at either of them. "The police know Damien had some valuable information about your worthless gang. As soon as he's discovered missing, they're going to know you came for him. And they're going to track you down like the dogs you are."

Neither of the two accompanying Samoans seemed concerned. Fanua spoke, "It doesn't matter. In this great country, we are 'innocent until proven guilty'. If they can't find the evidence, they can suspect us all they want." He leaned forward in his seat, resting his head on my shoulder. I could feel his warm breath touching my ear. He whispered, "This isn't our first time, you know."

I shrugged away from him, glowering inside, waiting and wondering for the fate that would be mine.

We pulled up to a smaller lake, surrounded by a thicket of trees, and what looked like some vacant camp sites in the distance. My eyes scanned the dark woods in search of any sign of visitors—flashlights in the distance or voices carrying through the air—but there was nothing. We were all alone.

The gangsters stepped out of the car, slamming their doors shut. Fanua pulled open my door and hauled me out of the car. He dragged me towards the water. The lights from the truck lit our path and illuminated the calm, lapping water. I could hear Iona following behind, the items he carried clanking against each other.

"Here we are. Have a seat." Fanua shoved me to the ground. I landed on my rear, grunting on impact. I scowled up at them.

"See, here's what we're going to do," Fanua continued, tugging a beer can from Iona's full arms. He popped open the lid, pausing to take a sloppy sip. "We're going to make this easy on you. Give you a few drinks and, along with our magic pill—" He pulled a small, plastic package from his jacket, holding it up in the light. Inside were three small, white tablets. "—you won't know the difference between sleeping and drowning. How's that for considerate, huh?" He gleamed at me, exposing a missing molar.

Despite my efforts to hide my fear, I scooted backwards, pushing my bare feet against the dirt. My eyes widened, eyeing the men in front of me. They smiled as they anticipated my reaction, relishing in my fear.

They were going to make my death look like an accidental drowning. Too much alcohol and a swim in the lake...not a far-fetched story for a graduated teen— especially one who was suffering from the emotional turbulence of losing her cousin and dealing with her father's remarriage.

Even as I pieced their plan together, I watched Iona open another can and empty its contents along the ground. He crunched the aluminum in one movement, tossing it a few feet away from me.

"Drink up, little lady," Fanua said, squatting in front of me. He put the can to my lips and tipped the can.

I grimaced, wrenching my face away. The liquid spilled down my neck and soaked into my tank top. I spit in his face. "Get away from me!"

Fanua growled, wiping a large hand across his cheek. "We're doing this the hard way, I see." He grabbed my hair with his free hand, yanking backwards. I cried out as my head snapped back. Fanua poured the beer onto my face, spilling the vile liquid down my nose and into my mouth. I choked and sputtered, swallowing while I tried to breathe, gagging as the bitter drink trickled down my throat.

"There, that's a girl," he sneered. He poured another dose all over my face. I coughed, blinking back tears and alcohol from my eyes.

"Please—stop!" I managed to choke out. Fanua released my hair and I sat up with a gasp. I shook my head, still coughing. Through blinking eyes, I watched Fanua rip open the plastic package. He pinched two white tablets with his fingers.

"Painless," he promised, putting the rest of the bag back in his pocket. "It should take twenty minutes or so. It will make drowning that much easier. And much quieter," he added. He dropped the tablets into the can and swirled it around.

My body trembled. I twisted around onto my knees. Leaping to my feet, I tried to bolt. My balance staggered, and I fell to my knees. I made an effort to scramble to my feet, but with my hands still tied, I wasn't fast enough.

Fanua grabbed me with his free arm, throwing me into a headlock from behind. I squirmed against him.

"No! Let go of me!"

Again, Fanua bent me backwards, digging his knee into my back. He poured the concentrated liquid down my throat. I gagged and sputtered, resisting the drug. I wrenched my face back and forth, struggling against my captor's arm, but every breath I fought for allowed a flood of tainted beer to trail down my throat and into my system. I could hear Iona laughing in the background, crunching another beer can. He egged his buddy on.

My mouth found a chunk of Fanua's arm. I clamped down with my teeth, biting down like a vice.

Fanua bellowed, dropping the can and releasing his hold on me. I launched to my feet, wobbling as I found my balance. I didn't look back. I took off running towards the trees, ignoring the deep hollering behind me.

I ran, my breaths heaving in my chest. Dry pine needles pierced my bare feet, but I ignored their prickling sting. My feet dug into the dirt, dodging trees and bushes. Without the truck headlights, lighting was scarce, but my eyes adjusted to the dim moonlight above the trees.

Footsteps thundered not far behind me. "Get back here!" Iona was yelling.

Branches flew by my cheeks, etching my skin with their callous touch. The muscles in my thighs ached at the sudden demand of strength, but they responded on instinct.

I altered my path, hoping to create enough distance between the oversized thug and myself. Perhaps he would not find me in the dark.

Perhaps he would decide I wasn't worth the fight.

And perhaps the drug would not make its way into my system, allowing me a fighting chance at escape. Minutes were all I had.

My lungs burned for deprived oxygen. I pressed on, begging my limbs to pick up the pace. I didn't know where I was going, but I had to keep moving. I didn't want to think about what they would do once they caught me.

As I dodged a tree, the ground beneath me sloped without warning. I tumbled down the hill, sliding a few feet along the loose dirt. My body rolled over brush and pinecones. I moaned, my shoulders and face having absorbed most of the impact. Looking back up the hill, I listened for the approaching footsteps. They were coming closer.

Scooting my body behind a bush, I hoped it would shield me from the top of the hill. I held my breath, afraid to breathe and give away my position. The footsteps were right above me now. I could hear the heavy breathing. But his steps carried on. Then there was silence.

I couldn't tarry too long. I jumped to my feet with effort, my legs beginning to wobble while I squinted at the bottom of the slope. It took me a few moments before I dared believe my eyes, but my spirits lifted.

There was a dirt road at the bottom, and approaching headlights in the distance. Help was on its way at last.

Slipping and sliding my way down the hill, my eagerness to escape almost threw me off balance.

"I'm here! Please, help me!" I yelled out, almost reaching the bottom of the incline. The headlights came to a stop a short distance away, blinding me. My eyes searched for my rescuers through the light. Imagining my appearance, my thoughts scattered at what I would tell them. With any luck, maybe their phone picked up service, and the police would be on their way in minutes. I couldn't let these men get away. Hopeful, I cast my eyes at the opening car door.

The familiar, large shape of Fanua stepped out of the vehicle. He stared at me with anger in his dark eyes.

Surprise and fear forced me to a halt, mid-step. My sudden jolt catapulted my body forward. My head slammed into a tree trunk, and I collapsed with instantaneous throbbing in my forehead.

"No..." I moaned, unable to move. I closed my eyes, wishing I could silence the drums in my head.

"You really know how to make things difficult," Fanua's livid voice said. His callous hands touched my skin, and I winced. His strong arms slung me over his

LINGERING ECHOES

shoulder. Thrown into the back seat of my suburban, I grimaced as the seatbelt buckle dug into my cheek. I wriggled my numb hands from inside the ropes, but the movements felt slow and uncoordinated. Helplessly, I rested my head against the seat of the car.

"Ah—there she is," I heard Iona say, slipping into the passenger seat a couple minutes later. "Bro, I think I can check off my exercise goals for the year," he said, still panting. "That's more running than I've done my whole life." I felt the car flip around, heading back the way we came.

Once again, I was yanked out of the car. My head danced around and around without my consent. My feet stumbled, unable to keep up as I was pulled towards the lake. Coming to a stop, my knees gave out, dropping my body to the floor.

"What's the matter? Feeling a little...dizzy?" Fanua's voice seemed to skip through the air, almost blending together in confusing tones, mingled with laughter.

The drug! You have to fight it!

"Damien..." I murmured. Images of his face infiltrated my mind, strengthening my senses.

"Damien's long gone, honey," Fanua said. "Afona should be back with the car any minute now. Maybe he'll be kind enough to bring the body for you. If you're still awake, that is."

I looked up at him from where I was slumped, noticing the tender, red marks on his right arm. Even

332

half-drugged, I could detect the bloody bite marks I had left as a souvenir for him. A sloppy smirk escaped my lips.

Fanua followed my gaze. He glowered at me. "You're going to regret that," he informed me. "Real soon."

CHAPTER 26

Fanua lifted me to my feet and towed me after him. Cold water bathed my legs as we trudged a couple yards into the lake. He shoved me to the ground. I landed on my knees, splashing into the pool beneath me.

I knew I should be scared. I was about to die—death by drowning, after all. It didn't matter that Damien had saved me once. This was my fate. Water, the conquering enemy, would have me at last, but the fear that should have fueled me was numb—unresponsive, just like the rest of my body.

"Have a nice swim," he said.

He placed his massive hand on my head, shoving it downwards into the water. Tranquilized or not, my body responded on instinct. I thrashed against the water, allowing my right hand to slip out from the stretched and waterlogged knots around my wrists. My fingers found Fanua's hand on top of my head. I dug my nails into his skin, scratching and clawing.

The pressure on my head released just enough. My head popped out of the lake, and I inhaled both water and air. My clumsy kicking managed to contact something of importance, because Fanua buckled over with a deep groan.

I lunged for the shore. Urging myself towards dry land, I crawled through the water. Frantic sobs erupted from my throat. A hand grabbed my ankle, pulling me back through the water. Dirt caught under my nails as I raked the ground with my hands. A tangle of slippery weeds braided between my fingers.

Shrieking, I rolled onto my back and kicked at Fanua's face with my free leg.

His arm came down onto my head. I was gurgling in the water again, blowing out precious bubbles of air.

Whether it was the drug or lack of oxygen, I didn't know, but the dizziness was winning. The world was growing bleaker around me, darkness absorbing my mind and body. I couldn't open my eyes, but I could feel the bursting pain in my lungs.

My head was pulled out of the water. I coughed against the water sliding down my throat.

"I have an idea," Fanua said, his fist full of my tangled hair. "Even though you've made this very difficult on us, I'm going to give you a choice. Option one: You can sit here and let the drug finish knocking you out, and you won't feel a thing when we leave you face-first in the water. Or..."

Fanua paused, enjoying his dramatic effect, while I shivered next to him. In the distance, I could see the Samoan's black car approaching the lake. Iona stood a mere twenty-five feet from us, waving it in. Afona was back, just in time to watch me die. I looked at Fanua, waiting for his final choice. He continued.

"Option two: If you can make it across the lake before the drugs take you, then—you're free to go." He shrugged. "No strings attached." But his features twisted into a cruel smile. I looked across the span of water, calculating the distance. It was a much smaller lake than Hidden Pines, but not enough to fool me into false hope.

With either option, the result would be the same. Fanua knew that, and he knew I knew that.

But one way allowed me to die fighting. I thought of Damien again, winning strength from his memories.

Fanua seemed to detect the determination in my eyes. "I hoped you would choose that one. It will be much more fun to watch." He pulled a knife from his pocket, flipping it open. He sliced the remaining knotted rope from my left wrist.

My hands wrapped around each other, massaging life back into them. I could feel the tingling sensation of blood absorbing through them again. At the same time, my knees wobbled, threatening to give out on me.

"There's just one more thing," Fanua said. "For all the trouble you've put us through tonight, I think I deserve a little farewell celebration." He pulled me close to him, wrapping his hands around my shoulders. I twisted my head away, reeling at the closeness of his foul breath, and his lips almost touching mine.

A shot fired into the night air, echoing against the mountains.

My eyes turned to see Iona squirming on the ground, holding his right bicep. He was lying at the foot of the Samoan's open car door, looking inside at the driver in disbelief.

Fanua pulled my back against him, whipping out his gun and holding it against my temple. I could feel the cool metal pressing against my tender skin. Both of us squinted to see through the tinted windows of the vehicle. My heavy eyes blinked at the strain, struggling to focus.

"I'll kill her. I'll kill her *right now* if you don't show yourself!" Fanua demanded, squeezing my arm.

The driver complied. He stood up behind the open door. I sucked in a breath of surprise, seeing the spikes of his gelled, sun-bleached hair before I saw his face.

Steadfast, Aaron stood before us, aiming an identical nine-millimeter at Fanua, both hands securely locked around his weapon.

"Aaron." I murmured his name in confusion. I looked at the passenger doors, waiting and hoping for one of them to open, but the doors remained closed. He was alone.

I looked back at Aaron, worried and concerned for his safety, but Aaron held his stance, while keeping an eye on the Samoan at his feet. I touched my throbbing head, fighting to shake the pain and dizziness from my mind.

"Allie...What have you done to her?" he said with

337

anger, noting my lethargic appearance. His sharp eyes glared at my captor.

"Nothing she didn't deserve," Fanua responded. He tightened his grip on me, pushing the gun harder against my head. His voice lowered. "What have you done with my brother? I'm assuming he didn't offer you his car and gun."

"Let her go," Aaron demanded. "Or you can join both of your friends. And this time," he continued, glancing down at Iona by his feet, "it won't just be a warning flesh wound."

Fanua gave a short, humorless chuckle. "You must truly care about this one to so carelessly risk your life."

Aaron's eyes met mine once again, securing our gaze for one long moment. The fear he tried to conceal edged its way out from its hiding place, coupled by something more indistinguishable. He swallowed hard.

Fanua spoke next to my ear. "Interesting. Looks like Damien's heart isn't the only one you've won over, is it? It's a shame we don't have more time together. I'd like to figure out what's so intriguing about you." He spoke up, directing his comments at Aaron. "Come on, now, bro. You're just a boy. You can't win! Put your gun down or your lady friend is dead." Fanua cocked his gun for emphasis. Aaron hesitated. I could see the indecision in his eyes.

And I saw the quiet movement before anyone else.

Look out! I screamed in my head, but my voice

was not cooperating. From where he lay on the ground, Iona had used the distracting standstill to reach for the gun inside his jacket. He pulled it out with his left hand, rolling onto his back.

I made an indistinguishable noise, my eyes wide, but the sound was enough to alert Aaron. He looked down at Iona, kicking the gun out of his hands. Iona brought up his own leg, nailing Aaron in the back of his quad with the toe of his shoe. Aaron fell to his knees, grunting in pain. Iona reached for the gun, almost wrenching it from Aaron's grip. Aaron tightened his hold, his face grimacing in the struggle. The gun twisted back and forth between them, both sets of hands fumbling over the loaded weapon with their bodies a foot apart.

Fanua released his grip on me, shoving me aside, into the water. He rotated his aim at Aaron's head. I looked up in desperation.

No, not Aaron, too.

Panicked tears blurred my vision. Fearful, I looked up at Fanua's aimed hand. A cruel smile formed on his lips.

"No! Don't do this!" My choked voice caught in my throat.

A sudden eruption of splashing caught our attention. From our left, a tall, thick figure was sprinting through the shallow water towards us. Fanua's face twisted from determined anger to surprise.

He growled, swinging his aim around. He wasn't fast enough.

Damien hurled himself at Fanua's torso, tackling him to the ground. The gun fired once behind Damien's back as both bodies plummeted into the water beside me. The gun slipped from Fanua's hands, landing in the muddied water. Damien and Fanua wrestled, the Samoan's massive hands wrapping around Damien's neck. Damien spun on top of Fanua, clubbing his jaw. Twice more he pummeled Fanua's face with his good arm, until Fanua released him.

Beside them, my hands scrambled beneath the water for the gun, my fingers groping the gravel. I looked behind me at Aaron and Iona, both of whom were still engaged in their battle for the weapon.

Without warning, Fanua pulled the knife from his pocket, stabbing it near Damien's wounded shoulder. Damien cried out in torment. Fanua leaped to his feet, kicking Damien onto his back in one motion.

"Sorry, Uso. No more second chances." Fanua yanked the knife from Damien's shoulder, smiling with pleasure as Damien's face contorted in agony. Eyeing Damien's neck, Fanua held the knife in the air.

With the last of my strength, I leaped onto Fanua's back, clawing at his face. My nails caught his eyes, his cheeks...anything I could dig into. Fanua roared. He grabbed one of my arms and hurled me off his back and into the water. Exhausted, I panted at his feet, unable to move anymore. I looked up at him.

Fanua growled, tightening his grip on the knife. In one swift motion, he swung at me. I closed my eyes.

A shot was fired.

And then another.

For a moment, there was silence.

Then Fanua fell down beside me. His massive body weight splashed me with water as he landed face-first into the lake. Bright blood swirled around his still body.

With water dripping from my hair and along my face, my mouth fell open with a small gasp. I looked up at the shooter, but Damien was already aiming the nine-millimeter towards the shore, struggling to keep it steady as his strength wavered. The circle of blood from his wound seemed to be growing larger every second, contrasting with his paling face.

A third shot sounded through the air. But it was not from Damien's gun. Terrified, I looked to where the sound originated, from where Aaron and Iona's bodies lay on the ground. Only one of them was moving.

My eyes widened.

The sobbing that ruptured from within was the first cries of relief I had shed all night. Aaron pulled himself off Iona, dropping the gun beside him. He leaned his back against the wheel of the car, blowing out a heavy breath of air. Dirt caked his sweaty face as he looked back over at me. I tried to smile at him, but my lips were quivering too hard.

"Allie." The low voice that spoke came from my left. I turned my head, my eyes locking on Damien's. He stood ten feet away, the revolver resting along his thigh.

He was leaning to the side, where the shoulder of his gray T-shirt continued to stain with fresh blood.

"Damien." His name escaped from my lips. The quiet moment allowed comprehension that he was truly alive. The flood of euphoria was so vivid that I wondered if all of this was just the drugs playing with my mind after all. With trembling legs, I rose to my feet, stepping over Fanua's dead body. Damien staggered over to me, wrapping his right arm around me and pulling me close. He dropped the gun, placing his hand along my back.

With a shaking hand, I traced his face with my fingers. He was real. And he was here with me.

"Are you ok?" he asked, resting his cheek against mine. The day-old stubble gently scratched my face, reassuring me of his presence.

I murmured a satisfied reply with a deep sigh, closing my eyes. My head was spinning, and my knees threatened to buckle, but none of it mattered now. I simply held onto Damien, clinging to him like a lifeline.

CHAPTER 27

My heavy eyelids resisted, but I forced them open. I became aware of the airy, unfamiliar blankets tucked around me, my cheek resting on a firm pillow. As I moved my head, I grimaced at the dull pain in my neck. My movements caught someone's attention, and I realized I wasn't alone. The face across from me, sitting in an uncomfortable-looking chair, widened his eyes and leaped to his feet. Aaron hurried to the edge of my narrow bed.

I rolled onto my back and pulled myself into a sitting position, looking around the white room. Dazed, I rubbed my face with my hands, trying to remember where I was and how I had come to be here. Aaron stood at my side and placed a hand lightly on my shoulder.

"Allie, how are you feeling?" His eyebrows arched up, studying my face. I paused, taking a moment to evaluate myself.

"Tired, and a little dizzy," I admitted, rubbing the stiffness from my neck. I inhaled, filling my lungs. Smells of disinfectant and rubbing alcohol drifted through the air. I wrinkled my nose in distaste.

Hospitals. I never did like hospitals, especially

remembering the last time I was in one.

"You ok?" Aaron asked.

I took in Aaron's disheveled appearance. He was wearing yesterday's polo and shorts, both now wrinkled and dusted with dirt. His ruffled hair sat flatter than its usual gelled touch. Light shadows smudged together beneath his eyes, quietly aging him.

"You look like you've been here all night," I commented, for lack of a better conversation starter.

"Yeah, I might have." Aaron stretched his long body up towards the ceiling, stifling a yawn. Something told me he had not slept as long as I had.

"Well, hopefully I look better than you do," I teased. I pulled at my knotted hair, still tangled with lake residue. I looked away in embarrassment.

Aaron smiled back at me, tucking a strand of hair behind my ear. His warm hand lingered against my cheek. "Always."

My face turned against his unexpected touch, eying his hand. Pulling his hand away, he put both of them in his pockets.

He shrugged, looking at the floor. "Sorry. I'm just happy you're ok."

"No, that's ok." I took a deep breath, distracting myself by inclining the bed. I shook my head. My sluggish mind was trying to run a mile a minute—like those dreams I'd had where I needed to run somewhere, but was anchored down by some imaginary force.

I looked around the quiet room, eyeing the

monitor beside me, and noting the empty bed across the room. I glanced through the open door. A nurse walked briskly down the hall, pen and clipboard in hand. A wave of panic attacked my chest.

"Um, where's—"

"Damien's in another room," Aaron answered, as if expecting the question. He turned to follow my gaze outside the doorway. His expression changed. "Don't worry. He's ok. Or at least, he will be."

I breathed a quiet sigh of relief, relaxing against the firm bed. I rubbed my eyes, fighting the lingering grogginess behind them, releasing a sleepy yawn.

"They said you'd feel drowsy and a little out of it for another twenty-four hours," Aaron informed. "I guess that's normal for being drugged."

Drugged. The word injected terrifying emotions into my body. Last night's events flashed through my mind, the nightmare of it all sending a tremor down my spine.

Dark images of Aaron wrestling with a gun. Damien's face twisting in pain. Deep, hateful eyes and a taunting, throaty laugh. My head submerged in cold water, while the desperation for oxygen burned in my lungs...

"Aaron," I said. "You could have been killed." Gunshots rang in my ear, almost audibly through the quiet safety of the hospital room. I blew out an anxious breath of air. "We all could have."

Aaron sat down beside me, pulling me into him. I

wrapped my arms around his neck, burying my face into his shoulder. Fresh tears of fear and relief dampened the dirty stripes of his shirt. Aaron pulled me tighter against him, securing me with his grasp.

"It's ok," he soothed, rubbing my back. "Everything's going to be ok."

I inhaled, sniffling back the last of my tears while Aaron held onto me. I felt safe in his clutches, knowing he wouldn't let me go until I asked. And I couldn't ask yet. My reeling emotions still yearned for the refuge.

I sat back against the bed, trying to sort out the last thing I remembered from yesterday, but the fragmented pieces refused to be made whole.

"Did we come straight here?" By "here", I knew we were in Sonora, a small city just forty-five minutes outside of Hidden Pines. It was the closest hospital to the lake, and one I was becoming well acquainted with.

Aaron nodded. "Yeah, once we got you inside the car, you passed out. We drove you straight to the hospital. Besides, Damien was bleeding pretty badly and had lost a lot of blood. He wouldn't have made it much longer."

I looked Aaron up and down.

"And you're fine?" I asked. He shrugged.

"Yeah, nothing more than a few scrapes and bruises. Can't complain really."

"But other than injuries, I mean, Aaron, you shot someone. Killed him."

Aaron caught me with a pensive gaze. "Allie, it wasn't a difficult thing to do. When someone you care about is being threatened, the choice is simple. The action itself is instinctive." His eyes met mine. "And obviously, you're worth it."

A moment of silence passed between us. I dropped his gaze and fiddled with my fingers. There they were again. Those emotions I wasn't quite sure what to do with just yet. I crinkled my eyebrows, attempting a different avenue.

"Aaron," I started. "What were you doing there last night?"

"I ran into Brooke. When she told me you had gone to see Damien, and you still hadn't returned, well, I got worried."

"Damien would never hurt me," I insisted.

"I know that now," Aaron continued. "But at the time, I couldn't stand waiting around, wondering if you were safe or not with him. So, I asked Brooke if I could borrow her family's car. It took me a while to figure out how to get to the back roads and to his cabin. But I knew the general direction, and once I found the bridge, I just followed the trail.

"When I reached the cabin, I didn't see your suburban. Something didn't seem right. And if you weren't there, then I didn't know where you could be. So, I walked right in, ready to confront Damien about what he'd done with you."

I listened to Aaron with wide-eyes, imagining what he was about to see—remembering the last time I had seen Damien, with a gun pointed at his head, before

347

I was hauled out that very same door just a minute earlier. Aaron continued.

"It all happened so fast. The gunman spun around in surprise with his gun now pointing at me. Damien jumped to his feet and tackled him. The gun went off when the Samoan guy fell. And then another shot was fired while they both fumbled for the gun. I jumped in and helped Damien pin him to the ground, just long enough for Damien to get the gun."

"Is he dead, too?" I asked, memories of the other two bloodied, dead bodies surfacing in my mind.

"No," Aaron answered. "Damien didn't think it was necessary—not yet, anyway. He held him at gunpoint, while I tied him up to a chair. Then we cleaned up Damien as best we could with some bandages and the little time we knew we had left. Damien had heard them talk about, well, drowning you up at the lake." Aaron grimaced in thought. I was sure my expression matched his.

"So we took the guy's car keys and his gun and drove up to the lake. It was Damien's idea for me to drop him off by the trees, and for me to drive up to the lake by myself. He thought a surprise attack might be more effective. Seems he was right."

Even though I knew how the story ended, I found myself clenching my fists so hard that my nails were digging into my palms. "And everyone's ok," I concluded, skipping the rest of the story that I remembered all too well now. "Has anyone contacted my parents?"

"Nick's on his way to the airport right now. I

talked to them on the phone before they took off. They're anxious, I can tell you that much."

"Can't imagine why," I mumbled. "What about the police? You must have talked to them, right?"

Aaron nodded. "They met us at the hospital and took my statement, and then told me they had another squad picking up the one gang member who was still alive at Damien's cabin."

"Do you think this will be enough to clear Damien's name, and convict them for Tommy Miller's murder?"

Aaron shrugged. "I don't know. You never know how these things will play out in the trial. But at least the process is underway. It will be a long time before all of this goes away."

"I assume they're going to want to speak with me," I stated, not eager to relive my encounter with the Samoan gang.

"They tried to talk to you this morning, but I insisted they let you keep sleeping. They should be back later today."

A petite figure danced her way into the room. "Hope you're ready to see your ultimate favorite gal-pal!" Brooke lugged an oversized, pink and yellow duffle bag onto the bed. She threw her arms around me. "Allie! How are you? Oh, I'm so happy to see you!"

My wide smile welcomed her positive energy that lit up the room. "I'm fine, Brooke. What are you doing here?"

She put her hands on her hips and tilted her head. "Well, that's just a silly question, now isn't it?" With one quick motion, she unzipped the bag and flung the flap open. "I brought you hospital essentials."

I eyed the bag, casting a sideways glance at Aaron. He smiled, shrugging his shoulders. Brooke emptied its contents along the bed.

"First," Brooke informed, "a change of clothes." She held up a stern index finger. "But, not to be worn before showering with my can't-do-without spa kit." She pointed to the shampoo and conditioner, an apricot body scrub, and a large, fluffy loofah sponge. Next came the manicure and pedicure set, lotion, deodorant, a bulging makeup bag, blow dryer, hair straightener, and hair products.

With the conclusion of her presentation, Brooke smiled at my overwhelmed expression. "Hello, Aaron, by the way," Brooke continued, flipping her hair over her shoulder as she tossed her head in his direction. She toned down her perkiness. "Like I said over the phone, I'm glad you're ok, too."

He leaned over and gave her a side-hug. "Me, too, Brooke. I don't suppose you brought any 'hospital essentials' for me?"

Brooke's expression appeared offended. She stepped away from his side and returned to her magical Mary Poppins bag. At the very bottom of the bag lay a blue towel and a familiar pair of Aaron's clothes. She held them out towards Aaron with one hand, placing the other on her hip and looking bored.

"Thanks, Brooke," Aaron laughed, accepting the items. "You never cease to amaze me."

"I know. You're welcome," Brooke stated.

"Well, on that note," Aaron said, walking towards the door. "I'm going to go change and let the nurse know you're awake," he said, addressing his comments towards me. "I'll also check on Damien and see if they're allowing visitors."

I smiled at the thought of seeing Damien. "Thanks, Aaron. You're the best."

He slowly nodded his head as he turned his back. He pursed his lips together as he hesitated with one hand on the doorframe, about to say something, but he didn't turn around, and instead, continued out the door and down the hallway. I watched him leave, with a tinge of guilt tugging at my heart.

Showered, dressed, and wearing less makeup and hair product than Brooke approved of, I followed the nurse down the hospital corridor. I ran a nervous hand through my hair, playing with the ends of it as we walked.

"That's a good friend you have back there," the nurse commented.

"Oh, Brooke?" I gave a good-natured laugh. "Yeah, she's one of a kind. Definitely keeps life interesting."

"That's not who I was talking about," the nurse

said. "Actually, I meant the tall, blond boy who never left your side the entire night."

My mouth dropped open into a silent "oh", realizing I had misunderstood her.

"He must care about you an awful lot. That much is obvious." She smiled to herself, noting the pink blush that escaped against my will.

I racked my brain for the right thing to say, to explain that he was just a friend, in a complicated kind of way...I stuttered, failing to put into words what I could not even describe inside my head.

The nurse seemed to ignore my efforts, keeping further thoughts to herself.

"Here we are. But just for a few minutes," she instructed, moving to the side so I could step past her. Damien's head turned towards me from where he lay propped up in the bed. I hurried to his side, all thoughts of complicated emotions brushed aside.

"Hey, beautiful," he said, reaching out to take my hand. I wrapped both my hands around his, bringing the back of his hand to my cheek. My heart surged to be near him again, to see and feel him alive. My stomach hurt, recalling how close I had come to losing him.

"How are you feeling?" I asked. I surveyed his face, wincing at the purplish bruises developing just under his left eye, and the mild swelling along his jawline.

"Like I would go through last night all over again, if it meant I'd get to see your face again." He brought my hand to his lips. Releasing me for a moment, Damien's face twisted as he moved to reposition himself.

"Here, let me," I said, adjusting the pillows behind his back. I moved around his left side, where his arm sat wrapped in a sling.

"I heard you were lucky," I said, "as far as gunshot wounds go."

"Yeah, I guess I am. The bullet shot just beneath my clavicle and out through the back, just missing my left scapula. Didn't hit bone or anything. So, no surgery, fortunately. They still won't release me for a few more days though." He frowned in annoyance.

"Well, this is one time I'm glad your dimpled smile won't win you any favors," I teased. "You need to stay put."

Damien looked disgruntled. "If I'm just going to be sitting around in a hospital bed, I may as well as sitting around at home, and with a much more pleasant nurse." He winked at me.

I sighed, sitting down beside him. "I can't help but feel responsible for what happened. I should have let you go last night."

"Allie, if I had left as intended, I would still feel like a coward. Sure, I planned on testifying about my involvement with the gang, and their threats against Tommy Miller. But I'd still be running. And the Samoans weren't the only thing I was running from." He softened his voice as he stared into my eyes.

I trembled with anticipation of his words.

Damien's large hand cupped the side of my face.

I couldn't help but lean into his touch, nuzzling against his palm.

"Allie, I've never felt this way about anyone else. I mean, not ever. And it scared me, you know? I thought it'd be easier to move on than to risk roping someone else into my life."

I looked back at him with glistening eyes. "Yeah, I know what you mean."

"But I was wrong." Damien squeezed my hand. "Spending that time with you last night was the happiest I've felt in a long time. I've never told anyone about my involvement with the gang, or losing my family. And sitting there talking with you, I felt like a weight was lifted—a weight that I didn't know even existed until I couldn't feel it anymore. I wouldn't trade our time together for anything."

I wanted to photograph the adoration on his face reflecting so much love back at me. I leaned down, brushing my lips along his. I slid along his swollen jaw, testing its sensitivity.

Damien murmured, closing his eyes and breathing in my fragranced hair that fell across his face. His full lips slipped over my own. The curve of his palm enclosed around my neck as he slid it back and forth along my heated skin.

A female voice cleared her throat behind us. I jumped back, my face flushed with both passion and embarrassment when a nurse I'd never met shook her head at us. "I think that's quite enough excitement for Mr.

Michaels," she chastised, her thin arms folded against her chest. The nurse eyed both Damien and me from behind her clipboard, frowning at us.

Feeling like a child, I looked down at my feet, avoiding her disapproving eyes. Damien seemed unperturbed. He wrapped his hand around mine, pulling me closer to the edge of his bed. He looked back at the nurse with a charming smile.

"Aw, come on, now, Nurse B. This is Allie, the one I told you about. You wouldn't want to prohibit the best medicine a guy could get, would you?"

The nurse looked me up and down. "Well, I don't know about that," she mumbled. "And stop calling me that," she said to Damien. "I told you, it's Brenda."

I released Damien's hand and moved out of her way, while she examined the monitor beside the bed.

"I better go," I said, resigned, shrugging at Damien. "I'll come see you later." I kissed him on the side of his head, whispering in his ear, "We'll be together again before you know it. In the meantime..." I threw a furtive look towards the nurse, grinning. "I'd watch your back if I were you."

CHAPTER 28

*K*nowing what awaited me, I hesitated for one moment with a nervous hand on the doorknob. With a deep breath, I twisted the handle and stepped inside. The hinges creaked as the door swung open, announcing our return.

"Hello?" I called.

The slamming of drawers from my bedroom came to an abrupt halt, followed by hurried footsteps.

"Allie!" Dad exited my bedroom. He barreled towards me with such force that I took a step backwards when he collided into me and swallowed me up with his bear hug. I returned the embrace. Peering over his shoulder, I caught sight of Nick stepping from around the corner.

Dad released his impossible grasp, but kept his hands on my shoulders. His eyebrows rose in concern, and his anxious eyes met mine.

"Are you ok? I'm so sorry I left you. It won't happen again. That was selfish and stupid of us—"

"Dad," I interrupted, shaking my head. "Dad, it's ok. It's not your fault. And you can't plan on not leaving me alone again. I'm going to college, remember?"

"Not for another month, you're not. And until then, I'm not letting you out of my sight."

I sighed at the adamant look in his eyes. This is what I was afraid of. Perhaps it wasn't fair to consider it an "overreaction," all things considered, but there had to be another way than falling prisoner to my father's watch.

Nick caught my eye as he and Aaron stepped away from a quick hug. He slipped his hands in his pocket and glanced at his feet. Looking back up, he said to me, "So, you're ok then, right?"

I smiled at his quiet awkwardness. "Yeah, I'm fine. Thanks."

Nick nodded. "Good to hear." He paused, and then he held up a closed fist in the air.

Laughing, I knocked my knuckles against his. A moment later, I surprised Nick by pulling him into a quick embrace, but he returned the tight squeeze before letting go, followed by a shy smile. It was going to take some getting used to before we both felt comfortable with the new boundaries we were exploring.

Dad's phone rang. Chasing after the muted ringtone, I followed him into my bedroom.

I gawked at the disaster that awaited me. My large, blue suitcase was pulled out from under my bed, lying open in the center of the room. Clothes from my drawers were thrown on top of it, almost hiding the suitcase. The top of my dresser was cleared from my small collection of hair and makeup products, lying in a toppled heap on the floor. Even my basketful of dirty laundry was sealed inside a Hefty garbage bag next to my bed.

"Hello? Hi, Holly. Yeah, she's back. She's right here. I was just finishing packing up her room. Uh huh. Of course. We can get her a flight for tomorrow afternoon."

"What?" My jaw dropped. Dad had his back turned towards me, standing by the window. I swung him around in one swift moment, my hand gripping his shoulder. "What do you mean tomorrow? You're sending me away?"

Dad put his hand over the phone, making a "shh-ing" noise with his lips. "No, I understand. Here, I'll let you talk to her."

Dad shoved the phone into my hands. "Talk to her," he whispered back. "She'll explain." He stepped away from me, lingering by the entrance doorway. I stood helplessly with the warm phone in my hands.

"Hi, Mom."

"Allie, it's so good to hear your voice! Your father said you were ok, but I just needed to be sure. Are you doing all right, honey?"

"Yeah, Mom. I'm fine. I've got some cuts and bruises," I admitted, knowing she'd be suspicious if I completely sugarcoated the incident. "But I'm fine. We were all lucky."

I could hear Mom let out a bitter laugh, hinting of anger. "Luck. Ha! That's the problem, Allie. You *were* lucky. What if luck had not been on your side last night? You could be dead, lying in some shallow grave up there, or floating head-first in some lake from the sounds of it."

I could hear the hysteria forming in her voice. I flinched at the images her words brought to my mind.

"I don't know what your father was thinking, leaving you alone like that," she continued, pausing just long enough to catch her breath. "I mean, honestly, Allie, when he called me to tell me what happened, it was all I could do not to take the first flight down there and pack you up myself. Of all the irresponsible, reckless things for him to do, leaving you alone like that. . ."

I glanced up at Dad, who still stood at the doorway. He wasn't looking at me, but the pained expression on his face told me he could hear every word streaming from the phone.

"It's not his fault, Mom," I interrupted in a hushed tone. "It might have happened any other night of the week, whether he was here or not. I was with this guy and—"

"And that's the other thing," Mom cut in. "What are you doing dating some older guy, with some crazy gang history that would get you into this kind of mess in the first place?"

My mouth fell open in surprise, and I glanced at Dad. He must have told her the small summary that he knew from Aaron, but not enough for either of them to understand.

"Mom, it's not like that. You don't even know the whole story." I could feel my defenses rising, seeking to protect Damien's name. "Why are you getting so mad and attacking everyone, anyway? It's nobody's fault. I told you, I'm fine. He and Aaron saved my life!"

"I almost lost you again, Allie! Do you understand that?" The high pitch of my mom's voice cracked as she choked on tears. "You are my daughter. I have felt twice over now, what it might be like if you weren't in my life. And I can't bear the thought."

We were both silent for a moment. When she spoke again, her voice lowered. "And that is why I have asked your father to send you back home. You're leaving for college in the fall and you'll be gone for months. I would just like a little more time with you."

I looked around at the tornado in my room, at a loss for words. I couldn't leave now. Damien needed me. We had been through too much together for me to leave like this.

"Mom, I can't." There was a brief silence.

"What do you mean you can't? Is this about that boy?" The annoyance weighed in her voice.

"Sort of."

Mom huffed unhappily from her end.

"There's just a lot you don't know. About what happened last night. And about what happened last summer." I chewed on my lower lip, fumbling on how to continue. The silence on the other line returned. I waited.

"Ok, explain to me what you're talking about," she said, maintaining her calm. I looked over at Dad, who listened with interest. I sighed.

"Dad, you may as well have a seat, too." He complied, sitting down at the end of the bed. I contemplated how to begin.

Relationships were difficult enough without having to explain them to your parents, especially over the phone. I had just figured some of this out myself only twenty-four hours ago. I wondered at my ability to express it to my parents—parents who didn't believe in first loves lasting forever. I feared they wouldn't understand, but I had to try. If not, I would be on a plane tomorrow, back in Portland.

"Damien saved my life last night."

Mom scoffed. "Well, it's the least he could do, considering he seems to have started this whole thing," she muttered. I could feel the skepticism seeping through the phone. I sighed in discouragement. She wasn't going to hear a thing I was about to say.

Dad took the phone from my hands.

"Holly, you need to just listen to our daughter. We both do. If she has something important to share with us, I think it's the least we can do, considering all she's been through."

I could hear Mom start and stop a number of times, failing to put her thoughts into words. Then there was silence.

Dad handed the phone back over to me. I smiled in nervous appreciation, putting the phone on speaker.

"Last night was not the first time he saved my life," I continued. Dad raised his eyebrows, tilting his head to the side.

"It was him. Last summer. He's the one that pulled

me from the river." Damien's dark features played in my memory, giving me strength to speak. "I would have been dead a year ago if it weren't for him."

The powerful, private moments we shared together in his room emerged in my mind. My heart pounded, in remembrance of last night's conversation. "And I love him."

CHAPTER 29

*A*n hour later, I found myself unpacking my belongings, folding and stowing my clothes back in my drawers. I had told my parents everything: explaining Damien's rocky past and losing his family in the fire. How he pulled me from the river that rainy day last June and played the anonymous hero.

I even shared with them, for the first time, the details of what happened in the river with Maddie—voicing aloud to them the heavy emotions they knew I carried around with me this past year. My voice shook and my body trembled as I spoke. It was the most I had spoken to either of them of Maddie's death, making them the second and third person to hear the full details.

But the tremors that shook me felt different this time. It wasn't guilty emotions that played with my nerves. Rather, my body was reacting to the palpable honesty I shared with them. My heart pounded, urging me to continue, to express the once-encumbering emotions. And with it, I offered each of them the remaining, broken pieces of an old shield.

I felt lighter. I wanted to keep talking until it was all out, until my parents heard everything, and I knew that they wanted to know. They had always wanted to know.

I could hear Mom sniffling on the other end. I tried not to notice the tears in Dad's eyes as he wiped them away, but I did acknowledge the proud smile he shared with me when I was done, matching the proud tone in Mom's voice.

A knock on the door made me jump. I dropped the shirt in my hands.

"Sorry, I didn't mean to startle you." Aaron was leaning against the doorframe, still standing in the hall.

"Aaron, hi."

"What are you doing?"

"Oh, just unpacking." I motioned towards the remaining scattered items by my bag. "My mom's letting me stay for the next two weeks. As you can see, I've got some reorganizing to do. My dad sure did a number on my room."

"Well, how about a break from all this? Want to go for a walk?" Aaron held out his hand.

I took one more fleeting glance at the mess around me. It wasn't a hard decision. "Sure. That sounds refreshing." I placed my hand in his, and he pulled me to my feet.

We ambled along the shoreline of the lake in quiet companionship. Our slow footsteps imprinted into the dirt, recording our path. It was still light outside, with the remaining glow diming.

Aaron's voice broke the comfortable silence. "So,

are you ready for it?"

I squinted at him in confusion. "Ready? For what?"

Aaron shrugged. "You know. College. Change. It's all coming your way in a few weeks." His words brought a wave of images to my mind: Chaotic, cramped dorm rooms, campus cafeterias, oversized classrooms with a sea of unfamiliar faces surrounding me...I cringed at the thought.

"Whoa, didn't mean to scare you," Aaron interrupted, squeezing my shoulder. "It's exciting. It will be different, at first, because it's all so new. But you'll do great out there."

"Let's hope so," I commented, looking over at the darkening lake. Change was a scary concept. Whether you were ready for it or not, sometimes it crept up on you, ambushing without warning, and no matter if you wanted it or not, you had to figure out how to accept it and adapt to its insistent nature.

"I'm not sure I'm ready for more change," I said. "I've had about as much of it as I can handle, I think." I chewed on the inside of my cheek for a moment. "So what about you?" I asked, diverting the attention. "Are you looking forward to your sophomore year?"

Aaron shrugged. "Sure, why not? Nick and I have plans to room in an apartment together. We might have two other roommates, but it beats the dorms. Oh, not that living in the dorms is a bad thing. You'll enjoy it. But after a year, it's definitely time to go. You'll see."

"That must be nice having your best friend around

all the time," I said. "Must be easier making friends, I'm sure. Not that you're the type to have any problems in the social arena. I'm sure you'll have girls lined up the minute you move in," I laughed.

Aaron slowed his pace. I mimicked his tempo, watching his features alter.

"Did I say something wrong?" I asked.

We had reached the observation dock. I followed Aaron as he stepped onto the dock and slipped between the metals rails. Sitting down beside him, I let my feet dangle over the edge, and rested my forearms on the rail in front of me. I looked over at Aaron, waiting for his words.

"Is that how you see me?" he asked, not looking back at me.

"What do you mean?

"You know, just one of those guys who hooks up with the next girl in line?"

My mouth opened and closed a couple times as I struggled with how to respond. This was Aaron we were talking about here. I shrugged with guilt. "I don't know what you want me to say, Aaron. I mean, I guess so. It doesn't seem like it's been a hard road for you in that area. You'll never have a hard time getting the girl you want."

Aaron was silent for a time, his eyes washing over my face. His eyes connected with mine with such sudden intensity that I felt my cheeks redden with warmth. "Except for the one that matters," he disagreed.

My mouth fell open, but my throat tightened

shut, sealing my voice. Aaron lifted a hand to my face, his fingers brushing the stray hairs falling beside my eye. I swallowed hard.

"You're different than any girl I've ever met, Allie Collins," he said, sliding his fingers down my face as he dropped his hand. "You're genuine. And brave. You've faced so many fears in just the few weeks that I've known you that I know how strong you are. Allie, when I'm with you, I don't want to be *that guy* anymore. You've shown me that there is something more to be felt—something that makes a relationship real."

The wind picked up in speed, stirring the air between us. I breathed a sigh of relief as it cooled my heated cheeks. It gave me a moment to sort through the tornado of thoughts and emotions whirling inside me. I cleared my throat, unable to hold Aaron's gaze.

"I'm sorry. I didn't mean to say that's the only way I think of you." I paused. "You've been there for me during all of this. Whether it was making me get up on that stupid wakeboard, or talking about my fear of love and relationships...you've made a difference in my life. And you're important to me, Aaron."

Aaron lifted his eyes to meet mine. "But just not as important as someone else," he concluded.

My face scrunched together. I didn't know how to respond. With a sigh, I looked up at the sky, seeing just a hint of stars beginning to shine through. I thought about all the constellations. Even the stars grouped in meaningful patterns. It was nature's purpose in life for all things to connect—to be together, but why did it have to be so difficult to define?

Aaron looked like he was struggling to say something. I waited with nervous anticipation of his words.

"Allie," he began, taking his time. "Do you think, well, do you think maybe, if you hadn't met Damien again, that somehow things would be different? Maybe we would have met and become friends like we have... and then maybe that might have developed into a little more, like it sort of did. The summer would come to an end, and we would go our separate ways. But we might have kept in touch while we were both in college. And I would go home to Danville with Nick on holidays when you would be visiting your dad. And we would see each other. And things would be the same between us, but with the potential to be even better."

I listened to his musings, with a twinge of guilt digging into my heart. There was no doubt I cared about Aaron. He had forced his way into a shielded part of my life, supporting me when I pushed everyone else away. Hearing him ponder about what could have been, had circumstances been different, played wistfully in my heart.

But Aaron was not the only one who had collided into my life.

"It's ok," Aaron spoke, squeezing my hand as he read my thoughts. "I know he means a lot to you. We can't live happily on 'what could have been', can we?"

There it was again. The timeless question of

"if only." I shook my head back and forth with slow movements.

Aaron let out a half smile, shaking his head with a hint of regret. He stood up, dusting off the back of his shorts. "Come here." He reached out his hand and took my own, pulling me to my feet.

I stepped into him, hugging him. "Thanks for everything, Aaron. And for understanding."

Aaron returned the embrace, playing with my hair against my back. "You're a good person, Allie. You deserve to be happy. Don't ever forget that."

As I pulled away, Aaron put a hand on the back of my head, looking down into my eyes. His own eyes flickered back and forth between mine. He smiled, and then leaned down to kiss my forehead. His lips lingered a moment too long, pressed against my warm skin. I took another step backwards, placing a hand against his chest.

Aaron put his hand on top of mine. I could feel his heart beating, its quick tempo matching my own. After a moment, he sighed, releasing my hand.

"Come on, pretty girl. I'll walk you home. I hope you know it's completely out of my way though."

I laughed, able to breathe again as we walked side by side along the shore, back the way we came.

CHAPTER 30

I looked back and forth across the streaming river. It flowed serenely towards the lake with its shallow waters. The river played a gentle melody, popping against the rocks and trickling its soprano voice.

I placed my bare foot on top of the rock, feeling the cool water splash against my ankle. I took another hesitant step onto the next rock.

And then another.

Halfway across the river, a flicker of a memory blanketed my vision, but it wasn't the one I feared would return. Instead, I saw Maddie's jovial face, swinging her pale hair as she leaped from rock to rock. She looked back at me, egging me on beneath the sunlight. I followed her eager footsteps across the river. It was just as it had always been. Fearless and fun.

My bare feet touched the soft dirt of the river's edge. Feeling triumphant, I looked back at the gentle current. The river was no longer taunting or threatening me with jeering memories—it was just a river, flowing from mountain to lake as it had always done, sweeping through the land at nature's bidding.

A warm hand touched my shoulder. I turned

around and smiled at Damien. He watched me, intrigued by the expression on my face.

"Do you hear that?" I asked, looking at the forest around us.

"No. What?"

"Nothing. It's quiet," I informed him. He looked at me as I smiled to myself. In perfect honesty, it wasn't truly quiet. Nature never was, with the birds, the crickets, and running water orchestrating its authentic sounds, but this time, something was missing.

The once-haunting laughter was gone, no longer echoing off the trees—no longer taunting me with painful memories and guilty emotions. I inhaled, letting the relief exit my lungs. I almost felt weightless, like I could hold my breath and, if the wind blew just right, that it might pick me up along with it and carry me above the trees.

Damien slid a long, thorn-less stem into my hand. I put the delicate petals to my nose, breathing in the sweet fragrance one more time. We walked to the river's edge, hand in hand.

"I love you, Maddie," I whispered, releasing the red rose. It fell into the river, gliding along with the current, running its course. We watched the rose move on until we could no longer see its vibrant color.

Damien dropped his weight to the ground and pulled me down beside him. He kicked off his sandals and dangled his feet over the embankment. I scooted closer to him, following his lead and dipping my toes into the water. Linking arms with him, I rested my head against his good shoulder.

"I've been meaning to ask you," I said, not moving from my relaxed position. "What's going to happen to your land and your family's cabin?" I thought back to the scorched skeleton of his vacation home, (or what was left of it), feeling like it was forever ago that I trespassed onto his property—back when Damien's identity was merely a disturbing ghost story.

Damien remained thoughtful before answering. "I've thought about rebuilding," he said. "I hadn't wanted to touch it before. I felt like it was all I had left of my family, and I couldn't bear the thought of tearing it down, but now...." Damien shrugged, returning my smile. "I think it'd be fun to build a vacation home and rent it out for a while—let some other families make some memories around here."

I nodded my head. "That sounds perfect. I think your mom would be happy about that."

"Now let me ask you something," Damien said. I waited expectantly and he continued. "Do you believe everything happens for a reason?"

I turned my head upwards in thought, taking in the calm, clear sky above us. "I don't know about all things," I said, "but certainly some."

"Even hard situations?" Damien questioned.

"Maybe especially the hard situations. I think it helps make us stronger, and helps us connect to the right people. I didn't always believe that, but I do now."

I looked up into Damien's marble eyes, seeing the image of myself reflecting back at me. Somehow, the reflection had changed from what I remembered. The frightened, self-tormented girl was gone, and in her place was someone else—someone standing taller, more confident, and with a touch of a smile on her face.

Damien leaned towards me and played with a loose wave of hair beside my cheekbone. He curled it around his finger before he released it and slid his fingers along my jaw. His hand pressed against my left shoulder, pushing my back against the ground. I looked up at him as he leaned over me, placing his face just above my own.

His face lowered, and I closed my eyes. Damien pressed his full lips against mine, tender with his touch. A surge of emotion wrapped around us like a blanket, shielding us both from the past and the future. All that lay between us was the present.

The demons we had battled lay peacefully at rest, and the future before us was unplanned and unwritten. For now, it was just the two of us, living in the moment.

ACKNOWLEDGEMENTS

To my sisters, Pawnee and Jen: Thank you for pushing me to turn what I thought was going to be a "short story just for fun" into a novel worth publishing! Your love for my characters and the storyline fueled my writing, and I will always be in debt to you for reading my long-winded first-draft, chapter by chapter. Thanks for every gasp of anticipation and shock, tears, and twitterpated giggles from start to finish.

To my husband, Dan: The plot to Lingering Echoes would not be the same without you. You are the most stalwart sounding board a writer could ask for! Thank you for your unique contributions to the storyline, the inspiring drive to Pine Crest, my laptop, Publishing for Dummies, answering my questions at random intervals, "truth bombs!" and most importantly—for never doubting that my dreams to be published would be realized. In everything I do, you believe in me and bolster my confidence. I love you!

I am beyond grateful to the members of Clean Teen Publishing for taking a chance on a newbie like myself. Rebecca Gober, Dyan Brown, Marya Heiman and Courtney Nuckels: Thank you for your friendly welcome and enthusiastic efforts to publish Lingering Echoes. I have been nothing but impressed with your efficient, professional and personable natures.

Cynthia Shepp: Thank you for cleaning up my manuscript with your thorough editing skills and for helping me realize I have a problem with over-hyphenating! I appreciate your educating tips and the time you spent to help my manuscript shine.

Finally, I very much appreciate my family and friends, who took the time to read, edit, brainstorm titles, and stand by my side with encouragement throughout this process. Your support means everything to me!

ABOUT THE AUTHOR

Erica Kiefer was born on Christmas Eve in Southern California to an American father whose ancestors arrived from Europe during colonial times and a Thai mother who moved to the US during high school. Adding to her rich and varied heritage, Erica grew up living abroad in Asia, including Taiwan, Fiji, Thailand and Indonesia. She gained a great respect for the beautiful mosaic of cultures found in various parts of the world. After graduating from International School Bangkok, she attended Brigham Young University in Utah, where she earned a degree in Recreation Therapy. Her career as a Recreation Therapist has allowed her to work with at-risk youth since 2007.

Erica made the best decision of her life by marrying her husband in 2005 and is currently a mother of three, one of whom awaits her in heaven. Erica also loves singing, reading, writing, and satisfying her sweet-tooth with chocolate-chip cookies.

Clean Teen Publishing

CPSIA information can be obtained at www.ICGtesting.com
Printed in the USA
BVOW07s1019261113

337063BV00007B/12/P